To Jan.

Hope you enjoy the read

I've Got Your Number

David E Merrifield

Best wishes

David

November 2016

I've Got Your Number

©David Merrifield 2016

Published by MindsEye,

an imprint of

Catberry Press, Lowestoft

ISBN 978-0-9954781-3-8

A catalogue record of this book is available from the British Library

Acknowledgements

I would like to thank Gorleston artist Paul Pascall, whose painting The Numbers Game is reproduced on the front cover.

paulpascall232@gmail.com

Thanks also to Jo at Catberry Press for her help and support in getting this book to publication.

www.facebook.com/catberrypress

Chapter		Page

Chapter 1
Sad Beginnings

As Matt pulled the heavy drab curtains aside, the morning sunlight flooded into his bedroom. He gasped. The bright light almost knocked him back a step as he first covered, then rubbed, his eyes to try and wake himself up. He quickly tugged the curtain back to give himself adjustment time before he made another attempt at looking out to see what sort of weather London was offering. He yawned, then stretched, and stepped nearer to the window. He cautiously looked to see exactly what things were like outside. Rubbing some condensation from the glass with a couple of fingers, he could see raindrops on the outside, but no indications that it was actually raining. He viewed the London landscape, trying to pick out The Gherkin in the distance, but it was too misty. Although the sky was quite grey it was still far too bright for his eyes.

Matt sat back down on his bed and momentarily thought about getting back into it. It was still warm and inviting and surely a few more minutes' sleep wouldn't do any harm. But it was Wednesday; one of those days when he just had to get up and kick himself into action. He sat for another couple of minutes arguing with himself before concluding that he must make an effort to get dressed and get out. He briefly considered whether it was really necessary to visit the Job Centre at all, but that would risk his

1

benefit money if he didn't go and register, which was the last thing he needed right now.

Another rub of the eyes, and Matt finally stood up with a purpose. The day was beginning and he pulled the old heavy curtains fully aside. He stood in his three-day-old jockey shorts and checked his mobile phone for overnight messages. He hoped Mikey might need him but no texts had been left. He walked over to the mirror and stared right into it as he moved his fingers up and down his unshaven face. He checked out various poses, wondering if he might look good with a beard. The answer was always no, but he just couldn't face shaving in the morning, at least not before a coffee and some food. As he moved from his bedroom to the lounge he spotted a letter on the side. He couldn't recall what it was, so picked it up and glimpsed inside to remind himself of its contents.

It was addressed to Matthew Ellington Briswell, his full name, so it was obviously official. He pulled the letter out of the envelope and read: '...required to pay £65...' and gave a number of dates by which the fine had to be paid or it increased each time. 'For travelling on London Transport without a ticket...' he read again. "Shit and bollocks," he said angrily. He thought back to the incident. A wet rainy day at Bank. He was annoyed he'd been caught but laughed proudly to himself at the fact that it took four of them to catch him that day. He had no way of paying £65 but probably still had another week or so before he would have to go to court and ask for time to pay. He quickly wondered if he could borrow the money from someone but nobody came to mind. He owed fifty quid to Nigel down the pub. He was in debt to a number of people in fact. He put the letter back on the side as he caught sight of his discarded jeans hanging over the back of an old armchair. A dirty t-shirt lay over the chair arm and a trainer protruded from underneath it. Matt's head drooped and he sighed.

From the lounge he went straight to the kitchen on the hunt for breakfast. There were two slices of stale bread in a plastic bag, which looked promising. Removing them from the bag for closer inspection revealed that they were both covered in mould spots. Matt sighed again, shrugged, and put the bread back in the bag before opening a cupboard. There was an old box of breakfast cereal standing proudly on the top shelf, which he grabbed and shook, but there was no familiar sound of moving cereals. A look inside the box showed about half a bowl of cereal remaining, although it was stuck together at the bottom of the bag. Matt retrieved a bowl from the pile of unwashed crockery in the sink and rinsed it before placing it on the work top.

'Milk,' he thought, 'have I got any milk?' He opened the fridge door. The smell that greeted him said it all. There was milk but none that even he was prepared to drink. The remains fell as white lumps into the sink. He made an attempt to wash them down the plughole with hot water and threw the empty carton into the bin.

"I must get some milk." Matt spoke to himself as if he was having a conversation with a friend as he briskly walked back into the lounge and searched through his jeans pockets to see how much cash he had. He slammed down a few coins on the table in the lounge. There was just over two pounds in total. He grimaced and sighed again.

"That's not enough," he said, moving the coins around on the table in the hope that it would produce more money than he had first identified. It didn't. Matt clenched his fist and rubbed his chin hard as he tried to think of ways he might get some money. I need some food, he thought, as he paced around the lounge fully aware that his benefits money wasn't due to be paid until tomorrow. He searched various hiding places in the lounge in the hope that a memory of previously hidden cash would come back to him but nothing came to mind.

The idea of breakfast was going rapidly down the pan when he spotted a coffee jar at the back of the cupboard with some granules left in it. He considered his reflection in jar. "A coffee will have to do," he told himself, despite realising it would have to be black coffee and without sugar. He shook the kettle and added more water to it before switching it on. He relaxed a little, glad that a coffee would give him time to complete his waking up and prepare for the day ahead.

As the kettle made working noises, he returned to the lounge and pulled on his best pair of jeans then picked up last night's t-shirt and gave it a sniff. He pulled a face as he did so and walked back to his bedroom where a pile of used clothes sat in the corner next to a black plastic sack which operated as his laundry basket. He threw the grubby t-shirt on to the pile and retrieved another reasonably clean one from a drawer. Pulling it on, he moved to the bathroom and swilled down some mouthwash to freshen himself up a bit.

Matt still did some of the little things his mother had religiously got him to do to look after his health. A quick face wash and toilet and he was finished. The kettle had boiled so he made the coffee. He downed a couple of mouthfuls of the bitter drink to take away the mint flavour of the mouthwash before grabbing his money from the table, slipping into his trainers and picking up his flat keys.

Matt shut his flat door behind him and glanced quickly out of the window to his left looking at the traffic and the various people moving along Church Road far below. Living on the fourth floor meant that it was easier to take the lift but it was usually slow and rarely near to where Matt wanted it but he pressed the button as he passed just in case before he went through the door to the stairs. Four lots of stairs could be hard for any man but bright and early in the morning and taking them down was never as bad, Matt thought. There was nobody else on the staircase and he didn't look through the entrance doors to the floors as he passed them on his way down but just kept on going.

At the bottom of the stairs he moved through another door and into a narrow corridor where at last there were some signs of sunlight. Matt took a quick look at the notice board but there were no obviously new posters on display so he continued to one of the exit doors. As he opened it he held out his hand to confirm that it wasn't raining, checked that he had his wallet, and continued on his way.

The weather wasn't brilliant but fine enough and Matt felt comfortable in just his t-shirt as he left the block of flats. He momentarily considered going back to put on a jacket but the thought of having to climb the stairs again made his mind up. There were the usual two big rubbish bins standing either side of the flat gates which gave a sort of comforting guard to the place. He turned right on to Riverley Close and then Crescent Road, and with a few quick strides he was on Church Road and on his way to Leyton town centre. At the first junction he came to he crossed the road and made his way past one of the many local corner shops in the area. The thought of milk came to mind again. He stopped and looked at the shop and in particular the food it had displayed outside on the street. He checked to see where the fridge was positioned but he recalled it was a fair way into the store. As he was considering his options and weighing up a possible opportunity, Matt became aware of a figure walking from inside the shop towards the door.

"Oi, you bastard," the Asian man spoke in Matt's direction. "You're barred from here, so don't even think about it." Matt looked up at the shopkeeper. He recalled having been half caught nicking something from the shop in the recent past but the exact details had escaped his memory. From further inside the shop came another male voice. "Is he the one, Dad?" A youngish Asian lad came towards the door holding a baseball bat.

Matt didn't hang about, but immediately turned around and started walking, reaching the edge of the pavement and running across the road despite the traffic crossing in front of him. A car horn sounded. There was a screech of brakes as a couple of cars stopped suddenly. The young Asian man ran out of the shop and shouted in Matt's direction: "You show your face round here again and we'll have you," as he waved the baseball bat above his head. Matt stuck a finger up at him and laughed from the other side of the street. Numerous busy commuters stared at Matt and wondered what was happening. He looked back at them defiantly. Many of the commuters showed signs of carrying their own stress, perhaps at being late for work, but annoyingly they all seemed to be wearing fine clothes and bright expensive watches. He cursed at them all.

Matt allowed some time to pass and things to cool down in the expectancy that the Asian shopkeeper would eventually go back inside and when the coast was clear Matt walked past the shop and on his original route to the town centre. Further down the road was yet another corner shop, and he wondered about checking his bank account at the ATM in the store, but decided against it knowing full well it would be empty. Matt carried on walking, occasionally looking at the people making their way to work. He looked up at the football stadium on his left. Leyton Orient, it said in big red letters. Matt liked football but thought of it as a pastime only for the rich.

A couple of corners further down next to the park was the burger man and his mobile stand. Matt walked over to him. "Hi, John," he said.
The burger man recognised him instantly. "Matt! How's it going?" His reply was professionally friendly and cheery. Matt would often stop and say something to the burger man just in case he would offer him a free bun or roll here and there. John did on occasions.

"You know, not so bad."

"Have you had breakfast this morning?"

Matt's mouth started to water at the thought of a burger or a bacon roll but he knew he couldn't really afford one.

"Yeah, had a bite before I came out but if you've got any of those broken or free ones behind there I'll help you get rid of 'em."

"Sorry, Matt, no freebies today, my man."

As the two chatted, Matt spotted a familiar sort of face heading towards the stand. It was the girl who worked in the sports shop two doors down. She was in a type of uniform which made it easier to identify exactly where he had seen her before and he knew he had spoken to her a couple of times previously. As she reached the cart Matt moved a step away to allow her to speak to the burger man.

"Hello, John, I'll have a bacon roll please," the girl put in her order as she lifted up her handbag to search for some money.

"Hi, will that be with anything added? Egg or sausage and would you like a white or brown roll?"

"I'll just have bacon in a white roll today please John, with some ketchup."

"Do you want anything to drink, my dear?"

"No thanks, just the roll."

As the burger man prepared the order Matt puffed out his chest and then took a casual stance before starting to talk to the girl.

"Hey, how you doing?" Matt flashed one of his

biggest smiles in her direction.

"Er, okay, thanks." She gave Matt a quick inquisitive glance before answering politely but curtly.

"Hey, Sabrina," the girl's name drifted back to him, "you still busy in the Sports shop?"

"Busy? Oh, I guess so."

"I came in after a Manchester United shirt the other week, remember?"

"Oh right, yeah, United," she replied hesitantly.

"Yeah, you tried to get it sorted for me so I said I'd owe you one, babe." Matt tried to give her a romantic look as at last he had caught her eye.

"It's nothing, just part of my job," the girl replied as the burger man finished her order and started to wrap it ready to hand to her. "How much, John?" she asked, looking away from Matt.

"That'll be one seventy-five," John replied as he took her money and handed her the prepared bacon roll. He pointed to where the sauces were situated on the end of the shelf. Matt's stomach rumbled at the thought of the taste of the bacon roll he wasn't going to get as the girl started to turn and go on her way.

"Just wondered if you fancied coming out for a drink on Saturday?" Matt spoke before the girl could get fully under way and he moved with her slightly so she couldn't ignore his offer.

"Thanks, but no thanks," the girl politely replied without even looking at him, "and the name's Sarah."

The girl turned and quickly walked away as Matt shrugged his shoulders and looked back to John.

"She just needs a little time," he said to John, who scrunched up his face. From a distance both could make out that the girl was still talking to herself as she walked away. "Jerk," she said, a bit louder, at the end of the sentence.

Hungry, Matt continued on his way to the underground and as he often did, found his way on to the platform without buying a ticket. All the time he kept watching out for either uniformed inspectors or plain clothed fraud officers and unless they had a big force out again he wasn't going to get caught today. The train was as busy as usual with a large number of suited workers and the occasional tourist to watch as he was travelling. He knew that they were the most likely to leave valuable things on seats, so he would always check if the opportunity arose. Two such tourists were having a conversation right next to him. They complained about how much they had to pay to go in to St. Paul's Cathedral, and the cost of their theatre tickets, but concluded that 'It's only money!'

Matt clenched his fists and bit his lip as he listened. He needed something to take his mind off what they were saying, and the encounter with Sarah was a start. Hmmm, thought Matt, not a bad looking girl. He tried to imagine the two of them going out. He thought about when he had last been on a date. He yearned for some female companionship. A kiss, a cuddle! Even more, he yearned for sex. He cursed himself for how little he had tried with Nancy. He thought back and decided he should have worked a bit harder with her. If he had, they might still be together. Perhaps life would be a bit more bearable if he had someone to share it with, but he rarely saw Nancy nowadays. If he were to see her again he would try a lot harder when they went out but he would actually have to see her first and that hadn't happened for ages. Matt had concluded that his life was crap and going nowhere as the train pulled into his station.

The journey was only one stop and as passengers moved towards the doors ready to alight Matt noticed that there was a uniformed person walking down the carriage checking tickets. He calculated that the doors would be open well before the inspector reached him but it would be close thing. The train seemed to struggle slowly into the platform and take ages to come to a standstill, as the official moved ever closer. Matt watched him as the inspector looked up to see what station they were arriving at. He caught Matt looking at him and seemed instinctively to know that he should try and check his ticket.

"Sir, can I see your ticket?" There were at least three people between him and his target but they all appeared to move aside to give him full access to Matt, who ignored what was being said as the doors hissed open. "Sir, I need to see your ticket." The inspector moved nearer as Matt joined the rest of commuters getting off the train. Without looking back, and as if he hadn't heard anything at all Matt quickly and swiftly made his way through the crowd, but without running. This was a bit of a practised art but Matt was quite used to crowds. The inspector got off the train and Matt glanced back over his shoulder then checked his route ready to make a run for it. "STOP! Show me your ticket!" The uniformed officer half shouted at Matt, but another passenger, thinking he was the one being shouted at, stood between them and displayed his ticket. Matt ducked down and moved towards the edge of the platform. The inspector lost sight of him and couldn't be sure if he'd doubled back on to the waiting train so he too got back on the train as Matt sat on a bench on the platform, watching. The train started pulling out of Leytonstone station just as the inspector caught sight of Matt who watched the train leave the station before making his way over the barrier and down through a tunnelled walkway to the station exit. He knew there was a possibility that a radio message might be passed back to one of the staff to try and apprehend him, but he was far too quick for them and within seconds was out of the station and into a small square. It was full of commuters and there was a number of people sat down at tables outside of a café drinking teas and coffees. Nobody would easily pick Matt out here.

Matt walked along the pavement ducking and

bobbing in between various people on the busy streets just in case anyone had been despatched to follow him as he made his way to his first destination. Nobody seemed to be following as Matt arrived. It was quite a big grand building with an entrance door to the left of the frontage, overall pretty smart except for a cheap plastic sign over it. Job Centre Plus, it read. Matt went in and was immediately approached by a suited male. "Can I help you?"

"I'm here to sign on, mate," Matt replied curtly.

"Do you have an appointment?"

"Yes," Matt replied, with a bored tone in his voice. Every time he was asked the same questions.

To his left were a couple of rows of computers known as the Job Points where claimants like Matt were supposed to log in and look for what work was available. He had looked many times and occasionally it was true, there would be a job that he thought he could apply for but more often than not, by the time he did apply for it the job had been taken. It was a very depressing process. Matt looked at the clock on the wall and he could see he had more than fifteen minutes before his appointment was due and they were usually late anyway. He sat down at an empty computer and went through the motions of searching. He only half concentrated on what he was doing but he'd entered the required information so many times before he felt he could do it in his sleep anyway. There were a good number of claimants stood around that Matt assumed were waiting to see their advisors, with only a few of them actively using the computers to look for jobs. In the far corner of this room was a big notice board which he checked to see if there were actually any jobs he could apply for. He had a quick look at all the cards that were pinned to the board, trying to identify any new adverts but as usual there didn't seem to be anything that he was suited to.

Matt's mind wandered a bit as he looked around the place. The place was full. Not just Caucasians but Asians, Blacks, Turks, Greeks and Eastern Europeans, all of whom seemed to congregate in their own little ethnic huddles. Matt nodded at one guy who half nodded back. Matt knew the man's name was Diego and had worked out that Diego was important amongst the Eastern Europeans; not someone you could just approach and chat to as if you were his friend, though it was useful not to be on the wrong side of him.

Matt wasn't even sure how well Diego would be able to speak English. Whenever he had heard him talking, it was in Romanian or some such language, or at least that was what Matt assumed. Matt thought he might have met one or two of the Eastern Europeans through his father when he was a very young child but he couldn't recall any faces or names he recognised. He was just pleased that Diego had acknowledged him which gave him a feeling of acceptance amongst Diego's other associates.

The time had come for Matt's interview and he waited to be called before going to a very smart desk where a young man in shirt and tie sat looking through some papers and checking things on a computer screen. "Good morning, Mr. Briswell, can I have your sheet please?" Matt handed him his list of job search activities. The young man gave it a cursory glance then placed it on top of the other papers he had been reading. "You need to call back same time tomorrow." This was said as a way of dismissing Matt. "Tomorrow!" Matt exclaimed. "Yes. Eleven o'clock." The young man spoke without looking up.

Matt's jobsearch continued as he made his way from the desk back to the noticeboard to take a closer look at the different cards that were pinned up. There were some showing immediate vacancies for skilled engineers and another couple advertising for trainee roles or some other sort of work in accountancy. Matt looked at them with a pained expression. Most of the cards were very similar, and all of them required qualifications or diplomas. After a few minutes he moved on to another noticeboard which he knew advertised the sort of low paid casual work where at least he would be likely to get an interview.

The title at the top of the board said 'Workers Wanted' in big bold letters, with notices giving brief descriptions of the exact types of job underneath.

They were generally warehouse type businesses looking for packers or factory workers. Many of the jobs were zero hours or casual short term contracts. These were just the sort of jobs he had applied for loads of times before and he knew that there would be many applicants for probably no more than a couple of positions, but he took down the details so that he could tell the Job Centre that he had applied. As he finished taking the addresses, an old man entered the agency and spoke to him.

"Hey son, what's going down?" Matt had often seen the old man while looking for work and the guy always spoke to him. Matt seemed to recall his name was Bill or Bob or something short like that, but he really couldn't be sure.

"Usual Mickey Mouse," he replied, indicating with his eyes towards the board. The old man just laughed. Matt suddenly looked back at the board as he thought he had glimpsed an interesting card. He had noticed an advert for a full time position as a car wash operative. "Hey, this could be just what I want," he said as he removed the pin and took a closer look. The old man showed some interest as well, just as one of the Job Centre staff moved in and snatched the card from Matt's hand.

"Sorry," she said, "that job's gone," as she ripped up the card, turned, and made her way back to the office. "Nuts!" Matt kicked the wall in anger. It was time for him to move on.

17

Matt also kicked at a free-standing advertising board outside the Job Centre, hurting the top of his foot as he did so. This only made him angrier and he let out a short yelp of pain. His stomach was grumbling with hunger and he looked around for a clock. It was approaching eleven thirty and a good time to check out some of the restaurants and cafes that he knew. He made his way round to the back of the first restaurant where a man in a blue and white chef's outfit was sitting on the step smoking a cigarette.

"Hi, Geezer, been a busy morning then?"
"What? Yeah, and hot," the man replied, without looking up at Matt. He took a long last drag on his cigarette before flicking it away.
"Many tourists in this morning?"
"Eh?"
"You know, rather than locals."
"Oh right, no, just the usual." The man rose to his feet and wiped down his apron to remove any ash.
"I just wondered if you had any jobs going?"
"Not really my side of things guv, you need to ask the manager."
"But you would know if there were any vacancies surely?"
"Nothing that I know of. We're well staffed in the kitchen, that's for sure."

Matt felt a bit more demoralised. He wouldn't mind giving working in a kitchen a go. How hard can it be, he thought to himself. There was a brief pause.

"Is there any leftover breakfast?" Matt hated saying it but he was hungry.

"Oh right, I thought you were after a job."

"Well yes, but if you had a piece of bacon or a roll that would be good, mate."

"We're not giving any food away here. Try Riches around the corner," the man said hurriedly as he disappeared back into the kitchen. Matt stood motionless, briefly bowing his head before turning towards the next café.

Matt knew that a lot of these places had left-over food after breakfast had finished, and if he could only find a chef he had previously chatted to who might remember him then he might get some, but he seemed to be out of luck today. He got the same answer from the next couple of restaurants and he was getting hungrier. Things were getting a bit desperate so his next plan was a visit to a corner deli to help himself to some food, which he had become quite proficient at. He knew it was wrong, and it could be risky, but he had seen his mother doing it when he was growing up so believed that when things were really bad and you were starving, it wasn't quite as wrong. Also, he had become quite clever at talking his way out of trouble if he needed to, which wasn't that often anyway.

After creating a distraction with another customer in the store he grabbed himself a sandwich and cereal bar and swiftly made his way out onto the street, before walking quickly away to get as far as he could from the shop. He risked a quick glance over his shoulder to see if anyone was chasing him but there was nobody in sight. At last he could have something to eat.

Matt turned right into a dark alley and paused to catch his breath. The adrenalin rush always excited him a little. He hurriedly unwrapped the sandwich before taking a couple of mouthfuls. It tasted fantastic. Another mouthful and the first sandwich was gone, with the second not far behind. He was left with the cereal bar, not his favourite food but it went down quickly as well. Eating it so quickly left Matt with stomach cramps, but some deep breathing helped. It reminded him of childhood when his meals weren't always that regular.

He thought back to how his mother had tried to bring him up. He could picture her face, and the way she used to look at him, but struggled to do the same for his father who he never really knew. He was sort of aware that his father was from Eastern Europe, and living in the UK illegally.

Matt had picked up what little he did know about his father from overhearing his mother talking to the police or visitors about him, whilst doing her best to deny as much knowledge of him as she possibly could. She had once told him that his father was from a country called Lithuania, or something like that, but she didn't know much more and it was obvious that she didn't like to talk about it, or him. By the time he was old enough to ask her what his father's name was he got several different answers. He was never sure if his mother simply didn't know, or had since forgotten. He remembered being told his father's name was Ramus, and once Ramanus, or Ramunas, but he was often referred to as plain Ram and so that was the name Matt picked for him. As for the surname, his mother could never manage any sort of answer and so, after many times of asking, he gave up worrying about it. He had his mother's family name, Briswell, and that was that. He knew a little bit more about his mother but when it really came down to it he didn't know a lot about her, either.

Matt spent that afternoon walking around parts of London watching tourists and city workers, all of whom appeared to have plenty of money. He also kept an eye out for opportunities in case anyone dropped anything of value. Money, a wallet, anything he could sell or trade. No such luck came his way. He knew that he really should be trying to find himself a job and he took out his piece of paper with the warehouse address on it. It was over in Stratford. It would mean a bit of a walk but working out a route, he set off. Matt suddenly thought to check his mobile phone.

'Blast!' he said out loud to himself, seeing that he had missed a call from Mikey, but there was also a text. 'Need you for a job will ring later' the text read.

He was pleased to receive the request even though he didn't really like doing the sort of jobs Mikey put his way, but it was an easy way for him to make a quick buck. It had so far been quite a long walk to the warehouse and his feet were beginning to hurt a bit. He really needed some new shoes but he knew he couldn't afford to buy any. On actually reaching the warehouse, Matt was a bit happier. He walked into the front office and waited at the reception. A smartly dressed man got up from behind a desk and walked over to him.

"Can I help you, sir?"
"You've been advertising for workers at the Job Centre."
"You mean the packing line jobs?"
"Er, yes." Matt actually had no idea what the jobs were that were advertised but guessed they could have been.
"They're all gone for this month, we took five new people on this morning."
"Will there be any more tomorrow?"
"No, sir. If you come back at the beginning of the month we might be taking on some operators but you'll need to be here early, before eight."
"Okay." Matt sighed and left.

The day drifted on with Matt achieving very little. It was probably time for him to return to his flat but he should try and pinch some milk on the way back, so he could eat the rest of his cereal. He rechecked his mobile phone in case Mikey had left him another message but there was nothing. Matt hoped he might be needed this evening but he knew Mikey was unreliable. He also knew that he couldn't ask Mikey if there was a job for him because that wasn't how these things worked. If Mikey wanted him he would ring and if he didn't leave a voicemail message, then Mikey had other options. Matt would keep an eye on his mobile just in case, but if Mikey didn't ring before nine then the chance had probably gone.

Matt spent most of the evening looking out of his flat window watching people down in the street below getting on with their lives whilst he waited for his to start. He looked out at the London skyline. The Shard was very prominent, as was The Gherkin. Matt thought about all the people with jobs in just those two buildings and began to feel a bit depressed. He sat back down in his armchair. Tomorrow would be a better day he thought. At least he would get paid his benefits money.

Chapter 2
Looking for a Job

Thursday morning began with a jerk as Matt banged his alarm clock with the side of his hand to make it stop. His first attempt missed but his second was spot on and the clock slid across the bedside cabinet and shut up. Matt hated Thursdays with a passion, but he was up quickly without even looking to see what the day was doing behind the heavy curtains. He moved towards the bathroom to prepare for the day. He had a sudden thought about Mikey, and turned back to check his cell just in case there had been any messages through the night, but there were none. He looked at the clock. It was 7.35. He reluctantly began his journey to the bathroom.

Matt never liked getting up early but he could if he needed to. He glanced at the clock in the sitting room as he made his way to the bathroom. It was exactly one minute later. Matt sighed at the thought of the early morning, but knew he had enough time to get up and out, especially as there was no breakfast. He would have to think about that on the way. He thought that a bacon roll would be just the thing this morning though he knew he still only had less than three pounds on him. However, he was expecting to get paid today so things would be a bit easier. Not having any money didn't normally mean that he would go completely hungry. If he had nothing to spend there were always a few places he could get some food if he had time. A burger sounded great, and it was probably a good day to buy a train ticket after yesterday's experience.

Matt left his block and took the usual route along Church Road and Oliver Road towards Coronation Gardens. He studied the buildings as he walked. Each individual building seemed to have its own character but they all just stood and allowed everything around them to continue without getting too bothered about it. It was the people that lived in the buildings that caused any problems. Arguments! Shouting! Causing problem after problem! Matt's mind wandered as he continued along his regular route.

At the second little store there was an ATM where he could check his bank account and get some cash. There were still a few commuters hurriedly making their way to work even though it was already close to eight, but nobody really paid anybody any attention. Matt was no different as he tried to act normal and keep his head down. At the cash machine he got his card out to check that the DWP had paid him his unemployment benefit money. The machine was out of order.

"Drat!" Matt banged his fist on the ATM. He let out a groan in irritated realisation of his situation as he removed his card. This was doubly annoying. He didn't know if he'd been paid, but worse than that he still only had a couple of pounds in his pocket. Matt considered where the next nearest cashpoint might be, but he couldn't think of one within a reasonable distance.

He crossed back over the street to avoid the Asian corner shop and concluded that it was not going to be as easy a morning as he had hoped. He could afford either a roll or a train ticket, and he would have to decide which was more important. He hadn't eaten since the stale cereal the previous evening. He approached the burger stand with similar pangs of hunger as yesterday.

"Hi, John," he called out as he approached.

"Matt, hi, how are you this morning?" The burger man replied, waiting for his latest customer to ask if he had any stale rolls.

"Yeah, the usual," Matt replied without really looking. He was thinking. He was sure his money would have gone in and he really wanted a bacon roll so he pulled out his cash. There was a moment's lapse as he tried to work out just how much he had before he went for it.

"How much would a bacon roll be, John?"

"That'll be one seventy-five, my man."

"And how much for a sausage roll?"

"Same price, one seventy-five. A bacon and sausage is two fifty but you can have an egg roll for one fifty." The burger man moved his price list around so that Matt could see it a bit better but he wasn't really looking at the menu, just his money. Finally, after counting the coins a couple of times he concluded he only had one seventy-two on him. Not quite enough for a bacon roll.

"Look John, I'm three pence short for a bacon roll, I'll owe you?"

"I don't do discounts, what about an egg roll?"

"I don't like eggs."

"So, have a plain roll."

The burger man had to admit he was pleased to see Matt actually with cash in his hands because he knew that if he had had any stale rolls he would probably have let him have one. Matt wasn't going for the plain buttered roll but he pondered over exactly what to do.

"Hey, what's the big deal?" said John. "Give me what money you have and you can have a bacon roll." The burger man couldn't stand watching his customer in pain any longer and held out his palm as numerous coins were emptied into it. He didn't count it but placed it straight into his little cash box. He was happy that there was nearly enough money and got on with preparing the roll.

Matt felt his stomach rumble and his mouth water in anticipation of what he was about to get. He hopped around a little bit and rubbed his hands together watching every detail of what the burger man was doing. Although there were lots of people rushing along the pavement Matt could only see his bacon roll being prepared. The burger man placed it professionally into a wax sheet and handed it to him. Matt's mouth opened and his mouth watered as he reached forward to take hold of the roll just as a commuter, in a bit of a hurry, pushed passed Matt, who was a bit off balance, and knocked the whole bacon roll out of his hands. Almost in slow motion, he was torn between catching the roll or preventing himself from falling into the road. A second or two seemed like minutes as the whole roll twisted around and finished up on the pavement mostly in one piece. The commuter continued on his way oblivious to what had happened.

"Oi! You stupid bastard!" Matt shouted angrily and with a lot of frustration at the sight of his breakfast on the floor. The commuter was oblivious to what he'd done and was one of a number of people who turned back to see what all the fuss was about. He could see Matt on his knees but was just not aware of what had happened, so immediately turned back and continued on his way.

"You absolute WANKER!" Matt shouted as the commuter disappeared into the crowd. The burger man didn't want any physical incidents happening at his stand and was rather pleased that the commuter had gone on his way. He popped out of his stand and picked up the roll from the pavement and blew on it as if to clean it somewhat before handing it back to Matt. It was pretty much still intact although the pavement showed signs of some droppings.

Still fuming and cursing under his breath Matt held the bacon roll close to him. He looked at every inch of the bread roll as the smell of the bacon became too much to resist and he took a mouthful as another customer seemed to appear out of nowhere.

"I'll take a coffee to go please," he said, in a strange sort of accent. It wasn't a British accent and it wasn't quite American but it wasn't quite anything else either. He was in his thirties by the look of him, dark haired and smartly dressed in what looked like a suit under an overcoat, but somehow not over-dressed. He paid John for the coffee and turned to Matt who was still cursing whilst eating. "Try not to get too stressed, it'll do you no good."

"Huh, who are you to tell me to cool it?" Matt was initially aggressive in his response.

"Okay, please don't get angry; I'm just trying to help." The stranger's voice was soothing and calm and there was something about his demeanour that Matt couldn't help reacting to. He very quickly found himself quite relaxed.

"If you had my life you'd be angry too." Matt turned towards John as he spoke, but was really answering the stranger's comments. "No job to speak of for ages, no girl to speak pretty to and no real home. It's a downer; a total bummer!"

John was just keeping quiet whilst he prepared the coffee in a takeaway mug but shrugged his shoulders as a way of answering Matt's comments when the other customer spoke again.

"You never know what's around that next corner, and I think the signs are good for you." The stranger smiled briefly and looked up to the sky whilst cocking his head as if to wink at Matt. "Someone up there is looking down on you. Your luck will change for the better, and probably quicker than you think." The stranger spoke like he was one of those religious doom-mongers but his tone also had a sense of truth about it. He then touched the top of his hat as if to pardon himself before leaving. He almost disappeared into thin air as he went nippily on his way down the crowded pavement. Matt's expression was quizzical as he absorbed what the stranger had said. Certain words like 'luck' and 'change' seemed to resonate louder than others, but he quickly concluded that the stranger was talking bull. Matt looked at his watch. It was already half past eight.

"I need to get going," he said to John as he went on his way still finishing off what remained of his bacon roll. He thought over the words he could still remember: "the signs look good for you," Matt repeated as he whispered them to himself. "You never know what's around the corner," he continued.

"Huh!" he said, out loud, and nodded his head. A passing woman gave him a strange look and detoured away from him, making them look like two magnets with the same poles.

Matt only went the one stop on the underground this morning, and once again without paying. He kept a close eye out for any inspectors but things were quiet and he didn't have to avoid anybody. After the tube, he had a short walk which he just got on with. Thursday mornings were normally quite busy and he still needed to check that his money had gone in, but he had time to stop at a newspaper stand, chat briefly, and sneak looks at the papers as others bought them.

"Hi, Matt," the paper seller called out as he saw him approaching. He recognised Matt as an occasional customer and knew that he would spend a few minutes passing the time of day with him talking absolute nonsense but this was the same for a number of his regulars.

"Hi, what's up then?" Matt put his hands in his pockets and stood casually next to the newspapers looking at the headlines.

"How's your search for work coming along?"

"No jobs to speak of. I go to all of the usual places but for an unskilled man like myself there's nothing." As Matt was explaining his woes to the paper salesman another customer interrupted their

31

conversation asking for a paper. This happened every twenty seconds or so and Matt tried to read bits of the papers they purchased as they were laid on the stand whilst the sale was being rung up. It wasn't easy but gradually Matt would work out various headlines and then try and read an article that took his attention. A new customer perused the papers as if he was deciding which one he would buy and counted out his coins from one hand to the other but seemed to be listening to the conversation between Matt and the paper salesman.

"Perhaps you should try down at Luger's warehouse in Temple Mills, they're often looking for people." The paper salesman passed on what advice he could.

"Luger's!" Matt exclaimed. "Bloody Luger's!" He gave the paper salesman a look of disbelief at coming up with such a suggestion. "He doesn't pay a lot of his workers and they have raids down there on a regular basis. You've got to be mad if you think I'm going to work there." "Just a thought." The paper salesman thought better of saying anything further as Matt left.

Matt looked at his watch again as he approached the bank where he had his account. Barclays Bank. His mind wandered briefly as he remembered walking into the bank in Leytonstone a number of years ago to open up his first account. He often recalled special things he'd done as a young teenager with a nice feeling inside. He tried to think back to his schooldays but it wasn't easy. He didn't like school and he didn't attend that much. In his early teens it was only when he could be bothered to go or wasn't required to deal with his mother. His very early years at school showed some promise as he was a quick learner and seemed a very nice lad, but his home life prevented him from mixing socially with the other kids and he grew up very much a loner. Matt still thought of those early days with his mother as happy days.

Yet another glance at his watch, and Matt saw that it was just past nine o'clock. Matt looked at the ATMs outside the bank but went right past them and into the building. He thought of himself as being so much more important being in the bank, rather than standing around outside with all the other plebs. He went straight to the cash machine, inserted his card and keyed in his numbers to check that his money had been paid in. He withdrew twenty pounds before making his way to his next port of call, back to the Job Centre.

He arrived on Lemna Road a little later and waited his turn to be interviewed. There only seemed to be one person doing the interviews and she was the good looking woman behind the desk. She was probably in her late thirties and very well turned out. Okay, she was probably married, he thought, but he was sure she might succumb to a bit of charm. As other customers and staff came in Matt looked to see who else was in the building. Most of them either entered through the staff office door or just checked the notice board for jobs, so Matt refocused his attentions on the woman behind the desk. There was a name card on the desk but Matt couldn't read it properly, though he was certain that her name was something like Sonja Wright, or was it Samantha, he couldn't tell exactly.

Matt watched her as she crossed and then uncrossed her legs and imagined how the two of them might be together in bed. He imagined her in stockings and suspenders as he slowly undressed her in his mind but then the picture turned ugly as he realised that the two of them were together on his grotty little bed in his flat with the wallpaper hanging down in one corner, and almost immediately the whole image disappeared. The woman had straight dark brown hair, and Matt concentrated on that for a while. It was lovely looking hair, and her glasses made her look intelligent which was very sexy. As Matt daydreamed he failed to realise that his name was being called by the woman.

"Mr Briswell."

The woman spoke without looking up, expecting everyone to be ready and waiting for their name to be called. Nobody came to the desk so she checked her paperwork to confirm that she was calling the right name.

"Mr. Briswell," she called again, as she got Matt's file out ready but still nobody came to her desk. This time Sonja looked up and identified the man she thought was Matthew Briswell and raised her voice.

"Mr. Briswell!"

Matt heard this time and almost jumped as he got up from the chair and made his way across to the desk where Sonja Wright was waiting for him. He smiled at her and gave her a sideways nod which Sonja ignored completely. She had no time for niceties with nearly seventy customers to get through today, and Matt had already wasted precious seconds so all she was interested in was asking him the questions she needed to and getting on with the next customer. Matt pulled out the chair and sat down.

"Good morning Mr. Briswell. I'm your new Personal Advisor." "That's great, and you look a real fox if you don't mind me saying," Matt started with his opening line but Sonja blanked him out.

"Okay, Mr. Briswell," Sonja pushed her glasses up her nose as she looked down at her file. "Have you managed to get yourself a job yet?" All of this was done without looking at Matt so as not to make eye contact. He felt a bit put out that his charm had not caused a reaction, and had almost missed the question he was being asked.

"Er, no." He shook his head. "No I haven't found a job as yet, but I'm hoping that today will be my lucky day..." Matt couldn't stop himself from continuing with his sentence, "...someone said it might be my lucky day today and just being able to meet you has proved them right." Matt smiled at Sonja but she was still looking at his file. His reply made her want to laugh a bit but she held it back and kept as serious as she possibly could.

"You handed in a sheet yesterday, so have you started one for yesterday and today to prove that you've been looking for work?"

"Er, yes, sort of." Matt reached inside his coat pocket for his activity sheet which showed that he had been refused an interview at the warehouse yesterday but as usual, although he had it all planned, when it came to it, he couldn't put his hand on it. Matt took out his wallet and placed that on the desk, then his identity card and put it beside his wallet. Sonja watched patiently as each item was revealed. Eventually a scrunched up piece of paper appeared and Matt handed it to Sonja. She read it. Matt watched her as she did so.

Sonja checked the date written on the list, made a brief written note in the file. "You only seem to get one job interview each week Mr. Briswell -" Sonja started before she was interrupted.

"Please, call me Matt," Matt kept on the charm offensive.

"- you need to do more, Mr. Briswell -" this last part was said more loudly to make the point, "- to try and get a job or else you'll lose your benefits." Matt turned off the charm quickly. "Surely, Mrs Wright," Matt checked Sonja's name card as he said it, "it's your job to find me a job?"

"There are plenty of jobs, Mr. Briswell." Sonja looked him in the eye and pointed to the many boards around. Matt stared into her brown eyes which he thought were really gorgeous.

"I know you must be in your late twenties, but you do look extremely hot," Matt gave it one more try. Sonja gave him a quick sly look and then looked back down at the file on the desk. There was a brief pause as she gave Matt a last look before regaining her composure.

"Go and have a look on the notice board and see if you can get two interviews this week or else we'll have to look at your unemployment benefit payment again."

Matt came to terms with the fact that he had got nowhere with Sonja but thanked her for her time and made his way to the notice boards which he quickly glanced at. There were loads of jobs on the board but all wanted experienced people or qualified people so nothing that Matt could really apply for. After looking at about ten different job cards, which were for qualified people, Matt decided that enough was enough and that it was probably time to be on his way. He thought it might just be worth calling in to Falcon mini-cabs. They would sometimes have some work for drivers and although Matt wasn't a regular driver and didn't have his own car sometimes they would have a spare car that they needed someone to drive. He thought it might be worth a look.

Matt's mobile rang. He checked the display and saw that it was from Mikey, so swiftly answered it as he moved to a quiet corner of the room. "Mikey, how's it going?" Matt asked, surprised.

"Matt, are you free this evening?" Mikey sounded a bit stressed.

"Yeah, you know me Mikey, always free." Matt thought that sounded like the type of reply Mikey would want but there was silence. "This is a bit early for you Mikey, is everything okay?"

"Don't you worry about me!" Mikey's reply was quite abrupt. Matt wasn't sure if he'd overstepped the mark with his responses, or if Mikey was just ultra-stressed. Matt waited in anticipation. "Just be at Dysans at 7.30 tonight."

"Am I doing a job tonight, then?"

"No details now but be ready to do a couple of drops."

"Right," said Matt, cautiously. He considered how to word his next question, which was how much he was going to be paid, when the phone went dead.

"Ah, right!" Matt shrugged his shoulders and put his phone back in his pocket. He looked around to see if anyone had overheard his conversation, but nobody was paying him the slightest attention. The encounter earlier with the stranger came back to him as the words 'your luck will change' repeated in his head. 'It might mean Mikey has a big job for me,' Matt said to himself as he left the building.

Matt made his way towards Falcon. He took his mobile out of his jeans pocket and placed it in his shirt pocket just in case there were any more calls. He wandered along the street glancing at a couple walking towards him who were obviously tourists. They both held steaming cartons of drink as they walked along and Matt thought he would also treat himself to a coffee. He felt in his pockets to see what change he had but he had nothing. No problem, he thought, I withdrew some folding money. He felt for his wallet but couldn't easily locate it. He wondered for a brief moment if he had actually brought it with him, then remembered visiting the bank. Not only that, he vividly recalled putting the twenty pounds in it.

He cursed at himself for losing his wallet, and thought back over what he had done, when it came back to him. He had taken out his wallet whilst he was sitting with Sonja. Perhaps that was where he had left it. Matt quickly made his way back to the Job Centre.

He hadn't gone that far, so within ten minutes he was back. When he went in, he spotted Sonja Wright sitting at her desk talking with another client. There were probably others waiting to see her but as soon as this customer had finished he would go and speak to her. Ten minutes later, she was free.

"Sorry Mr. Willington, I'm not quite ready for you." Sonja said, not looking up, assuming that it was her next customer.

"Eh, man, I'm not Mr. Willi…whatever it was," Matt spluttered a reply. Sonja looked up and recognised Matt immediately.

"Oh, it's you." Her reply sounded somewhat disappointed at first but then she realised what Matt was there for. "You left your wallet behind, Mr. Briswell."

"You've got it?" Matt was happy to hear her talking about the wallet. "I knew you would have it."

"It's in the office. They have your name so just go and ask." Sonja spoke as if this sort of thing happened every day. "Oh yes, one other thing." Matt wondered what else Sonja might have to say. "I think I have a job for you. It only came in this morning but in my opinion it would be just right for you. Ask for Tom Grainger at the office, tell him I've sent you and ask him about the courier job. He'll give you the details," Sonja said, while continuing to look through her next customer file, and not once looking up at Matt.

"You've sorted out a job just for me?" Matt stuck his head forward, disbelieving. "A job! For me!" His voice went high as he spoke.

"Don't think I don't care about my clients."
"Hey, thank you." Matt touched Sonja's hand and she looked up immediately.

"Don't waste the opportunity," she replied as she pulled her hand away from under Matt's, giving him a stern look as she did so. "You won't get another one this easily so make the most of it." Sonja got straight back to sorting out the papers in her file for her next client.

Matt made his way to the office and asked for Tom who gave him his wallet back. Matt stood for a few seconds checking that all the money was still in it. Tom said nothing and Matt wondered what he should do next.

"I was told to come and ask about the courier job." Matt hoped he had heard Sonja correctly as Tom seemed oblivious to the situation.

"Oh, you're the guy!" The penny suddenly dropped and Tom turned briefly to grab some papers and a job card, then explained what the job was. It involved delivering packages for FedEx who needed a new delivery man. Matt picked up the job card and looked at the details. Although the initial work would be on foot, carrying small packages and some letters, there was opportunity to progress to a driving position in time. The company would pay for driving lessons if necessary. Matt was allowed to take the card and told to call in as soon as he could to arrange for an interview.

"Sonja seemed to think this job would be right for you," Tom said, as Matt turned to leave. Tom seemed to half expect some sort of reply but Matt said nothing. He wanted to thank Sonja personally but she was still busy with yet another customer. Matt waited in case he could catch her eye but decided it was unlikely so went on his way.

Tom stood in the office doorway watching Matt leave. He turned back into the office where his colleague Susan stood at a filing cabinet.
"I've just given that FedEx job to some arrogant jerk that Sonja thought should have it."
"Oh, good!" Susan replied, only half listening to Tom.
"Why did she think he was the right bloke for the job?"
"Er, who?" Susan gave herself away as not having

listened to what Tom had said previously, but Tom wasn't worried.

"That guy Briswell; why did Sonja think he should get the FedEx job?"

"Don't know," Susan shrugged. "She just thought he was right for it, I suppose."

Matt made his way to the FedEx offices on Orient Way. There wasn't much to see. A very basic sign on a colourful warehouse with the shutters down and a door that presumably led to some upstairs offices. Matt made his way in and found a small counter with a bell on it which he rang. A rather stressed and dishevelled old man came to the counter.

"You're at FedEx, do you have a receipt card sir?" The man stood there with his hand out waiting.

"Er, no..." Matt wasn't quite sure what he was supposed to say.

"Can I have your house number and post-code then please, sir?" The man was polite but obviously in a hurry. Matt gave his address and the man disappeared through a door on the far side of the office. It was nearly ten minutes before he returned. "I can't find any package for that address, when did the card go through your door?"

"Card through my door?" Matt still wasn't sure what was going on. "I've come about a job interview."

"Oh, the job!" The man scrunched up the piece of paper with Matt's address on and threw it into a bin. "The job!" the man repeated. "Can you come back in about an hour?"

"Yes I suppose so, I haven't much else to do."
"Good. We'll see you then." The old man looked over towards the corner where he had thrown Matt's details but there was a pile of scrunched up pieces of paper both in and around the bin. "What's the name again?" The old man tore off another sheet of paper and took Matt's details.

Matt returned an hour later and found himself being interviewed by a rather more smartly dressed man. The interview only lasted about fifteen minutes, but he was offered the job and told to report at the office on Monday morning at seven. Matt had got a job again. He was quite pleased with himself but also remembered he needed to thank Sonja when he could. He thought back to events earlier this morning and concluded that perhaps today *was* the day that his life might change.

As the staff back at Job Centre were packing up and getting ready to go home, Sonja collected her case files and returned them to the main office. Susan had Matt's file which she handed to Sonja.
"Oh thanks, Susan, is the letter from FedEx in the file?"
"Yes, Tom put it in there. He was asking why you picked this guy out for that interview."
"Was he now?" Sonja exclaimed, unsure whether she was more annoyed that Tom should question her decisions, or that he had discussed it with Susan. "It's none of his business really."

"No, I know that, but that's what he said."

Sonja thought for a few seconds. "Actually, he's quite cute in an unsophisticated sort of way." Susan nodded in agreement. "He's got no money, no prospects and I just felt a bit sorry for him. Don't ask me why. Something just made me think that he needed a bit of help."

Chapter 3
A Meeting in a Bar

It was still hard for Matt to take in that he had a job. As he made his way back to his flat he realised his walk had turned into a sort of skip and that he was sticking his chest out. "A job!" he said, proudly, to nobody in particular. "I'm a courier with a job!" He almost laughed as he said it. He continued on his way, walking with a real swagger. Nothing could upset him at the moment, he had a job.

Matt considered knocking on the door of one of the other residents in the block just to tell them his good news. There was a woman who always wanted to know everybody's business but Matt wasn't sure he really wanted to tell her because if he did everyone else would know before he had even got upstairs. Who could he tell?

There was always Nancy, he thought, but he wasn't quite sure where she worked nowadays. He also recalled that the last time he called her number it was unavailable, so perhaps she had changed it. Matt wondered if she might have lost her mobile phone. Even if he could contact her it was unlikely that she would want to chat to him now. True, she would say 'hi' if he saw her about town, which wasn't that often, but she never stopped and spoke to him anymore. There was of course Jed who ran the White Hart, a pub that Matt often frequented and considered as his local. Jed was a decent sort of chap and seemed the best bet so it would be the White Hart, in order to tell someone about his new job. He didn't want to go there during the day, so he started to plan the rest of the day.

He was already due to meet up with Mikey and Mop who had some jobs for him. They were bound to be reasonably simple jobs for which Matt would earn a few quid, but he had mentioned a couple of drops, so there might be a bit more cash coming his way. He knew it would probably be dodgy work, but he always had the thought in the back of his mind that if he ever got caught he could just plead ignorance and get away with it.

Mikey had told him to be in Dysans on High Road in Leytonstone at seven thirty. This was Mikey's current sort of headquarters. It was a bar-cum-club run by a couple of Turks but Mikey often laid down his job instructions here to whoever was running for him. Matt wasn't over keen on the place as it was also where married men would meet girls, many of them on the game, and the atmosphere wasn't to his liking but it was where Mikey ran his operation from. The extra cash would come in handy. He hadn't done much for Mikey recently and he was feeling it in his pocket.

Matt thought that if he could earn through his new job, then he could probably start refusing these little jobs. He was also a bit irritated that whenever he met up with Mikey or Mop they would try to sell him some gear. He just wasn't interested in drugs these days. He had worked hard to get clean and that was how he was going to stay. Matt was a little annoyed that he'd allowed Mikey to supply him with some blow a few months back when he was at a real low. He was proud though that he hadn't drifted since then. He'd seen what drugs had done to his mother and always kept an impression of her at her worst in his mind which seemed to do the trick. He also knew from experience that many others in his position had gone on to harder drugs and he'd seen what it did to them. Fortunately, he managed to just keep one step away from addiction. Anyway, he thought, Mikey knew he never had enough money to buy anything much, so he probably wouldn't push him too hard.

Matt thought about what he would tell Jed about his new job, not that he knew that much at the moment. It occurred to him that he owed Jed over twenty pounds for an unpaid bar bill. "Damn!" he said, looking at what money he had. He probably could pay off the bar bill but then he'd have nothing left. The trip to the White Hart was cancelled. His thoughts switched to how he could thank Sonja for getting him this job. He could take her out for a meal and a drink, then realised he probably wouldn't have quite enough money for that. "Just a drink, then," he said to himself, before concluding that she was probably married and that she would never go for a drink with him anyway. She was well out of his league and he knew it. Perhaps I'll just get her some flowers. It seemed a bit of a poor effort, but it would have to do unless he could think of something better.

He returned home to the flats and pressed the button to call the lift but it seemed to be out of order. Matt waited for a couple of minutes and pressed the button another couple of times but it definitely suggested that the lift was not working. Matt started to climb the stairs. He saw another bloke making his way down the stairs. It wasn't anyone that Matt had seen before. As they came within view of each other they both kept their heads down so as not to make eye contact and passed on a landing without a word. It wasn't appreciated to talk to the neighbours and everyone kept themselves to themselves. Matt could hear the usual babies crying, and shouting from anguished mothers and tired fathers, as he made his way up to the fourth floor. There was also the occasional smell of dinners being cooked which made him feel a bit hungry. The whole scene reminded him a bit of his early childhood and made him smile inside.

Once inside his flat Matt sat down on his bed and looked around at the few possessions in his room. There was a small wardrobe unit in one corner with his clothes in it, not that he had many, but it contained a few t-shirts and a couple of pairs of Levis, and he had a decent shirt and tie just in case he needed it. He wondered what to wear for his new job. As he briefly picked up each piece of clothing he considered whether it would be okay for work. He thought about what other couriers usually wore. He was convinced that he would get some sort of uniform with the FedEx logo on it. He would definitely go and show Sonja how smart he looked, hoping that she might just go for a man in uniform. He knew it was frivolous thinking that he could ever impress her properly.

In the living room Matt turned on his small television, and tuned into the news channel. He tried to catch up with how his beloved Manchester United were doing. Having been a fan right back from his schooldays he was always keen to hear if his team were doing as well as they used to but they rarely seemed to be favourites for any titles recently and this year was no different. Matt had always wanted to go and see them in the flesh but it had never happened. He imagined going to watch them at Old Trafford. Matt did a few pretend kicks before nipping through to his bedroom to look at his poster of Wayne Rooney on his wall. He thought about when he and some mates went to Wembley stadium when Manchester United were playing in a cup final, just to see what the atmosphere was like.

Matt dreamed of the day he might be able to buy a ticket to actually get in and watch a big game. He knew it was very much out of his reach but the thought of it happening one day never left him.

Very soon he had daydreamed away an hour or so. Looking at the clock by the side of his bed, he saw it was nearly 5.30. Matt sat up on his bed and stretched. "I suppose I'd better think about what I'm going to eat," he said out loud, talking to himself. He looked in the kitchen cupboard where there was a tin of soup he had taken from the corner deli, and a tin of peaches which for some reason he had actually bought, but not much else. He looked in the fridge which contained a used carton of old milk and some butter. He checked the remaining two slices of bread, which had now turned more of a blue colour. He threw them in the bin and concluded that soup was the only thing on the menu. 'I must get some food in,' he thought to himself, as he prepared and ate his soup.

After dinner, Matt thought about what he was going to wear, not that he had a great choice. Even if he did choose the shirt it was unlikely to be clean. He needed to save up some change and get to the laundrette as he was beginning to wear some things for the third or fourth time. It depressed him a little. He knew that the bar he was meeting Mikey in was a reasonably smart one, so he checked how clean his best pair of jeans were before finding the smartest pair of shoes he had. None seemed really appropriate. He found a decent button-up shirt and smelt under the arms to see if it was clean. It smelled acceptable, and he checked that he had deodorant and aftershave he could use to cover up any lingering odour. Matt looked at his watch. It was just about six, and although he wasn't due to meet Mikey until 7.30 there wasn't much time before he needed to change. He hung his shirt near an open window where he could leave it for fifteen minutes or so in some effort to give it an airing.

By 7.15, Matt was in sight of Dysans. He didn't want to go straight in, walk up to the bar and order a drink, as he didn't have enough money to do that for the whole evening, so he just pushed the door open slightly to see if Mikey was there. The place was pretty empty and with a quick glance he was able to identify a group of office workers at the far end of the bar, a middle-aged bloke at the nearest end of the bar watching the television screen and a couple in a booth who were obviously finding it hard to keep their hands off each other. Another woman, suited like an office worker, emerged from the washroom and joined the other workers at the bar as Matt turned away. It was clear that Mikey wasn't there yet. As he turned around, a young woman making her way in blocked his exit.

"Excuse me," Matt said, as he gave her one of his best smiles, and stepped aside to allow her through the door. He paused and considered what he could say to her, but in the end just smiled at her as he backed off further to allow her through. The good looking woman smiled back briefly and made her way into the bar. "Thanks," she said, as she passed Matt and entered the bar.

Matt looked her up and down as she went in and looked around the bar. It was obvious she was also looking for someone, and he guessed she was here to meet the middle-aged bloke, but she looked in that direction with no reaction at all. Matt continued to watch her as she walked up to the bar and moved a stool out of the way as the barman came to serve her. Matt gave her legs one last look as he finally left.

Across the road were some old Victorian terraced houses in front of which a group of youths were standing, generally doing nothing. He thought he would keep an eye on them as he wandered up the street from Dysans. He hadn't got more than about twenty yards from the door and was still considering how to waste some time when he spotted the courting couple leaving from the door to the bar. This could be an opportunity, he thought.

Matt went back into the bar checking that everyone was still where he had seen them last. The young woman had moved from the bar, although he couldn't see to where. The middle-aged bloke was still in the same place, as were the office workers, and Matt clocked that the couple's booth was still empty as he made his way over to it. He had noticed that the bloke had been drinking from a bottle which seemed quite full, and as he had guessed, the bottle was still half full on the table. Matt picked it up and casually wiping the rim, held it as if he had been drinking it for the last half hour. He checked out the rest of the tables. The woman had obviously been drinking white wine. There was some left in her glass which Matt downed in one to quench his thirst pulling a pained expression as he did so. He didn't really like wine but it felt good to get some alcohol down his neck.

Bottle in hand, he looked around for a fruit machine and noticed that there was a small glass still almost full at a place on the bar. Matt guessed it was the young woman's drink and he made his way over and stood right next to it. The barman came over almost immediately and gave Matt a strange look as he saw him holding the half-finished bottle of beer.

"Can I get you another drink?" The barman nodded his head in the direction of the bottle of lager. "No, chief, I'm just waiting for someone," Matt said, in a way that suggested he was with the young woman, but in fact he meant "Fuck off and leave me alone". The barman obliged.

A couple of minutes later the young woman returned. Matt wasn't sure where she'd come from as she hadn't returned from the direction of the toilets, but regardless of that, she sat back on her stool near where Matt was standing and turned away from him slightly.

"Fancy meeting you again," said Matt, casually, but the young woman didn't react.

"Hey, do you know if they have any live music in this place at all?" Matt spoke a little louder to try and catch the young woman's attention. She turned towards him.

"Are you asking me?"

"Yes sorry, I just wondered if the place livens up at all later."

"Oh, right, yes, they usually have some sort of music after eight I think."

"Oh, so you're a regular in here then?" Matt turned his head to one side as he spoke to try and make the comment a funny, rather than an accusing, one.

"No, not a regular." The woman laughed briefly as she turned away from Matt again. This didn't put him off and he continued chatting.

"I always like a bit of music when I'm in a bar, I hope they have someone playing some soft rock." Matt hoped this would be the sort of music the young woman liked, but she didn't reply. There was a brief pause, and Matt decided to go for it.

"So, are you meeting up with the girls tonight?" Matt put on his poshest voice. "You know, for a proper girls' night out." Matt was confident she wasn't from the way she was dressed.

"No, I'm meeting my boyfriend, he'll be here soon." She turned to face him as she replied. "Are you here to meet your girlfriend?"

The question took Matt a bit by surprise.

"No, I don't have a girlfriend, and certainly never had one as good looking as you."

"Oh!" The woman screwed up her nose and mouth by way of reply to show that Matt's reply was a bit naff. "That's a shame."

Matt went over in his head what he had just said and felt a bit stupid. He hadn't made sense let alone sound cool, but he'd said it and that was that. The woman turned away from Matt again and took out her mobile to check for messages.

Matt turned and leaned back against the bar. He looked around the room as the young woman got up, picked up her drink, and made her way to a booth. Matt took this to indicate that her boyfriend's arrival was imminent and she didn't want to be seen chatting to a strange bloke at the bar when he arrived. He watched her as she sat down on the bench and looked again at her body. She had great legs, he thought.

The barman came over to Matt again as he drank from his liberated bottle of lager. "Are you actually going to buy a drink?" The tone of his voice said that he was annoyed, but it wasn't rude. Matt felt he ought to oblige.

"Yes, another lager," Matt replied. The barman duly opened up a bottle and placed it on the bar.

"And another gin?" The barman continued.

"Er, what?" Matt hadn't quite caught what the

barman had said but he could think on his feet. "Is that what Molly was drinking? Another expensive night for me then." He nodded in confirmation that he wanted another gin. The barman brought it to the bar.

"Has Molly started a tab?" asked Matt. It wasn't in too many places that bars would open a tab for you without first seeing you had the ability to pay but Dysans was trying to be a little bit more up market. "No, do you want me to start one for you?"
"Yes, that'll be good." Matt drained the first bottle, grabbed the new one and the gin, and walked over towards the young woman.

She saw him approaching and fidgeted around at the thought of having to ward off Matt's chat again. Matt knew she was uncomfortable and looked at her with his saddest face.

"Hey, look, I'm not one of those nutters you read about in the papers, and if you tell me to go I will, but I'm sorry if I annoyed you at the bar. As an apology I've bought you a drink. No strings, and as soon as your boyfriend arrives I'll clear off and you can tell him," Matt paused briefly to try and think of a perfect line, "that I'm one of those nutters." The woman sort of laughed and then took a deep breath as she smiled at Matt's comments.
"I don't usually take drinks off strangers, but thanks."

She lifted the glass she already had on the table.
"Cheers, here's to meeting the ones we love." She tried to think of what to say next. "And I hope you find a girlfriend soon."
Matt lifted his bottle.
"I'll drink to that."

He stood and chatted to her for a few minutes, then his phone rang. It was Mikey, and Matt didn't want to talk with an audience, so he made his excuses and walked away to answer his phone.
"Hey, Mikey!" Matt was never quite sure how to speak to Mikey, but didn't have to worry as Mikey was doing all the talking this evening.
"Don't worry about meeting this evening, Mop has found someone else to do the jobs, so you can take it easy instead. I'll be in touch if I need you again."
Matt didn't get a chance to say anything else as Mikey disconnected. He had only just got outside the bar when the call was over. Matt sighed. Then he cursed to himself.
"Shit, man!"

He looked at his mobile as he shook his head slowly, then glanced over to where the youths had congregated. They were looking back at him. Matt bit his bottom lip and clenched his fists in anger. All in all, this evening was looking like a washout, but then he thought about getting a new job and was pleased that Mikey wasn't putting work his way. It would be good to turn a new leaf. Matt walked back into Dysans, his thoughts turning to the luscious Sonja and he considered how she helped him get his new job. Things didn't look too bad again.

Matt made his way back over to the young woman who was still sat at the table composing a text on her mobile. She looked up to see who it was and wasn't surprised it was Matt. In fact, there was even a certain relief that it was him.

"What a bummer, eh!" Matt said as he sat down.

The young woman continued texting as she pressed the keys ever harder and then pressed the send button.

"What's your problem?" She asked him, noting that Matt wasn't completely happy.

"My mates have just called off."

"That's a shame." She sounded sympathetic. "I thought it was your girlfriend."

"No, I said I haven't got a girlfriend, remember?" Matt glanced over towards the bar where he had said it.

"Oh yes, you did," she replied. Her mobile buzzed, indicating a text message. She opened it and read it briefly, then clenched her fist and looked angry.

"Bastard!" she exclaimed.

Matt was surprised at her language. "You've got a problem too?"

"Yes, I've just been dumped." she told Matt. She wiped away a tear. "No need to worry about that bastard now," she said, sounding a bit more positive.

"He's just dumped you by text?" Matt tried to stop himself from asking the question but it was too late, he had said it. Immediately he put his hands up in apology indicating that the young woman didn't have to answer it. Zoe downed her gin and tonic then looked at him with wet eyes.

"Hi, I'm Zoe," she held out her hand as she spoke. He shook her hand.
"And I'm Matt." He looked around and noticed that the barman was out of sight. "Let's get out of this place and go somewhere else." He took Zoe's hand and almost pulled her out of her seat. They left the bar and he led her down rapidly the High Street into a crowd so anyone who might consider chasing after them wouldn't be able to see which way they had gone.

"Can I walk you back somewhere?" Matt thought he would try his luck.
"Maybe," she replied. Then had a thought. "Or we could go for a drink somewhere else."
"Okay, to another pub. Let's get happy."

Matt knew that there were a couple of pubs nearby but he needed to get out of the area in case anyone from Dysans was out looking for him.
"Let's find a decent bar and I'll buy you another drink to cheer you up."
"No, you're not to buy me another drink before I buy you one in return." Zoe was insistent. "Christ, you

might yet turn out to be one of those nutters!" She laughed and put her arm through Matt's as they set off down an alleyway.

They found a pub where they had a couple of drinks, then stopped at a fast food place for a burger. They seemed to do a lot of walking and talking through parks and along streets. Zoe appeared to know where she was going and Matt was happy to walk wherever. He occasionally tried to put his arm around Zoe's shoulders but just in case she wasn't happy with that, he never left it long. Walking through a park, Matt took her hand to help her climb over a bench. They held hands quite naturally and seemed to be getting on very well.

Matt talked about his current life in a very general manner, then told Zoe about his new job. He didn't explain who Mikey and Mop were in any sort of detail but told Zoe that they were two old school friends. She in turn told him quite a bit about herself. As their conversation paused naturally here and there, it seemed obvious that they both wanted to kiss but Matt worked hard at being a perfect gentleman and didn't push it at all. They had been walking a couple of hours when they stopped outside a lot of flats just two or three stories high.

"This is where I live," she explained, looking up to the top floor.
"Wow, this looks a nice place," Matt said as he

noticed that there was an automatic gated entrance. "This is proper posh, ain't it?" Matt forgot he was trying to sound more refined as he said it.

"No, not really," Zoe replied as she looked for her key card in her handbag.

"You see, you even have a posh key."

"It's just a key." Zoe wondered what sort of place Matt lived in, as she thought of her flat as being very basic and perhaps a bit cheap and nasty.

"Do you want to come up?" she asked, warily. Matt looked at her, and moved in for a first kiss. Their tongues touched briefly which encouraged him, but then Zoe retreated and he remembered his manners.

"I would love to come up but I'm not sure that's the right thing to do." Matt was hoping that Zoe would tell him he was being a jerk.

"Ah, Matt, that's so romantic." She kissed him again quickly. "So how about we meet again tomorrow evening for a proper first date?" She was excited about having met such a nice bloke. He was disappointed to hear that she agreed with his idea and her suggestion that they continued their relationship another day.

"That's great. We'll meet tomorrow evening." Matt resigned himself to the fact that he wasn't going to get to see Zoe's bed this evening but he felt she was worth waiting for. They swapped telephone numbers and agreed a time and a place for tomorrow evening.

I've Got Your Number

After a last kiss, which was a bit longer than the previous one, Zoe smiled at him and gave a little wave as she left him at the door.

Matt's heart was pounding. "Wow!" he said out loud, feeling as if he could walk on water. Zoe was so nice, he was sure she could be the one for him. He looked up at the windows in the flats hoping to identify hers, waiting to see a light go on. None did. He stared for ages until he realised that there were more windows around the other side and that she probably lived in one of those. He walked around trying to see her but he couldn't. He imagined what she would be doing in her flat and what she looked like naked. He couldn't wait to see her again tomorrow.

Matt thought back to everything that had happened to him today. A new job, and a new girl. It was all a bit much for him to take in. He then remembered the stranger at the newspaper stand, and how he had said that Matt's life would be changing. "Perhaps the man was right," he thought. Things were going right for him for once. He stood for nearly an hour and a half looking up to where he imagined Zoe might be, just in case he could catch a glimpse of her. He considered trying to knock on her door but realised not only that he didn't know what number she lived at but that he wouldn't be able to get into the building that easily anyway. He was also a bit drunk, he supposed, but didn't care, things were looking good for him. He would see her again tomorrow evening when they could carry on where they left off.

Matt noticed a clock over a shop building and saw that it was nearly three in the morning. "Perhaps I'd better get home," he said quietly to himself, still with Zoe on his mind. He even started singing as he turned and made his way in the general direction of his own flat. The rest of the world was totally oblivious to him and in particular the driver of the speeding car approaching him as he meandered across the road. A desperate late attempt at braking wasn't enough to stop the vehicle from hitting Matt, sending him spinning to the kerb. The shaken driver got out and saw blood flowing from Matt's head. He shook him gently, but there was no sign of life. Then, the driver looked around, decided that nobody had seen the accident, got back in his car and sped away from the scene.

In fact, a shadowy figure stood in an alcove of the adjacent Methodist Church had seen the accident. A man, dark haired and wearing a thick dark overcoat, walked calmly towards where Matt lay, as the sound of screeching tyres receded in the background. Before he reached Matt's body, he saw a passing couple turn the corner. They had also seen the body lying in the road after hearing the screeching tyres as the car disappeared. They ran over to Matt and prodded him to see if there were signs of life, and called 999. They hadn't seen the accident, but they told the emergency services that they guessed he had been knocked over by a car.

The man retreated back to the church, where he watched and waited for the outcome, but he was fairly sure that Matt wouldn't recover from his injuries. He slowly walked up and down muttering quietly to himself. "This wasn't supposed to happen," he said, and "the Forces won't like this." Every now and then he glanced over towards Matt while the paramedics did their work. As Matt was stretchered and placed gently in the back of an ambulance, the man knew he had just a little time to find a new plan.

Matt was taken to a nearby hospital, unconscious. The doctors and nurses worked hastily to try and stabilise him. Things didn't look good, and most of the experienced staff knew that Matt was unlikely to survive his injuries. It was probably just a matter of time.

Chapter 4
Waiting for Matt

Zoe awoke in the dark, turned over and looked at the clock on her bedside table. It was 03:20 according to the bright digital display. She turned back and tucked herself under the comforter in an effort to try and get back to sleep but Matt was everywhere in her head. After a sleepless half hour or so, Zoe looked at the clock again but sleep was seemingly avoiding her tonight. It was just after 4am as she sat up and surveyed her bedroom. She smiled briefly to herself as the thoughts of last night's events went over and over in her mind. She just couldn't believe her luck at being chatted up by such a nice bloke as Matt. Zoe smiled again as she realised that she had enjoyed last night so much. She felt good. It wasn't as if they had done very much but she just knew immediately that Matt was possibly going to be the one. Suddenly the thoughts of the disappointment of the earlier part of the evening came back to mind.

"Wow!" she thought to herself as she remembered just how angry and annoyed she had been, and amazed at how Matt had managed to wipe that totally from her mind. "I'll have to tell Ruth just what a poor choice she made," Zoe said to herself, "I never thought going out with a friend of a friend was a brilliant idea," she continued, and was actually happy that her date had let her down. Matt was much more her type anyway. He was simply gorgeous.

I've Got Your Number

The sound of police sirens and screeching cars outside the flats was quite normal, and often a hindrance to sleep, but tonight it seemed even more so. She looked at her clock for a third time. It was now 4.30 and she was no nearer to getting to sleep. There was still a lot of noise coming up from the street. Car doors slamming shut, people walking about. There was also a reflection of some blue lights, suggesting emergency vehicles. It was likely to have been another gang fight or mugging down some dark alley, she thought.

She looked at her clock yet again, almost five. She had been awake for nearly two hours and wasn't used to being up at this time of the morning. She then thought of the busy day ahead, so she snuggled down deep in her bed trying to ignore the noise outside, and hoping to get some sleep before she needed to get up.

The alarm went off at six thirty and Zoe reached out an arm and turned it off. She rubbed her eyes a bit and was surprised at how quickly it had woken her. She stretched and yawned as she sat up in bed but was really quite awake for this time of the morning. She guessed that the late evening would catch up with her during the day. She got washed and had her usual light breakfast, and by seven thirty was leaving her flat for work. There were just a couple of flights of stairs to walk down to get to the lobby but as she walked down the final flight she could hear some people talking ahead of her. There were a couple of residents still chatting as she approached them.

"Yes, another hit and run, honey," said a woman in a green coat.

"Did the police get anyone?" Another woman replied. She was checking her post, the flap of her post box open with keys hanging from it.

"No," replied Green Coat, "I don't think so."

Zoe overheard the end of the conversation as she approached the two women and they both turned towards her, stopping their conversation but nodding in a neighbourly way.

"Have you heard that we had another accident last night?" Mail Woman asked Zoe. Zoe recognised her as living in Flat 8, to whom she had spoken a few times previously. Zoe also knew that she would always be one of the first in the building to pass on any gossip.

"No, what happened?"

"Some airhead kid no doubt, a hit and run, honey," Green Coat advised her. "Someone knocked down right outside the front here," she added, a screech of excitement in her voice. Zoe briefly thought of Matt. She thought of him possibly witnessing the accident. Her thoughts then suddenly turned to concern that Matt might have been involved in the accident.

"What time was this?"

"About three or four in the morning, we think," the woman from Flat 8 replied. Zoe sighed and her nerves calmed on hearing this was nearly three hours after she returned.

"It's a shame. I'm sure the law will catch them." Zoe carried on, leaving the apartments, and making her way to work.

Zoe found that time dragged during the day. She couldn't wait to finish work and get back home to start getting ready to meet Matt again. She wanted to tell Ruth all about him, but Ruth wasn't at work today which was frustrating. Zoe thought Ruth would probably want to know all about the date that she had set up, and Zoe was itching to boast that she had managed to get a date without any help from her friend. She thought about ringing Ruth to tell her about Matt, but remembered that she was out for the day, so she would just have to wait. She clenched her fists impatiently, but then smiled from ear to ear at the thought of meeting Matt again this evening.

She imagined the two of them walking hand in hand along a beach, and then him cuddling her from behind, keeping her safe. Her mind took her to another time and place and the smile on her face grew so wide that even she noticed it as she saw her reflection in the computer screen. Had anybody noticed that her mind had wandered? She looked around at the others, but they were all busy and nobody had realised where Zoe had been.

Eventually it was time to leave work and get on home. Zoe almost ran out of the office and made her way through the crowds of commuters back home. She was conscious that she was almost skipping as she made her way along the pavement. She felt like a teenager again. As Zoe got back to her flat she threw her work clothes off and made her way to the bathroom. She took time to shower and then pick each piece of clothing she was going to wear for her date. Her heart beat faster as she put each piece of clothing up to her body to see what she would look like in the mirror. She didn't want to come across as too keen or desperate but then she wanted to create a good impression and let Matt know just how much she liked him.

Zoe thought about where they had agreed to meet up this evening. It was a pub called the King George near to Ilford. It wasn't a pub that she knew but she would be able to find it easily. "How hard could it be to find a pub?" she asked herself, and laughed out loud. She didn't know why Matt had suggested this place, but it was obviously somewhere he had been before and not too far from where she lived, so she was quite happy to follow his lead. Zoe checked the clock, 6.05. They'd agreed to meet at 7.45, and she didn't want to be late, but she also knew that she couldn't get there too early or else she might be sitting around on her own like the previous evening.

That would never do she thought, as she imagined Matt walking towards her, greeting her as she entered the bar. She hoped that would be how the evening would start.

As she tried various different items of clothing on and stood at different angles in front of the mirror to find the right look, she glanced again at the clock on the table. It was half past six and she had calculated that it would only take about ten or fifteen minutes to get to the pub, so she still had an hour to kill.

A few more costume changes took place before Zoe settled on exactly what to wear. With the important decisions made she put on some of her favourite music and bopped happily around her bedroom and bathroom whilst getting ready and anticipating the evening to come. It was always a difficult choice to decide what look she needed for such an occasion but she ended up in her favourite skirt and a newish top.

She sprayed a little more perfume behind her ears before setting off for the evening. Without thinking, Zoe found herself almost running to the pub and the walk from the station actually took no more than eight minutes. She was there just after half past seven and annoyingly early. The King George was easy to find with a big sign outside. She looked at her watch in case she had misread the time but no, it was not even 7.35 yet.

She stood for a few moments outside the front entrance to the bar but felt that this wasn't the best thing to do so she wondered if she should go in. She took a few moments to rehearse what she would do and say and then spent another few moments wondering how she would cope if she found herself on her own again, but she was confident that Matt would be in there. She briefly considered waiting outside a bit longer, but then she thought Matt might be early and already in there himself, so why not just go in.

As she stepped into the bar she was a bit surprised to find that there were quite a few people inside. It seemed very quiet from the outside but there must have been nearly twenty people inside drinking. Nobody appeared to see her entering or even take any notice of her as she moved further into the bar so she looked around to see if she could spot Matt but he wasn't making himself obvious.

She could see there was space at the bar, but it wasn't as easy to see if there were any empty tables she could go and sit at, as suddenly the reality kicked in again that in fact she was on her own again, like last night. Unlike last night though, she had almost expected Matt to be there to greet her when she arrived, so hadn't prepared herself for having to wait a while but it wasn't a problem. She bought a glass of wine and looked for a vacant table that was near enough to the door. There were none free so she remained sat at the bar as far away from the rest as she could, but still within sight of the entrance. She glanced at her watch again and it was twenty to eight so she knew she wouldn't have to wait long. To pass the time she looked to see what sort of people were in the bar. Most were either in work groups or couples so she felt happy that there would be no unwanted guys harassing her tonight like Matt had the previous evening.

Fifteen minutes passed and Zoe looked at her watch again to see that the time was now five to eight. Her glass was half empty and she knew she needed to slow down a bit as she didn't want to be seen buying more than one drink on her own. She got out her phone and checked in case there was a text from Matt to tell her he was running late or something. Matt had given Zoe his mobile number which had in some peculiar way made her feel happier that he was genuine. It was almost a guarantee that he would be coming.

The clock on the back wall showed that it was now five past eight, and for the first time Zoe began to think that Matt might stand her up. This possibility had not even entered her mind before now as she was convinced that both of them just wanted to carry on from last night. She went over the events of the previous evening trying to analyse whether she might have come on to him too strongly but dismissed that idea. She then worried that perhaps she had not given him the right signals, making him think she didn't like him. She dismissed that idea too. As she looked at herself in the bar mirror she thought that any sensible bloke would know instantly that she had been attracted to him. Perhaps he was just another absolute bastard, or maybe it was she who had the problem. The barman looked questioningly in her direction, but she turned away to indicate a negative answer. Zoe looked at the wine glass and twisted it around between her finger and thumb. "Bloody men!" she thought.

At a quarter past eight Zoe decided that Matt had had it. She made her way to the toilets and rang his mobile number preparing to give him a real earful but it went to a recorded message which threw her slightly. She paused before she left her message.

"Where the hell are you?" Her breathing became short and fast as she spoke, before she tried to calm down and control her anger. "It's now a quarter past eight and you've not turned up, ring me as soon as you get this message." A tear ran down her cheek. She sniffed and then wiped it away with the back of her hand. She needed to compose herself. She controlled herself, and took some deep breaths. The whole episode lasted for just a few moments before she tidied herself, checked her make-up and decided she would make her way back home.

Zoe could feel the tears wanting to begin but she fought against them. She leant on the sink and stared aimlessly into it. Her eyes were watering but she was determined not to give in.

"Christ!" she shouted "that's two dates that have dumped me in two days." Then her resolve kicked in and she thought a bit more about her current situation. Matt hadn't dumped her; he just hadn't shown up. There could be all manner of reasons why he wasn't here. She looked at the address on the piece of paper that he had given her the previous evening with his address and phone details on it. She read the address out loud "Flat 37, Bolan House, Riverley Close, Leyton," just as another woman entered the toilets. She gave Zoe a quick glance before disappearing into a cubicle.

Zoe decided she would go and call at his door to see if he had any sort of excuse for not showing up. Without much more thought, she worked out which station would be nearest to his flat, and made her way to the address he had given her the previous evening.

It was a bit of a walk to Matt's street from the tube but Zoe found the address relatively easily and looked for the entrance. Flat 37 was clearly marked but there was no buzzer at the entrance. It was easy to gain access to the flats as there was a trade button that opened the door, but Zoe wasn't sure whether to go in or not. She hung around for ten minutes or so in the hope that Matt, or indeed anybody, might appear at the door but nobody did. Zoe rang Matt's mobile number again and once more it went to voicemail. Zoe left a half sobbing message: "I'm outside your block now so be a man and come down and explain yourself." She waited for a while hoping that Matt was up there listening to the recorded message but there was nothing. She ended the call aggressively. She stomped over to the other side of the road and looked up to see if she could see Matt but realised that she had no idea which window was his. In fact, she didn't even know whether his flat was on this side of the building, so she stamped back to the front door. Her evening was a disaster. She looked at her watch and was surprised to see that it was already nearly a quarter past nine. She looked for something to kick but there was nothing except the building. Zoe made her way back home.

It was another bad night for sleeping. Although Zoe initially laid down to try sleep she knew that she had to clear her mind first before she would have any chance of succeeding. She went over and over the events of the previous evening trying to work out how she had read the signals from Matt so badly...if indeed that was the case. He seemed really interested and such a nice bloke. She knew it was possible to misjudge someone, but she rarely got people so wrong. Zoe knew a lot of her own faults, but she knew she was fairly good at reading other people, men in particular. She spent a few hours going over what she had said, what Matt had said, how he had acted and how she read the situation, before finally falling asleep.

The next morning was Saturday and there was

nothing to get up for so Zoe didn't have an alarm set. She usually tried to make the most of her lie in at the weekend but this morning wasn't going to be a very long one. She looked at the clock every half-hour or so from about 4.30 until 7.30 by which time she had had enough. "I'm getting up," she said to herself. She walked slowly from the bedroom into her living room, and slumped down into one of the easy chairs. Her eyes ached as she blinked. She thought about making herself a hot chocolate but she couldn't be bothered to get up. She stifled a yawn and then stretched her arms out upwards. She picked up the piece of paper with Matt's address on it from the table and read it.

"Bastard!" she shouted vehemently, as she screwed the paper up and threw it across the table. She hated being in this state, and it wasn't one she allowed herself to get into very often, but Matt had managed it. Zoe started to cry again as she hit the arm of the chair with her fist. She didn't know what to do.

After half an hour of being slumped in the chair her back began to ache. She rubbed her aching eyes and stood up. She walked around her living room, stretching, to try and relieve some of the pain in her back. She eventually found herself staring out of her apartment window at the people outside getting on with their lives. She felt a sort of void at this moment, and it wasn't a feeling she liked but she wasn't sure how best to get out of the mood. She stood and stared at nothing but she felt her eyes aching again. Maybe a bath was the best solution. Zoe didn't have the best of baths, or bathrooms for that matter, but she could still run enough water to lay and relax a bit. Yes, she thought, that might do the trick. She ran herself a bath and with some music playing she managed to deliberate on the whole event and determined that she had read Matt right. He was either a brilliant liar with a girlfriend or he had come across some sort of problem that had stopped him from keeping their date last night. Her conclusion was that it was more likely to have been the latter. She had only known him a few hours but that was enough to think him worthy of another chance so it was obvious what she had to do. She would go back to his flats and wait until she saw him.

Zoe considered her decision. It was the right thing to do and she wouldn't give up on him. First, though, she would ring him again in case he was brave enough, and available, to answer it this time. She stood wrapped in her bath towel and with her hair in another she dug an ear out so that she could hear what he had to say. The phone just went to the same old recorded message. This time Zoe didn't say anything.

Her contemplation had worked. She hadn't had much sleep during the night but things were much clearer in her head and she was able to move on and think about other things. She had a bit of shopping to do today, just to get a few cosmetics, so she made her way up town and scrutinised the shops she needed. It was her intention to go straight from her shopping trip to Matt's so by one o'clock, Zoe was ready to make her way back over to his flat.

She made her way up to Flat 37 and rang the doorbell but, as she half expected, there was no reply. There was another door, number 35 just along the corridor and she thought about knocking on that door but couldn't think what she would say to whomever answered it. As she walked back and forth between Flats 37 and 35 she saw an Indian family appear from the stairwell and enter a flat on the other side. She moved to a position where she could not be easily seen.

After five or ten minutes and another couple of rings on the bell at Flat 37 it was becoming more and more obvious that nobody was going to answer. Matt either wasn't there or he was fast asleep or maybe worse, had seen her and was refusing to answer the door to her. As she walked slowly up and down she could hear various noises coming from the flats on the other side of the stairwell. Television or radio music, some talking and a dog barking. Every type of noise was there. She looked up and down the corridor again and fiddled with her fingers. She thought again about whether or not she was doing the right thing. She didn't know Matt at all, and probably had no real cause to be annoyed with him, and she began to think that she might just be best to leave it to him to contact her. She looked at her nails. She then looked at Matt's door for one last time as she considered her next action.

Zoe was on the verge of leaving and started to make her way to the stairwell when the door of a flat opposite opened, and a woman appeared. She was in her forties and wearing probably more make-up than was good for her. Zoe and the woman looked at each other and it seemed obvious to Zoe that she looked out of place.

"Er…good afternoon," was all that Zoe could manage.

"Are you after me?" The woman looked Zoe up and down with an aggressive stare. "Are you selling or something?" The woman continued curtly.

"No, I'm waiting for Matt to come to the door." Zoe hoped that by mentioning Matt's name it would put the woman at ease.

"Matt!" The woman shrugged her shoulders and pulled an expression on her face suggesting she didn't understand. "Who's Matt?"

"From 37."

"I don't know who lives there, I keep my own business."

"The young man, he's about six foot and has fair hair." Zoe started to describe Matt, but the woman wasn't listening. She either didn't know Matt or didn't want to know why Zoe was looking for him and, as quickly as she could, made her way along the corridor to the stairs.

Zoe sighed and turned back to look at Matt's door. It seemed that nobody knew who he was, if this was indeed where he lived. She decided that this was getting her nowhere and therefore probably not the right thing to do so started to make her way back down the stairs. She turned her head for a last look just in case she never saw Matt again, and then continued walking down. She hadn't seen the old man walking up the stairs in her direction, and she briefly bumped into him as they passed each other. Zoe paused and wondered whether or not she should ask one more person but he was past her and gone before she got the chance.

"Ah, well," she thought to herself, as she took a step further down the corridor, but then heard knocking at a door, which she assumed was the old man. Curious, she slowed her walk to listen to what was happening.

"Matt, are you there?" the old man said.

Zoe stopped in her tracks.

Zoe turned back and walked up the few stairs towards Matt's flat and the old man just as he turned too and saw her approaching.

"Is Matt in?" Zoe asked him. The old man looked at her rather oddly.

"You know Matt?"

"Yes, sort of."

"Are you his girlfriend, or a sister perhaps?" The old man seemed friendly enough, but obviously didn't know who Matt's girlfriend was, or if indeed he had one. Zoe wasn't quite sure how to answer so gave it some thought before replying.

"Sort of his girlfriend." Zoe's response was met with another strange look from the old man. "Do you know Matt?"

"Yes I know him." The old man didn't see any problem admitting it. "I don't know him that well though, and I'm sorry I've never met you before. I'm Jack."

"Hello, Jack. What time does Matt normally get up on a weekend?"

"He's normally up by now but I haven't seen him since Thursday morning and I just wanted to know if he wanted any milk."

"Milk?" Zoe found the comment a bit strange.

"Yes, I know he doesn't have a lot of money and can't always afford milk, so I buy him a carton on a weekend," the old man explained.

Zoe and Jack carried on chatting for a while and he told her how Matt never had any money or a job.

"But I thought he had just got himself a new job!" Zoe exclaimed.

"I never see him go to work," replied Jack.

"Yes, he told me he was starting on Monday."

Neither really knew what to say next as Zoe then added, "I might have got that wrong and he might even have started this morning."
She looked for some sort of confirmation from the old man that she might be correct but there was no response at all. Zoe wasn't quite sure how well this old man knew Matt so she tried to get a bit more from him.

"Matt is about six foot with fair hair?" she asked the old man.
"Yes that would be him. Matt. He's a good boy, you know."
"And you haven't heard from him today or last night?"
"No I just call in and see if he wants milk today."

Zoe still wasn't sure what to make of it all but was a bit concerned that the old man had not seen or heard from Matt this morning. She was convinced that Matt would have tried to let the old guy know that he had got a new job. She concluded though that this was probably the reason for Matt not being about, and tried to put the old man at ease by telling him so. Zoe and the old man exchanged pleasantries and said goodbye before he went back down the corridor to his own apartment.

Zoe decided that the best thing to do was to leave Matt a note, just in case his phone wasn't working or he had no credit. She had learnt a bit more about

Matt from the old man and in particular that Matt often didn't have any money. She decided that this might well be a reason why she had not been able to contact him by mobile phone, or more importantly why he had not been able to ring her back. She searched in her handbag for a pen and some paper but all she could find was a very small piece of card. She looked in her shopping bags but unless she actually tore a piece of paper out of one of the bags, the small card would have to do. She took the pen and simply wrote

Matt,

Please get in touch!

Zoe X

Zoe looked at what she had written and knew it probably didn't say enough, but it would have to do. She would have preferred to be able to write him a longer note, but she couldn't find anything else in her bags that she could use. She pushed the piece of card under Matt's door and left, hoping that eventually he would contact her.

Chapter 5
Missing persons

It was getting close to four o'clock when Zoe sat down on her settee in a good position to look at her phone as it lay on the table. She tapped her fingers on the arm of the settee about a hundred times and then another hundred times. She walked around the room and looked hopefully out of the window just in case Matt was looking up from the street below. The day was turning into evening and the clock showed six. Zoe stared at her mobile phone as if to put a spell on it and make it ring. It didn't. "He must ring," she said to herself. "Saturday evening, and whatever he's doing he must be finished by now." Nothing seemed to make that damn mobile ring and the stress of it all was becoming extremely tiring.

Another walk across the room to the window to look outside, but nothing had changed. It had got a bit darker making it more difficult to see the people below as they walked past, but Zoe was hoping to just see Matt standing there, gazing up. He wasn't there. "Perhaps I should go and visit his apartment again," Zoe thought to herself, but didn't want to bump into the old neighbour again. If Matt was going to contact her, then he would contact her. She just had to put him out of her mind until then. It was all far easier said than done, though.

Zoe grabbed her phone and found Ruth's number. It

seemed like the best way to try and get her mind on something else. Ruth was probably Zoe's best friend and always willing to have a chat. The line rang for a few seconds and Zoe flopped back down on the settee.

"Hi Zoe, what's up?" Ruth spoke excitedly, waiting to hear Zoe's news.

"Hello Ruth, how did Friday go?" Zoe started the conversation by asking about Ruth's day out so she didn't think that Zoe had just phoned her to discuss herself. Ruth explained how boring a day it had been but that she had done her family duties, and waited patiently for Zoe to get to some far more interesting gossip.

"Ruth, I met someone on Thursday."

"Ooh, great," said Ruth with an excited giggle.

"I met this absolutely beautiful guy in a bar."

"Yes, you were going to meet that bloke Linda knew." Ruth knew a bit more about him than she was prepared to say. "I hope you made out with him!"

"No, not him, the twat! He stood me up." Zoe took a short breath before realising exactly what Ruth had said. "You mean Linda from Accounts?"

"Yes, Linda from Accounts. But if you didn't meet up with him, who are you talking about?"

"Well on the same evening I met another guy in the same pub and we got on brilliantly." Zoe explained.

"That's bloody fantastic. Have you shagged him

then?"

"Ruth, what sort of girl do you think I am?"

"One that's desperate for it, Zoe!" Ruth laughed and Zoe didn't have the courage to argue.

"So, give me the gory details, girlfriend. Shape, size and does he know what he's doing in bed?"

There was a silence as Zoe tried to compose herself. Ruth could hear what she thought sounded like tears. "Zoe, are you alright?"

Zoe inhaled deeply and wiped away a few tears that were escaping down her cheeks. "Yes, I'm okay, just need some advice."

The conversation went on for a few more minutes before Zoe got round to asking Ruth whether or not she thought that she should try and find out what had happened to Matt on Friday evening or should she just leave it alone. Ruth of course told her that she should never chase a guy but although Zoe listened to her older, more experienced friend, and of course knew that this was the correct advice, she also knew she wasn't going to follow it. The girls talked for about another twenty minutes before Ruth said she had to go and do something and the call ended.

Zoe reviewed the whole situation. Her chat with Ruth had given her a chance to put all that had happened to her in the last couple of days into some sort of order. She nodded to herself and felt the strength of self-confidence rush through her body. It was such a relief. Zoe had made up her mind whilst talking to Ruth as to what she was going to do next. As for Saturday evening Zoe knew the best thing to do now was to have a long bath and get some sleep. It was early to bed tonight.

Sunday morning Zoe was up reasonably early and she had a quick shower before getting into her track suit. A visit to the gym was in order. This was a good way in which Zoe could release any pent up anger inside of her and she had some to get rid of, that was for sure. She looked at herself in her tracksuit and grabbed at her stomach, pinching it thickly and realising how untoned she was. She felt that a good long session at the gym would be just right.

She spent two hours at the gym and felt a lot better for it. Her iPod and the television screens took her mind off everything as she worked out on several machines, and as she showered afterwards a feeling of positivity shone through. All that exercise did have its downside as she now felt very hungry, so from the gym it was straight to lunch. The feeling of hunger temporarily dissipated but a call in the convenience store on her way home enabled her to top up with chocolate bars in case of emergencies.

Whilst soaking in the bath last night, and during her work out in the gym this morning, Zoe had finalised her plan. This evening would be make or break time with Matt. Whatever his situation might be, if he was working or had simply just made himself scarce for some stupid reason, Zoe concluded that six or seven o'clock on a Sunday evening would be the best time to catch him at home. She had got to the point where self-respect had told her that she needed to bring this to a conclusion and she so wanted to see Matt again even if it was only to hear him tell her to get lost. By a quarter past six, Zoe was outside his block of flats again, and within five minutes had gained access to the building. She made her way to Matt's door and was about to knock on it when she spotted the edge of her note still sticking out from under the door. This was evidence enough to prove to her that Matt had not been home over the weekend at all. She still knocked on the door and waited but nobody answered.

Zoe worried a little bit initially, but then realised that she didn't know much about Matt at all. He might have a family to visit on the weekend, or friends he would go to, to discuss his personal situation for example. She imagined Matt chatting about her to a pal of his but then shook her head and sniffed as she realised that this was a silly idea as men just didn't do things like that. Not that she knew much about men, but it was just accepted that men didn't discuss personal problems.

She made her way back down the corridor wondering how long it might be before Matt would get back in touch. She was still annoyed with him for not showing on Friday but she was prepared to forgive him if he had the right excuse. Zoe had reached the stairwell door when the old man, Jack was making his way up. He recognised her immediately.

"Oh hello, is Matt in now?" The old man seemed pleased to see Zoe and smiled.

"Hi. No, Matt still isn't back by the looks of it but I've assumed he's gone to his parents, perhaps?" Zoe made this as much a question as a statement hoping that the old man might remember what Matt did most weekends.

"Oh, right." The old man had a quizzical expression as he took in what Zoe had just said. "Does he have any family then?"

"Well I don't know. I assume he has!"

"He told me long ago that he didn't know his father. I believe he just upped and left when Matt was a baby, and I think he lost contact with his mother so I don't know where he would go. He's never gone to any family since I've known him."

The old man looked at Zoe still with a quizzical expression on his face. "Has he never told you this before?"

"Well, I don't know him that well." Zoe admitted, as she began to feel sorry for Matt.

They continued chatting about Matt for a little while longer but were unable to come to any real conclusion as to where he might be. Jack did mention that he had heard from others in the flats that Matt owed rent and they thought he may well have done a runner but the old man didn't agree with them. Zoe wasn't in agreement either but believed the old man when he said that this was not normal for Matt. She had only known him for a short while but she was convinced knew enough to believe that he wasn't the type to just up and go. Matt obviously led a far more difficult and complicated life than he let on, but Zoe didn't think he came across as someone who would just run. She was also pleased to get the impression that he didn't have a girlfriend.

Zoe began to reconsider the accident outside of her flat, and immediately wondered if indeed that it could have been Matt who was involved. The neighbour who told her about the accident had said that it happened around four in the morning and she knew that she had left Matt outside at just after half past one, which was a time lapse of two and a half hours, so it was very unlikely to be Matt, but she felt she should just go to see the police anyway.

There wasn't a police station exactly on her route, but it wasn't too far out of the way so Zoe made her way there on foot. She climbed the steps to the front office and spoke to the officer at the desk.
"Hi, I just want to know if I can find out if a friend of mine was involved in a traffic accident on Friday morning?" Zoe asked. The desk officer took some details of who Zoe was and who it was she was

reporting missing. "I don't know that he's missing exactly," Zoe told the officer but this seemed to be the only way that she could get him to take any notice and listen to her.

Next she was given a big form to complete asking for loads of details about Matt that she just didn't know. Zoe got quite frustrated looking at the simplest of details that she was unable to fill in. Surname and date of birth were obvious things that she thought the police would expect her to know but despite her annoyance she completed the details she could, like height and hair colour, and handed the form back to the desk officer. Zoe was asked to sit and wait whilst the form was passed on to a detective who would then come and speak to her. Zoe just hoped they would quickly be able to confirm that it wasn't Matt in the accident, and then she could go home.

It was a Sunday evening and there wasn't a lot going on in the police station. Zoe expected to see officers coming and going but there was nobody about at all, so time dragged a bit. She thought she had got to the station about seven thirty and it was now a quarter past eight but she had no other option but to wait. Eventually a detective came out, showed Zoe into an office and invited her to sit at a desk. There were files piled high, looking as if they were in no particular order, and Zoe wondered how on earth anyone ever knew what was going on. This gave her another frustrated feeling as she sighed at the thought of having to go through all of this for nothing.

"You want to report Matt as missing then?" the detective started.

Zoe knew all her efforts to explain to the desk officer what she was trying to do had gone to waste.

"No, not exactly."

"So what are you doing here?"

"I just thought you would have details of who was knocked down on the junction at Lister Road in the early hours of Friday." Zoe tried to explain. The detective seemed unsure of what to do so Zoe thought she ought to explain a bit more. "On High Road, Leytonstone." Zoe thought some more, "Vernon Road is opposite." There still seemed to be nothing coming back from the police officer so Zoe continued. "I don't know who it was that got knocked down but Matt was there earlier and he has now sort of gone missing and I just wondered if it was him." The officer looked up and down at a report he had and nodded his head in thought.

"How do you know this man Matt, then?" The detective tried to get more out of Zoe.

Zoe explained all about Thursday evening as the detective made a few notes. She admitted that she didn't know his name, apart from Matt, but she knew where he lived and said that if it had been him involved in the accident she wanted to know. The detective said very little. He advised Zoe that the man who had been knocked down was still in a coma and that they really had no idea what sort of recovery he would make. Despite Zoe asking questions, the detective gave no further details of the accident victim, but took her full details, name, address, everything. Zoe was happy to give her details, but had hoped for a bit more in return. However, this was obviously going to be a one-way exchange.

There was an open report on the detective's desk to which he was referring, and Zoe tried to look at it without him being aware of what she was doing. It wasn't easy and she was really only able to make out the word Whipps, but that one word at least meant that she knew which hospital the casualty had been taken to. Whipps Cross.

The detective concluded their interview by saying that someone would be in touch and that if he was able to tell her anything about Matt that he would do so, but that if Matt didn't want anyone knowing where he was then the police wouldn't tell her anything. He placed his new report inside the accident file and thanked Zoe for coming in, but from his tone even Zoe could guess that it was unlikely that she was going to hear any more about it. She was shown back through to the entrance and thanked one last time before the detective returned back out of public sight.

Zoe thanked him as he walked off, and turned towards the exit repeating the words 'Whipps Cross' over and over in her head. As she got outside she actually spoke the word properly to help it stick in her mind. "Whipps Cross, Whipps Cross. Whipps Cross Hospital," Zoe repeated to herself as she looked at her watch again. It was 8.45. She knew exactly what to do next. Zoe made her way to Whipps Cross Hospital.

Chapter 6
The man in Room 375

Matt wasn't quite sure where he was but he felt weird. He was sort of floating, but was also able to move around where he wanted to. He could see Zoe's small block of flats from a high position as though he was on the roof of another block but he wasn't standing on the roof, he was just floating in that position. He was also aware of other figures floating around above his head, although he couldn't see them properly. They were just there, bright white figures that Matt knew were there but couldn't focus on. There were also some clouds higher still which Matt could see, but not quite. He wanted to look higher and concentrate on what he could see but found it impossible to lift his head properly so he was only ever able to just glimpse what was above him.

It was a really strange sensation and it took Matt a good five or ten minutes to come to the conclusion that he might be dead. Was this how it felt to go to Heaven, he wondered? Or was this actually his route to Hell? "It's far too late to start worrying about faith," he told himself. He tried to think about what he'd heard about what it would be like when he died but nothing was really coming to mind. A quiet voice broke his concentration.

"This is not how it's supposed to be," the voice said. Matt could hear that it was coming from above but still wasn't able to look up and see who was speaking.

"I have a plan," Matt heard, which he thought was a strange thing to say.

Without any sense of movement Matt looked down again to where Zoe's flat had been, only to find himself looking down on a completely different scene. He was in a hospital where he was able to see someone in a bed. There were electrical leads attached to the figure, and tubes looking like they were coming from every orifice possible. Also to the side of the bed were a stack of monitors. Matt couldn't immediately identify the person as he just floated around as if on the ceiling of a hospital ward. Suddenly the body in the bed rose up towards him before passing him and moving higher up into the sky.

Matt instinctively grabbed at the body to pull it back down, knowing that if he let go that person would die. Without any real explanation he just knew it was himself dying in the hospital. A big decision seemed to be lingering in his mind, as if he was able to simply admit death or fight for life. The voice from above spoke to him again.

"You're too young to die. There's so much still to do."

Matt pulled harder on the floating body to try to ensure it went back into the bed. It was hard work, as the body floated upwards with immense strength. The figures also floating around him, which he now identified as angels, weren't helping him or indeed hindering him either. They purely seemed to be there to watch and guide him to Heaven if that was the path he chose. The voice suddenly spoke for one last time.

"We can put this right."

It was peculiar as far as Matt was concerned. Although he had heard the voice a few times now, it suddenly became evident that he had heard it before. He couldn't put a name or a face to it but it was obviously one that had spoken to him before. It felt calming and relaxing, which was surprising considering Matt's current situation.

In reality, Matt was close to death in his hospital bed. He was still in a coma, and had been from the moment the car hit him. The medics at the scene had tried desperately to revive him as he was technically dead when they first reached him, and although they got his heart beating again they were not able to bring him round, and so here he was somewhere between life and death.

The doctors had done what they needed to, to tend to his injuries. A broken collar bone and arm, a shattered pelvis, but the most worrying thing for them was the brain damage that he may have suffered, and how strong his heart was. His heart seemed to have been beating okay but the doctors could never be absolutely certain just how well it would be.

Zoe had made up her mind whilst at the Police Station to go to Whipps Cross Hospital and see whether she could see the accident victim to check whether it was Matt.

"It would answer lots of questions if it was him," she thought to herself. Zoe looked at her watch and realised time was getting away, but she was pretty determined by now and nothing was going to stop her. She went over what she would do when she reached the hospital, even practising what she would say if asked by a doctor who Matt was. She had got some idea of what she might be asked from her experience at the police station, so she considered her plan again, but quickly realised that there was a pretty big flaw in it. She still didn't know Matt's surname so couldn't check any lists for him and if nobody knew who he was anyway then his name wouldn't be up there in the first place. It was all beginning to become a bit of a farce. Zoe went over various ideas for approaching her current problem but as she walked into the hospital she still had no idea what she was going to do.

There was a board up in the entrance lobby showing how to get to all the various wards but this was no good as she didn't actually know which ward she was looking for. Then an idea came to her. What Zoe needed was to ask someone where traffic accident victims would be found, but who could she ask? "Yes, that would do it" she said to herself. There was a uniformed nurse at reception but Zoe didn't want to ask her. There was a cleaner but Zoe didn't think she would know. A small cafeteria was just about open so Zoe looked around the tables. She saw a couple of nurses drinking coffee and she knew that these were the right ones to approach.

"Howdy, I'm looking for my boyfriend and I don't know what ward he's in, can you help me please?" Zoe asked both nurses at the same time. They looked at each other and then Zoe.

"If you give his name to the nurse at reception she'll be able to tell you which ward," one of the nurses told Zoe.

"This isn't going to be easy, is it?" Zoe said under her breath. "I don't actually know his surname you see as we've only been going out a few days." The nurses giggled slightly realising what sort of predicament Zoe was in.

"What's he in for?"

"He got knocked down by a car and is in a bad way." Zoe thought that this might help her cause a bit more. The two nurses whispered briefly before one replied. "You need wards 3 or 6 but I'm not sure how easily you'll find him."

"Thanks," Zoe said, making her way back to the

ward listings.

"Good luck." The nurses went back to their coffees and the conversation they were having before they were interrupted.

Zoe swiftly found her way to Ward 3, but this was where her problems really started. The entrance to Ward 3 opened straight onto a work station where there were at least three nurses and Zoe knew that she would be asked who she wanted to see as soon as she walked in. She peered through a large glass panel in the door, and could see that some bays had what appeared to be visitors by the various patients' bedsides, so it was a good time to arrive. She decided to just go for it.

As expected, as soon as she went through the door all three nurses looked up at Zoe and made a gesture waiting for Zoe to give a name of who she was here to visit. Zoe said nothing.

"Can we help you?" A nurse said.

"Yes I hope so. I'm here to see my boyfriend Matt but I don't know what bed or bay he's in. I've been told he's in Ward 3 though."

"Oh," was all the nurse could say. "What's his surname?" Zoe readied herself.

"I don't actually know his surname I'm afraid." All three nurses looked at Zoe after hearing her response, almost as if it was an alarm bell ringing. Zoe decided it was best if she continued to explain, "He was knocked down by a hit and run driver but the ambulance took him away without me being able to see him. I've been to the police and they said I should try at this hospital."

The nurse who was obviously in charge said nothing immediately but considered the situation. The other two stood upright as if they were guarding the nurse station and kept their eyes on Zoe.

"When was the accident exactly?" The senior nurse asked as casually as she could.

"Friday morning, about three or four." Zoe repeated what she had been told.

"I might know who it is you're after. Just take a seat please." The nurse pointed to some cheap plastic seats a bit further down the ward as she stood up. Zoe made her way there and sat down as the three nurses whispered again, and the nurse who seemed to be in charge went off.

As asked, Zoe sat patiently watching as the other two nurses went about their work. They occasionally looked in her direction and smiled when they caught her eye but Zoe was convinced that they were acting more like prison warders than nurses. It seemed like ages before the nurse came back bringing with her a man in a white coat.

"Hello, Miss?" The doctor made it sound like a question. Zoe didn't realise what he was asking to begin with.

"Hello," she replied.

"Can I take your name please, Miss?" This time she understood more, what was expected.

"Oh right, Miss Winfield. Zoe Winfield," she said it as casually as she could. The Doctor scribbled down something on his clipboard which Zoe assumed was her name.

"And who are you trying to visit?"

"My sort of boyfriend." Zoe felt a bit awkward. "Matt," she added although this still didn't sound like a great answer. The doctor also looked as if he was expecting more of an answer so Zoe continued. "He may have had an accident."

"MAY have had an accident!" The doctor looked surprised at the comment. "What do you mean MAY have had an accident?" The doctor scribbled some more notes as he spoke.

Zoe tried her best to explain the situation to both the doctor and the nurse but neither seemed totally satisfied with her explanation. "He might not be here, you see. I mean it might not be him who was in the accident," Zoe continued as the doctor and the nurse discussed the situation.

"Come with me!" The doctor barked out his order. He turned and walked off down the corridor and back through the exit from Ward 3. Zoe followed. A horrible thought then came to mind that perhaps she was being escorted off the premises or worse, taken to some other office where the police would be called. The doctor took a quick glance to make sure that Zoe was still following him as he turned sharp left and then right along another corridor.

"Don't be daft," she said to herself. "The doctor looks like a kind man. He only wants to help." Zoe just followed him. There was nothing said between the two of them.

As they were walking along Zoe could see that they were in a section of the hospital where there were private wards, although most of the doors were shut as she passed them. Abruptly the doctor came to a stop outside a door numbered 375. He turned to Zoe and nodded at her with his head to look through the window.

"Is this your boyfriend?" Zoe stretched up on her toes to get a good look at the patient in the bed but although she could see it was a man it was not easy to get a good look at his face.

"It might be, but I would need to go and speak to him really."

"I'm sorry, Miss…" the doctor paused and looked at his scribbled notes before continuing. "…er, Winfield, but you won't be able to speak to him as he's in a coma." Zoe didn't know what to say and looked around for some sort of inspiration. She noticed that the nurse had also made her way to Room 375. "Let's just take Miss Winfield into the room for a moment, nurse." The doctor indicated to them both that they should enter the room.

Zoe stepped in through the open door and the immediate noise of various monitors hit her unexpectedly. There were continuous beeps and buzzes which Zoe winced at when she first heard them. She scrunched up her face as if in pain before taking a quick peep at the man, and she knew it was him. A tear fell from her eye and rolled down her cheek, tickling her as it moved. She rubbed it with the back of her hand as the full realisation of just how injured Matt seemed to be hit her painfully. More tears fell and she gave out an involuntary gasp.

"It's him, then?" The nurse said, softly and knowingly.

"Yes, it's him." Zoe started crying. She imagined Matt being knocked down by a speeding car and possibly even dying because of it, and all she had thought about was what a bastard he was for not meeting her on Friday evening.
"You won't be able to get much response from him I'm afraid, but please hold his hand. He may recognise something that might help him out of his coma."

Sitting down by the side of Matt's bed, Zoe held his hand. She spoke to him and apologised for being angry with him but there was no real response. The monitors seemed to beep slightly faster as she held his hand for the first time but he just lay there and said nothing. She sat with him for about forty minutes keeping hold of his hand and wondering what else she could do. The nurse and doctor came back into the room and looked at the two of them sympathetically.

"I'm sorry Miss Winfield, but visiting time ended nearly an hour ago so you will have to go now." The nurse said. "You can come back tomorrow between ten and twelve or after two in the afternoon though," she added. As Zoe began to get ready to leave Matt the nurse spoke again. "The doctor would like you to answer a few questions about Matt please, to help us get in touch with his family." Zoe was led to a small room where the same doctor sat at a desk reading some pages in a file. He turned to see who it was entering the room. "Miss Winfield, doctor," the nurse announced as she pulled out a chair for Zoe to sit on.

Zoe was asked various questions about Matt including his name, date of birth, national insurance number and address, but she wasn't able to answer many of them. They were very much the same questions she had been asked at the police station. The doctor scribbled down a few notes then thanked Zoe for coming along. As she left the ward she made her way back to the main reception area. Zoe looked to see if the two nurses were still about as she wanted to thank them for helping her but the only person sat in the café area was a man in a dark coat. Zoe made her way back home.

The hospital prepared the information that Zoe had given them ready to pass on to the police when they made their regular visit. The hospital had reported a patient as unidentified and it was the police's job to identify him. In fact, it was the duty of a police officer from Lea Bridge Police Station to deal with this latest John Doe, and after making a number of enquiries with the landlord of the flat where Zoe told them Matt lived, and cross-referenced their findings with the postal service, they were able to name the patient in Room 375 as one Matthew Briswell. Having got over this initial hurdle, they then identified him as a previous offender confirming his address, but they still couldn't identify any next of kin nor ascertain much else about Matt Briswell. At least they had a name.

Zoe visited Matt for the following three nights in the expectancy or hope that he would be out of his coma quite soon but it was the same each evening. She would speak to him and hold his hand for a while but he would just lay there motionless. She found less and less to say to him as the evenings went on and after four nights decided that it was of no use to either of them for her to spend her evenings sat next to him. Zoe went to speak to one of the nurses on the ward.

"Just to let you know I won't keep coming in to visit but I would like to know as soon as he comes out of the coma please?"
"Okay Miss Winfield. We have your contact

details." The nurse checked the file "It may still be useful if you could visit every now and then though as you may not think he can hear you but we're sure many patients in comas do have some sense of who is talking to them." The nurse looked at Zoe.

"I will when I can, but I've really only known him a couple of days. Perhaps his family would be better for him?"

"We don't think he has any family, so you're probably all he has got."

This made Zoe feel sad again at the thought that Matt was all on his own in life. She then thought that she might go and see the old man, Jack, and see if he might go and visit Matt in hospital. She thanked the nurses and left. Zoe still cared about him but needed to get on with her life for now.

Someone else was also looking out for Matt, the man sat in the hospital café, dressed in a dark coat. He smiled with an inner confidence as he said to himself that he wasn't going to let Matt die today. Nobody seemed to pay the man any attention, in fact nobody else seemed to even notice him. It had all been agreed with The Force and he was pleased that it had been fully and properly approved in such a quick time. He knew what he had been instructed to do and he was now able to continue with his work and make sure that everything was put back on track. With luck it would all be back to his original schedule once this little saga in the hospital was over, but the next thing was to work out just what special power he could give. It had been discussed and agreed with The Force that a special power was probably needed.

Chapter 7
What's your number?

Zoe didn't stop going to visit Matt altogether, but tried to visit every other evening if she could. It had given her a chance to sort out where she was at in her life. Zoe thought back to her conversation with Ruth at work when she told her about her visits to Matt. Ruth sounded as if she understood exactly what the situation was. Added to Zoe's personal feelings Matt didn't appear to have had any other visitors so she felt that she must try and see him whenever she could. She weighed up her situation constantly. She didn't really know Matt at all. In the back of her mind was always the worry that somewhere out there he did have a girlfriend who cared for him but didn't know that he was in hospital.

All of these different thoughts and worries were swimming around in Zoe's head as she made her way to Room 375. It was a Thursday evening and Zoe's seventh visit to see Matt. The nurses more or less knew who she was now and never blinked an eye as she made her way around the ward. She had a bit of a routine when she visited. She would get a hot chocolate on her way up and by the time she got to Matt's room it was usually cool enough to drink. She was also able to use it to warm her hands so that Matt didn't get a shock from having his hand touched by her cold one. Zoe did think she was being rather ridiculous being as cautious like this but she found it helped. Her time with Matt each evening had also reduced to around an hour now and she would sit there and tell him things about her day and what was happening in the world, and this evening was no different. Zoe held Matt's hand as she started to chat to him.

"Hi Matt, you'll never guess what Ruth did today, I've got the whole shebang. She got caught kissing one of the maintenance men."

"Uh!" Almost unnoticed, there was a strange noise coming from Matt's direction.

"Yes, it's the one she's had her..." Zoe stopped suddenly and looked intently towards Matt. Had she heard Matt making a noise? She looked at the monitors then back at Matt. "Matt, Matt!" Zoe stood up over him to see if there was any sign of him opening his eyes or mouth but she couldn't see any change. After a minute or so, a nurse passed by the room door and Zoe called out. "Nurse!"

"What's the problem?" Nurse Maddock stopped to see what Zoe wanted.

"I think he made a noise when I was talking to him," she said. Nurse Maddock looked at Matt but saw nothing to indicate that there was anything different but when she looked at the monitors there was obviously something happening there.

"I'll go and get a doctor," Nurse Maddock said as she hurried down the corridor. Zoe felt good inside knowing that she would be there when Matt came out of his coma.

She kept looking at the ward door as people approached it from the corridor outside. Each time, she hoped it would be a doctor. She looked at Matt. She looked at the nurse. She looked at the monitors. It seemed like ages, but in no more than ten minutes a doctor appeared and started to check Matt over with various instruments. He did it all without speaking but Nurse Maddock stood there obediently awaiting instructions.

"I think we might be getting somewhere, Miss Winfield." The doctor spoke to Zoe without stopping whatever it was he was doing. Zoe looked at Matt and then noticed one of the monitors began to show indications of something new as the graph lines began to move up and down a lot more quickly. "That's good," the nurse advised with a smile.

Twenty minutes later, Matt opened his eyes. Everyone seemed to be holding their breath. They all looked at him intently. He looked at the doctor, then the nurse and finally Zoe. Zoe smiled back at him. "Ruth!" Matt uttered one word. The doctor turned to Nurse Maddock who looked at Zoe.
"I was just telling him about my friend Ruth at work." This seemed to please the doctor.

"Where am I?" Matt continued. Almost as soon as

he had finished his last word his face grimaced with pain.

"You'll feel quite a bit of pain, I'm afraid," the doctor said calmly. Matt didn't seem to have heard him. "You're at Whipps Cross Hospital, Matt," the doctor told him. There was no real response to this either from Matt but the Doctor took a torch and started to look into Matt's eyes. "Let's sit him up a little bit, nurse!"

Matt's next words were a bit slower than his first. "How did I get here?" Zoe waited for the Doctor to move away from Matt and sat herself next to the side of his bed. She looked towards the nurse and doctor for confirmation.

"You were involved in a car accident, Matt," Zoe took Matt's hand as she got ready to try and explain. Matt pulled his hand away, but then grimaced as the movement seemed to hurt him.
"Where is this place?" Matt began to talk slightly more easily, "Who are you all?" Matt looked from the doctor to Zoe and back again. "What are all the numbers for?" Matt looked at the nurse. The monitors began to beep a little faster as Matt just kept repeating the words "Where am I?" over and over before the doctor gave him a sedative which relaxed him back into some sort of sleep.
"He'll be out for a few minutes then hopefully when he comes round again he'll be more relaxed," the

doctor explained to Zoe. "You stay there holding his hand."

"Are you sure?" Zoe did as she was told.

About an hour or so later Matt began to regain consciousness again and opened his eyes. He looked at Zoe and smiled, which Zoe found quite comforting.

"You're safe now Matt, I was worried about you," she told him softly. Matt didn't reply but smiled again. Zoe wondered if it was still the effects of the sedative that made him slow to respond so she spoke again. "It's great to have you back with us, Matt." Zoe had been told to keep using names as much as she could as it would help him to recover his memory.

"What are the numbers all about?" Matt said quietly and slowly in a hoarse croaking voice.

"They're to help the doctors make you better, Matt." Zoe nodded her head in the direction of a monitor as she tried to speak as positively as possible. Matt didn't seem to hear her reply or at least not take it in. He just looked around at the doctor, the nurse and Zoe in turn with a confused stare.

Zoe frowned. She had imagined that Matt would just come round and then apart from the pain, everything would be alright again but he obviously wasn't finding it easy to grasp where he was or what had happened. She then worried that he might have some sort of mental damage that nobody would be able to identify straightaway. Matt tried to move his leg but his face showed that the pain was just too much for him.

"Ow," Matt exclaimed angrily. He began to breathe heavily before deciding to lay back on the bed.
"He's in pain, nurse," Zoe said.
"Yes, Matt will have a few broken bones to contend with but we'll get him through it all, won't we Matt?" The nurse smiled at him as she moved his bedclothes a bit to allow him some room to sit up a bit more. Matt looked at her as she adjusted the sheets.
"You have a number as well," Matt said, as if he was asking the nurse for her telephone number. Zoe gave Matt a hard stare. The nurse just continued with her work.
"Yes I have a number, but that's none of your business." The nurse glanced at Zoe and raised her eyebrows in gesture.
"Not your phone number," Matt tutted. "I mean the number above you, what does it mean?" The Nurse stopped and looked at Matt strangely. Then looked at Zoe and shrugged her shoulders.
"Oh, that number," the nurse replied, as she began putting the bedclothes straight and tidy again. "It's just a special number, Matt." She looked at Zoe again with a confused look.

As Matt tried to move again he showed immediate signs of pain.

"My arm!" Matt's face had a pained expression as he grabbed at his left arm.

"Try and lay still Matt, as anytime you move you're going to feel pain somewhere." The nurse tried to make him as comfortable as possible before leaving Matt and Zoe alone together. Zoe didn't know what to talk to Matt about so just told him about the weather, how things seemed to be at his block of flats and generally what she'd been told about the car accident he'd been in. Matt took it all in without saying anything. Matt looked at Zoe a couple of times and she touched his hand as he did. Matt seemed happier to allow her to hold his hand which gave her a bit more comfort.

The doctor reappeared and began to check Matt over. He looked at his eyes and got him to focus on an object, whilst he moved it from left to right.

"Matt, I think you're going to be alright." The doctor said in a confident tone.

"Doctor?" Matt replied as if he was going to ask a question.

"Yes?"

"You've got a number as well." Matt said calmly.

"Okay." The doctor half listened whilst he read through some notes on a clipboard.

"What does the number mean?"

"Er, the number?" The doctor replied, most confused. "It doesn't mean anything, Matt." The doctor wrote something on the notes and then returned the clipboard to its position on the wall

116

above Matt's bed. Matt didn't reply.

"I think Matt will need quite a bit of rest, Miss Winfield, so another ten minutes and then I think we'll try and let him get some more sleep," the doctor told Zoe.

Zoe held Matt's hand again as the doctor left them.
"You're going to make it, Matt." Zoe smiled and inhaled deeply.
"I'm okay," Matt replied. "I just don't understand all the numbers."
"What numbers?" Zoe replied, abruptly.
"The numbers over your heads." Matt waited for Zoe to reply but the silence made it obvious she wasn't going to or perhaps just couldn't.
"You need some rest, Matt." Zoe stood up. "Just concentrate on getting better."
"If I need some help will you come if I call for you?" Matt asked.
"I've got to go home."
"Oh right. So who takes over from you then?" Matt asked.
"Nobody takes over from me, Matt. I'll be back sometime tomorrow."
"It's okay, I'm alright now," Matt said before pausing. "At least I think I'm alright. I haven't kicked the bucket yet." Matt watched as Zoe collected her coat and prepared to leave. "Anyway, what group are you from?"
"Group?" Zoe gave Matt a funny look. "What do

you mean, group?"

"Well, you know, who do you work for exactly?" Matt looked at Zoe who just looked more confused. "I mean, who are you?"

"I'm Zoe," she replied, trying not to get angry. "Your girlfriend!" There was a short silence.

"Oh!" This was all that Matt could say. After a few moments had passed and nothing else had been said, Matt continued. "My girlfriend, of course."

There was a big sigh as Zoe sat back down in the chair. She was close to tears as she realised what was going on. "You don't remember me, do you?"

Matt pulled a bit of a strange expression and tried to be as kind as he possibly could. "I didn't think I had a girlfriend. I just don't remember that much I'm afraid."

"We met on the evening you had your accident," Zoe tried to explain quickly, aware that she might be moved on very soon by the nurses.

"I'm sorry, er...Zoe?" Matt searched for the name to complete the sentence. "I don't actually remember very much at all although I seem to recall I live in a flat."

Matt could visualise his bedroom in his mind but that was about it. "And I don't remember all these numbers before. They're new!" Matt continued.

"What numbers exactly?" Zoe asked.

"Well you have the number forty-three shining a nice bright orange colour over your head." Matt said. Zoe waved her hand around over the top of her head making the numbers become fuzzy and partly unreadable as far as Matt was concerned. Zoe couldn't feel anything herself.

"What numbers, Matt?"

"It's there over your head. Everyone seems to have one." Zoe looked at him with concern.

"You should try and get some more rest then perhaps when you wake up tomorrow everything will be back to normal."

The doctor then came back into the room and spoke briefly to Matt. Matt saw that he also had a glowing orange number above his head but his was number twenty-five. Matt decided not to say anything. He came to the conclusion that Zoe couldn't see the numbers, in fact at the moment nobody else had said that they could see them.

"How are you feeling now?" the doctor asked him.

"Pains everywhere, doctor."

"That's expected. What about who you are? Do you know your name?" the doctor continued as Zoe listened on intently.

"Err, yeah, my name's Matt."

"And your surname?" The doctor continued. Matt dithered over the answer. He tried to think if anyone had mentioned his surname as he was sure he had heard it, but nothing came to mind. He looked at his chart and it sort of seemed like a short word beginning with the letter D.

"D…D…Don, I think," Matt finally replied.

The doctor made no obvious response. He looked into Matt's eyes again. Zoe began to cry and the sound of her sobbing suddenly became evident. The doctor turned to her.

"I think it would be best, Miss Winfield, if you left us now. Visitors should have been away nearly fifteen minutes ago." His voice was authoritative but pleasant.

"Oh yes, that's it. Winfield." Matt interrupted giving the reply as if the doctor had said it to help him remember. "My name is Matt Winfield." Zoe cried emotionally.

As a nurse was passing along the corridor the doctor summoned her to come into the room.

"Nurse, if you don't mind could you assist Miss Winfield to leave the ward, please?" The doctor said all this without changing position or stopping his inspection of Matt.

"Matt, I'll be back tomorrow," Zoe said through her tears as the nurse escorted her away from the ward. Matt watched the nurse who also had a shining orange number over her head but this time it was twenty-nine. "Just what do the numbers mean?" he said to himself.

Matt was checked over again by the doctor and told that he just needed to get some sleep, as the nurse returned to the room. The doctor left the two of them. Matt looked at the nurse. She was dressed in a light blue one-piece uniform dress like the rest of them, but Matt could see she hid a fine body underneath it all. He tried to read her name badge but he was having some problems with smaller print at the moment so decided he would have to ask her.

"What's your name, nurse?" Matt just came out with it. The nurse gave him a sly look out of the corner of her eye.

"Nurse Simpson," she replied.

"No, what's your proper name, nurse. I can't keep calling you Nurse Simpson, can I?" The nurse continued with her duties as they chatted. She tidied up Matt's bed and put the chair back.

"You should respect my uniform and call me nurse so for now Nurse Simpson will do." She tried to sound as official as she could. Matt didn't argue he just watched her as she moved around and bent over his bed in front of him. He also watched the orange twenty-nine over her head as it moved with her.

"I would guess you're aged about twenty-nine," Matt said.

"Well, would you now?" The nurse neither confirmed nor denied Matt's guess. "And why would you guess that?"

"Oh I don't know, just a lucky guess I suppose." Matt smiled confidently at the nurse as she grinned back at him.

"Well you're wrong." Matt was a bit miffed hearing the nurse's reply but then realised that it couldn't be her age as the doctor certainly wasn't twenty-five.

"What do the numbers over your head mean, then?" Matt put the question as casually as he could, hoping that if it came across in a knowledgeable way he would be more likely to get an answer. The nurse just pulled a face and looked at Matt oddly. Matt guessed she also had no idea what he was on about and probably couldn't see the numbers either.

"Numbers?" The nurse replied as she looked at Matt with a strange look.

"Oh, it's nothing." Matt decided to leave the subject. The nurse continued to tidy down the bed and finally came to an end.

"Right that's it, Matt. Lights off in an hour," she said, as she left his room. A moment later she poked her head around the corner again and caught Matt's eye. "Janet," she said, as she winked at him and continued on her way.

That night Matt had a fairly good night's sleep and the next morning he began to remember a bit more about his life. He now remembered exactly who he was. Matthew Ellington Briswell. He could remember his date of birth and even more he could recall parts of his childhood, but not necessarily the better parts. Matt recalled moving out of his home after seeing his mother stoned and drunk too many times, but alas he still couldn't remember his address. It didn't matter too much as the authorities knew where he lived. Zoe knew where he lived. The doctor had told him it would take a while for his memory to come back so he guessed it would be okay in the end.

Suddenly Matt remembered those strange numbers again. "Perhaps they were all just in my mind and today they will have gone," he said to himself. He needed to see someone. He could hear some people just outside of his room but he needed them to come in. It didn't take long as within minutes a nurse opened his door and saw that he was awake. It wasn't Nurse Simpson, but to Matt's astonishment and annoyance she too had an orange figure, thirty-four, above her head.

"How are you feeling this morning then?" The nurse asked him.

"Still lots of pain but otherwise okay."

"Good. We might try and give you some food and drink this morning." And as if she had given herself the instruction, the nurse scooted off.

Matt was by now getting used to seeing people with these orange shining numbers over their heads. He still wasn't absolutely sure what they meant but noticed that although generally everyone had a different number, every now and then two people would have the same number. The nurse with the thirty-four above her head seemed to be spending most of her time looking after Matt this morning. She was probably in her mid to late fifties Matt guessed, and she appeared to be fairly senior. He knew that there was no way that she was aged thirty-four, so decided to stick with the idea that she had thirty-four years left to live. The idea of knowing that was quite weird and difficult to take on board.

"Is there any chance of me getting out of bed, nurse, do you think?" Matt asked.

"Yes, if you think you're up to it."

"I would like to feel the splash of water if that's possible. Can I go to the toilet please?"

"Okay. Let me get another nurse and a wheelchair and see if we can't get you up."

The nurse soon returned with another nurse and a wheelchair. They helped Matt get out of bed and tried to see if he was able to support himself on his own. It was quickly obvious that this wasn't going to be happening. However, using the wheelchair gave Matt the opportunity to move around and get to the shower as he had requested.

"I'll get Maddy to push you down to the bathroom and you can move into the disabled cubicle in your wheelchair and wash. How does that sound?" The senior nurse asked Matt.

"Sounds cool." Matt was raring to go. The senior nurse found Matt some soap and a towel and then left him to it.

As his nurse pushed him past other wards, Matt tried to look at the people there. Mainly patients of course, but also a number of nurses and hospital orderlies. They all had numbers over their heads with wide ranging figures from the high teens to the fifties and even sixties. However, he noted that several of the patients had lower numbers, many of them having just the number one over their heads.

Maddy chatted to him as she pushed him to the washroom and then lectured him on how to call for assistance if he needed it, and how to get back to his room if he wanted to try and push the wheelchair himself. He was also told not to try and get out of the wheelchair without supervision and no way was he to try and get himself back into bed. Matt half listened but found his attention being distracted by all the numbers. Maddy was happy she had done her bit and left Matt to it.

The shower cubicle was difficult at first as Matt was unable to stand up and wash in his usual way but after propping himself up against the sink he was able to run some water and then rinse his face a bit. It was surprisingly refreshing, he thought. The soap was new and hence hard to lather up but eventually he was able to get some suds on his face and hands. He considered trying to have more of a wash but decided that it was probably a bit too much to attempt today and satisfied himself with the light wash. He used the towel he had been given and started to make his way out of the cubicle. He was beginning to get the hang of pushing the wheelchair and although it was giving him some pain he wasn't going to give up his independence so quickly.

Matt had pretty much worked out how to get back to his room but he was curious to look into some of the other wards to see what he could see. The first ward he went past had six beds, of which four were occupied. They were very much all old men and all had the number one over their heads, although one of them was purple rather than orange. This was the first time that Matt had encountered a number of a different colour so he looked at the old man more intently. Matt wheeled himself down to the bed but the man was asleep. He had a number of tubes attached to him and he looked in a very bad way. In fact, it didn't look as if he had much time left in this world. As Matt said this to himself he became even more certain that the numbers indicated some sort of life expectancy. Matt looked at a nurse who was tending another patient and guessed that she was about thirtyish. She had an orange number fifty-seven above her head. If Matt was right, then she would die when she was eighty-seven or something around that age. It all started to make sense.

He moved to the next ward and things were very much the same. All the patients had either a one or a low number over their heads with a couple of the number ones being red in colour rather than orange or purple. This was yet another new colour for Matt to take on board. "Orange, purple and red," Matt said to himself. He then realised that he had only seen the different colours when there was a number one over someone's head. Perhaps the different colours showed the rate of deterioration in a person's last year. Matt looked at the numbers and then back at the patients trying to take it all in before deciding he should try and make his way back to his room. There was just one more ward to pass and in one of the beds Matt noticed someone sitting up in bed with a black shining number one above his head, but it was flashing rather than staying on permanently. This was yet another new sensation to take in and far too much to resist so Matt made his way over to the man.

"Hey fella, what you in for?" Matt asked the man.

"I'm waiting for a liver transplant, son. What about you?"

"Oh, involved in a car accident. Broken a few bones but I'll mend," Matt answered whilst checking the bloke up and down. "So when do you have your operation?"

"Hopefully tomorrow if everything goes okay."

The two of them chatted for a few moments as the patient told Matt about how risky his forthcoming operation was going to be. He also knew that there was always the chance that the new liver might be rejected by his body so it was obvious that he was well aware that his position was in the balance. Matt tried to get as much out of him about how he felt before a nurse came along and told Matt to get back to his own ward. He had made a bit of a friend though, and now knew him as Eric.

Matt made his way back to Room 375 full of all the new things he had taken on board regarding the numbers. These numbers did mean something and Matt felt he was working out just exactly what.

Chapter 8
The Forces Above

Looking down on the earth were the collective beings known only to themselves as The Force, or Forces to be more precise. They watch every incident they can, check on numerous individuals and try to keep the balance of everyone's lives on earth as level as possible. It isn't an easy job. However, nobody is aware of their existence and that is how it must always be.

Members of the High Counsel are continually meeting to discuss issues on how to deal with individuals or help situations and this never stops. Grand Counsellor Solon was in charge of the latest list of problems. "Counsellors, we have about twelve situations to look at currently and I will discuss them with you one by one," Solon said, in a deep commanding voice. He looked at the other Counsellors gathered. "We have an individual in Brazil who has now killed two other humans and we know he won't stop there." Solon paused.

"Why didn't we act after the first killing, Solon?" Counsellor Zeroun asked. Zeroun's voice was also quite deep but more soothing than Solon's.

"Thank you for asking, Counsellor Zeroun," Solon replied, then continued: "You may recall that this individual was discussed previously and we sent Angel Melkir to act purely as a watcher."

"Yes, High Counsellor, I do recall this," Zeroun

replied. The other Counsellors remained silent and still, awaiting High Counsellor Solon to continue.
"Angel Melkir provided us with an excellent report on matters as they were at the time and it appeared that the first killing was a one-off revenge. I instructed Angel Melkir to provide further details but alas a second killing has now taken place and it is obvious that we have someone disturbing the balance in a bad way." Solon turned to Counsellor Beathas and nodded slightly. "Counsellor Beathas has spoken directly to Angel Melkir if you wish to ask anything in particular."

The Forces of the High Counsel all muttered to each other for a few seconds except for High Counsellor Solon and Counsellor Beathas who remained still and silent. Every Counsellor was upright and in an arc with High Counsellor Solon more on his own. Each one was dressed in a sort of off white cotton robe which gave off colourful reflections as it wavered and moved in the slight breeze. They were all on clouds with the bottom halves of their bodies mainly obscured. In the middle of them was open sky and the Earth below. The muttering stopped. "Does anyone have any questions for Beathas?" Solon asked. Nobody responded at all. The other Counsellors all nodded their heads gently. "Then we must decide what course of action to take with this individual." Solon announced. "Unless anyone has any objections I feel that we should by-pass any sort of influence and go directly to determination." Solon looked around at the other Counsellors before continuing with the decision. "I would prefer a quick easy termination. It is known that the individual eats on a regular basis so some form of food poisoning would seem the easiest solution." Solon looked again at the Counsellors. "Are we in agreement?" The other Counsellors turned and looked briefly to the Counsellor next to them and then as if it had been choreographed to music they all turned and faced Solon and spoke together as one.

"Aye," was the only word uttered by the Counsellors. Solon's head nodded again gently as he held up both hands to face level.

"It is the decision of the High Counsel that this individual be terminated by food poisoning." Solon spoke commandingly.

"Aye," all of the other Counsellors replied together.

After a brief silence there was again some muttering amongst the Counsellors until Solon's hands were raised again. "I will ask Counsellor Beathas to oversee this and I am happy that Angel Melkir continues to be used." Solon's hands were lowered. A brief pause followed. "Next we have an individual moving around Europe trying to incite unrest and terrorism." Solon began to discuss the second individual that The Force needed to look at and so it went on.

Solon discussed each individual or situation making a decision as to what action The Force needed to take, who should oversee it and what Angel should be used to ensure that action takes place. "We now come to our individual in England whose life we wanted to improve." Solon spoke with a slight concern in his voice. Solon looked at all the other Counsellors before continuing. "This individual just needed a little influence from us to balance up his life. Counsellor Thaddeus oversaw this initial influence using Angel Luther to simply put our individual in contact with a woman who would bring his life into focus, and obtain him a job in which he would thrive and blossom."

As Solon finished speaking the other Counsellors muttered amongst themselves for a few seconds until all became silent again. "Counsellors, I remind you that once again human intervention beyond our control drastically changed the situation and we agreed to Counsellor Thaddeus' request that we prevent the individual from dying." Once again after Solon had finished speaking the others muttered to themselves. "It was also agreed amongst us that due to this latest unfortunate event bestowed on our individual that he should also be given a special power to boost his good luck." Again the Counsellors all muttered amongst themselves but it went on for a bit longer than normal this time.

"I still believe that it was unwise to bestow such a power on this individual." Counsellor Frode spoke. The other Counsellors muttered.

"Your concern has been noted, Counsellor Frode." Solon replied. "Angel Luther is acting as both a watcher and an influencer currently, and we will receive regular reports from Luther as to how the situation develops." Solon looked for any other comments from the High Counsel.

"How has the special power been accepted by the individual?" Counsellor Ahura asked.

"It is too early to know, Counsellor Ahura." Solon replied. "The individual is still getting over the accident and a lot has happened to him recently so let us give him time to take it all on board and see if we cannot get him back on the right track."

"Is there not a risk that the Golden Rule may be tested, High Counsellor Solon?" Frode asked.

"You mean that the individual may become aware of our existence?" Solon replied.

"It is a possibility, surely?"

"I have weighed this up and do not believe that our individual will have any idea of any outside influence. Angel Luther is a well experienced watcher and influencer and indeed if we need Luther to be a Determinator then Luther can supply whatever we require."

"I believe that we should keep a close eye on this situation, High Counsellor Solon," Frode replied.

"I agree, Counsellor Frode."

There was a brief pause in proceedings whilst Solon discussed some finer points of the situation with

Counsellor Thaddeus, which took place whilst the other Counsellors muttered amongst themselves and looked down on the Earth. Behind them was a bright blue sky which had occasional flashing lights all over it. There was no obvious pattern to the lights and some were blue, some were green and some were red. They would flash on for no more than ten seconds at the most and none of the High Counsel paid them any attention at all. Unnoticed by the Counsellors, a red flashing light remained on for more than ten seconds. It stayed on for more than thirty seconds. After a minute a thunderous noise was heard and all of the High Counsel stopped muttering and returned to their places on the cloud. Solon and Thaddeus also stopped their conversation and took their places in the circle.

"It would appear that we have another situation to deal with." Solon spoke as he looked at the red light that had remained on. "It would appear to be an individual in Mali," Solon announced. The other Counsellors made their usual mutterings. "I would like Counsellor Ahura to use Angel Drusilla as a watcher and report back to the High Counsel." Solon looked again at the Counsellors. "Are we in agreement?" The other Counsellors all turned and looked briefly to the Counsellor next to them before they all turned and faced Solon and spoke together as one.

"Aye," the Counsellors replied. Solon's head nodded, again gently both hands were raised up to face level.

"It is the decision of the High Counsel that Counsellor Ahura will use Angel Drusilla to watch this individual." Solon spoke commandingly.

"Aye." All of the other Counsellors replied together.

Chapter 9
Flashing black

Matt struggled as he wheeled his wheelchair away from Ward 5 and made his way haphazardly back to his room, but all the way back he went over in his head every different thing that he had chatted about to Eric. There had been a lot discussed between them. Matt pondered over the fact that it was likely that Eric was going to die in the next few months if things didn't go right with the operation, and from the number one Matt could see above his head, he surely didn't have any more than twelve months to go. It was all quite a lot to take in.

"Actually," thought Matt, "if the number one has gone through colour changes, it is likely that Eric isn't going to survive the operation at all." Matt considered what he had seen. Orange numbers! Red numbers! Purple numbers and black numbers! And now flashing numbers! It was all beginning to take shape, what the different colours probably meant. Matt wasn't too sure that he liked being able to see these numbers, and wondered why he could. "Can anyone else see them?" he wondered.

He'd already checked to see if he could see a number over his own head by looking in mirrors, and reflections in windows, but there was nothing there. Perhaps some other people could see them, not only him. It was very confusing.

By the end of the day Matt was able to move around in his wheelchair quite easily and for most of the afternoon he had been sitting out of bed watching the television in his room. An older woman knocked on his door and showed him that she had a trolley with drinks on it.

"Do you want anything to drink?" The old woman looked at her trolley. "I've got tea, coffee, fruit juice or water."
"I'll just have a coffee please, if that's okay?" Matt answered her.

The woman was again looking like she was in her fifties and sporting an orange twenty-two over her head. As she made him a coffee he decided to just slyly ask her about the number.

"So you must work in the hospital all the time?" Matt started slowly.
"Yeah son, that's right. Nine to five, every day of the week."
"So you see all the patients and their numbers?"
"Their what?" The drinks lady gave Matt a most confusing look.
"Sorry, I meant their names," Matt replied as if embarrassed.
"Oh, I don't know all their names, son, I just give them drinks," the woman replied. Matt paused briefly before changing the subject completely.
"So, if you were able to know when you were going

to die, would you want to know?" Matt was initially concerned as to how the drinks lady might take the question but her look told him she was thinking about her answer and that was fine as far as he was concerned.

"Well, I don't think anyone should know when they're going to die. If God wanted us to know that, son, he'd have found a way of telling us, wouldn't he?"

The woman seemed happy with her reply and nodded affirmatively as she said it. It was enough to convince Matt that she couldn't see the numbers that he could see. The drinks lady gave Matt a good stern look. "You don't wanna be messin' with God's work now," she said, as she wagged her finger in his direction. "You want milk and sugar with that?"
"A little milk and one sugar, I think." Matt replied as the drinks lady gave him another peculiar look, as if he was just weird.

Matt sipped at his coffee every now and then and decided that next time he would try two sugars. He hoped that Zoe would be coming to visit him again this evening as he enjoyed her company. He tried hard to remember exactly who she was, how long he had known her and how they had met but nothing was coming back to him. He honestly couldn't remember much after the age of about sixteen or seventeen at the moment, but he wasn't stupid and knew just by looking at himself he was probably in his mid to late twenties. It then came to him that he might have a job. If he did he couldn't remember what it was, but that meant nothing really in his current condition. He didn't think he had a girlfriend either but he obviously did, as Zoe had said she was his girlfriend. He then wondered if he really fancied Zoe at all. She looked okay, he thought, but he had seen plenty of other women around the hospital who he fancied more. Zoe was nice. Perhaps it was her personality he went for. This was all very confusing going around in his head when he suddenly had another thought. Perhaps Zoe knew if he had a job.

The clock on the wall said half past five and Matt worked out he had about half an hour before visiting time started. He wanted to go and have another chat with Eric. Matt used his wheelchair to get to Eric's ward and remembered that he was due to have an operation tomorrow. Eric was still in his bed but laid down rather than sitting up. Matt went round to the side of his bed to make sure he was awake, but he seemed asleep and almost right out of it. Matt wondered whether he should say anything when he saw some movement in Eric.

"Hey man, how's it going?" Matt said cheerily. Eric opened his eyes slightly to see who it was.
"Oh, Matt, it's you." Eric smiled and his eyes lit up a little bit as he tried to lift himself up. There was a lot of effort but without much success.

"No, don't struggle man. You probably need to rest." Matt didn't want any of the hospital staff to know he was there and if Eric started to fall out of bed he knew he wasn't in a position to help him very much.

"I'm not sure how I'll get on tomorrow Matt." Eric remained in a sort of laying position.

"It'll be fine, you'll see."

"No honest, I think it might be my time." Eric said rather croakily. Matt had to agree with him especially having seen the number one over his head but he didn't want to say anything to let Eric know what he thought, so made no reply.

Eric tried to move again and reached out towards his bedside cabinet. Matt wasn't easily able to stop Eric but tried to get him to stop moving.

"Matt," Eric said, "I have a letter I've written for my daughter. I need someone to get it to her just in case I die, you know." Eric seemed to struggle to get the words out. He was finding it difficult to talk generally, but he was obviously choked up about the whole situation with the letter. He tried to complete what he wanted to say. "I need her to know I loved her. I need someone to make sure she gets this letter." Eric fell back on the pillow exhausted with emotion. Matt tried to think what to say.

"Hey man, you'll be able to deliver the letter yourself, it'll be easy once you've had your new liver." Matt tried to think of ways of getting out of this personal situation, as he pushed Eric's hand back from the bedside cabinet. As this was going on a nurse spotted Matt and came over to see what was going on.

"You're not from this ward, are you?"

"No, I'm from Room 375."

"Well, Mr. Reynolds needs rest rather than chatting so perhaps you should make your way back there," the nurse said. This was Matt's excuse to depart.

"I'll come and see you later, Eric," Matt said as he quickly wheeled himself away from Eric's bed and back towards the vicinity of his room.

When Matt returned to his room the doctor was there to see him. "I'm hearing that you are getting the hang of this wheelchair and making a nuisance of yourself around a number of wards." The doctor was straight on to the offensive.

"Uh, well," Matt was taken aback slightly. "I'm trying to get around a bit I suppose."

"So, Matt, how do we feel generally?"

"I'm pretty beat and still aching all over, doctor."

"Yes, but what about your memory, has anything come back to you?"

"Not really."

"So if we call you Matthew rather than Matt does that help?" There was a brief pause.

"No. I think Matt sounds better." Matt was getting nothing. The conversation went on for a little while before the doctor advised him that thanks to his girlfriend they had managed to find out his address, and ascertain that his name was Matthew Briswell.

It didn't really mean too much to Matt at the moment.

That evening Zoe arrived later than usual and when Matt saw her he thought he noticed that her demeanour was different to what he had seen before. There were even indications that she had been crying and Matt knew this wasn't going to be an easy visit. "Evening, Matt, I see you're out of bed," Zoe said as she gave him a small hug and a little kiss. Matt tried to respond with a much fuller kiss but there was an obvious reluctance from Zoe to fully commit.

"Oh!" Matt said as he looked at Zoe. She just looked back at him. There was silence for almost a minute until Matt continued. "Thanks for coming to see me."
"Don't be daft."
"No, I'm very pleased to see you." The awkward moment after the kiss was subsiding but it hadn't quite gone. "You know I need you, Zoe, don't you?"
"Do you?" Zoe gave Matt a non-expressive look. She sighed before starting to chat about Matt's life, not that Zoe knew that much. Most of it was what Matt had told her that first night. For all Zoe knew she could have been telling him a load of crap. Zoe did tell him how they had met on that dreadful night when Matt had been knocked down by the car. Matt tried to be as honest as possible without hurting Zoe's feelings, but he had to admit in the end that he had no recollection of ever meeting her and in fact wasn't quite sure which bar she was saying they had

met in. He tried to tell her though that he still wanted her to come and visit him, and if his recovery went okay then perhaps they could start all over again. The whole evening visit was a bit fraught and conversation was guarded and intermittent but Zoe seemed reasonably happy when she left, Matt thought.

The next day was a Saturday and when Matt awoke that morning more of his past had begun to formulate in his mind. Matt all of a sudden remembered Mikey and Mop. He could picture them and knew exactly who they were. He still couldn't remember having a girlfriend called Zoe but guessed this memory would return sooner or later. Zoe had agreed to come and see Matt during the afternoon today rather than in the evening. The hospital had encouraged her to continue her visits, hoping that at the end of them Matt would be very close to remembering everything about himself and his life. The staff knew that it could take a while but hoped that every visit would put him back on track.

Zoe found visiting Matt rather difficult. He just wasn't the man she had fallen in love with back on that eventful evening, but she was determined to try and get that man back, back to what she had seen in him before. She knew it wasn't going to be a quick job but it would be worth it if she could find her Matt. On each of her visits she tried to remember to talk to him about everything she could, all sorts of things.

But she also tried to ask him some questions in the hope she could get details out of him that would point to exactly who he was and how he lived, but it was hard.

Matt was also trying to piece every part of his life together. No matter how hard he tried, lots of blanks remained. It hurt him as he clenched his fists and banged his head hoping to dislodge a thought or two but he failed to come up with anything. Matt was thankful for what Zoe was doing. None of the nurses spent as much time with him as she had and he had managed to talk about his childhood and tell her bits about his mother and her drugs, but he couldn't remember much else.

The other evening, Matt and Zoe had been talking about the sorts of things kids used to do at school and after school when suddenly a memory of his mother just came back to him. It was a strange memory. He had mentioned already that his mother smoked a bit of pot and Zoe had accepted this quite well. This particular evening though, Matt had some further revelations about his mum's drug habits, as after a few years she turned to harder drugs and Matt became aware of how to deal with needles. He was only about thirteen of fourteen but most mornings he would find his mother almost unconscious with a needle down by her side. He explained how he learned to pick the needles up and put them somewhere safe and then just check that his Mother was still breathing before leaving for the day. It had all sounded quite an ordeal as far as Zoe was concerned and she cried that night, but this afternoon she arrived full of smiles.

"Hello, Zoe," Matt tried to greet her in a way that showed he was pleased to see her. He had been meaning to call Zoe by her name for a long while and he was glad to have remembered to do it this afternoon. They hugged and kissed briefly before Zoe replied.

"Hi to you." She smiled back at him. Matt quite liked listening to Zoe talking, he found her voice soothing. It wasn't just that, he wanted her to help him to remember.

"So tell me again, what can you remember about your flat?" Zoe searched around in his bedside cabinet and retrieved what had been identified as his flat keys as she asked. There were actually only two keys. The two of them had previously discussed the keys and concluded that one was for the main outside door to the block of flats and another for his room. Zoe looked in the cabinet hoping to spot his wallet. She had looked for it before but it was nowhere that she had been able to see. She couldn't remember if Matt had even used a wallet during their evening. If he had, then perhaps someone had taken it after he had been knocked down.

"Well, it has three rooms altogether, I think." Matt could only really remember three rooms. He described them to Zoe as he felt they looked, but there was a slight nagging doubt that he was getting mixed up with other places where he had lived. Zoe had recited Matt's address to him a couple of times but it didn't seem to jog any further memories. They chatted for a few minutes before Matt asked Zoe a favour. "Do you think you could push me round to another ward, as I want to go and see how an old bloke I met is doing?"

"Sure, I suppose it's alright to do that, is it?"

"Yes, they don't mind."

"So who is this bloke then?" Zoe asked as she helped him into his wheelchair. She huffed and puffed and went a bit red in the face as she was doing so.

"I just know him as Eric," Matt replied.

"So you know what bed he'll be in then?"

"Well, maybe." Matt thought for a moment. "Do they move patients around that much?"

"Yes, sometimes I think." Zoe tried to give a convincing reply.

"Well, we might have to go to a few wards if they have."

"So you'll recognise him then?"

"Er..." Matt thought about going into an explanation of how he would recognise him by his flashing black number one but decided against it. "Yes, I'll recognise him."

"Oh, right." Zoe seemed happy with his answer.

When they reached the ward, Matt looked over in the direction of where Eric had been but the bed was empty. He looked around to see if he could see any flashing black numbers but most were solid and either red or purple. An orderly suddenly appeared looking to change the bed covers and Matt asked Zoe to push him over towards her.

"Where have they put Eric?" Matt asked the orderly who just looked at him in a strange way as if he had been talking in a foreign language. "The man who is normally in this bed, he had an operation yesterday?" Matt asked again but the orderly just shrugged her shoulders. A nurse in a dark blue uniform came over to Matt and Zoe to find out what was going on.

"Can I help you?" The sister asked politely.

"Yes nurse, I'm just trying to find out what you've done with Eric?"

"Do you mean Mr. Reynolds?" The Sister asked.

"Yes that's right. I just know him as Eric."

"So how well do you know him, then?" The sister asked. Matt pulled a face and stared back at the sister in annoyance. He banged his fist on the arm of the wheelchair.

"Just tell me where Eric is." Matt looked at Zoe. "Come on, let's go to another ward." Matt made movement motions as he sat in his wheelchair and tried to wheel the chair past the sister who was stood in his way.

"You do know Mr. Reynolds?" The sister looked at Matt sternly.

"Questions, always questions!" Matt raised his eyebrows in a furious gesture. Zoe knew that Matt was getting stressed and tried to intervene to help the situation.

"Matt, it's okay, the nurse just wants to know how you know him."

"Well I just got chatting to him, and I said I would come round and see how he got on after his operation. Have you moved him to another ward?"

"I'm sorry if you knew Mr. Reynolds."

"Eric," Matt interrupted.

"Yes, Eric. Well, I'm afraid he passed away last night." The sister looked at Matt, and waited to see what sort of response this brought. Zoe bowed her head.

"Oh," she said. Matt's reply was different to what was expected.

"Oh, right, I didn't know he would go so quickly." Matt seemed quite matter of fact about it all. "He was a nice bloke."

"Yes, and it was quite a sad ending really." The sister was upset.

"What do you mean a sad ending?" Matt asked her.

"Well, he never got any visitors all the time he was in hospital. None of them wanted to come and see him."

"But he had a daughter, he told me."

"Yes, we have spoken to her on the phone, but she was adamant that she wasn't coming to see him." The sister sounded annoyed. "And I guess she gets all his money." This was a comment that seemed to echo for a few seconds before Matt interrupted.

"Will she come and get his effects then?" Matt asked.

"Well I assume so but that's her business and not

yours." The sister was authoritative in her reply. "We'll keep hold of them for a while but if nobody claims them they'll be destroyed."

"There's a letter he wrote to his daughter that he asked me to pass on to her, can I see if I can find it?" Matt was beginning to wonder what Eric's daughter might be like and whether she would be happy inheriting from a father she wasn't prepared to come visit in hospital while he was dying.

"Sorry, but Mr. Reynold's effects are none of your business. The hospital will sort them out."

Matt thought about what Eric might have written in the letter. He wondered if the old man might have a lot of money stashed away somewhere that he was wanting to pass on to his daughter. If he had, he might have been telling her where he had hidden it all. Matt silently thought through all of this in his mind, not wishing to involve Zoe in any of it. Matt wished he'd agreed to take the letter now. Certainly given the opportunity again he would probably act differently.

"It's a shame, isn't it?" Zoe could see that Matt was deep in thought and guessed he was sad about the passing of Eric.

"Oh, yes it is, but I'm thinking more about his horrible daughter."

"His daughter!" Zoe exclaimed in a high voice. "You know his daughter?"

"No, I don't know her, but Eric was really upset that she wouldn't come and visit him." Zoe pushed Matt back to his room as Matt explained a bit more about poor Eric and how horrible his daughter must be. Zoe commented with her thoughts on the daughter, and Matt replied at the right moments, but was thinking more about how much money this daughter was going to inherit and how he felt she didn't deserve it.

After Zoe had left the hospital Matt went over how the two of them had been that evening and he was happier that they had found a sort of understanding between them. It wasn't easy for him finding he had a girlfriend he hadn't known about. Zoe was really nice. Matt liked her but he wondered exactly what it was that he had first seen in her to make him ask her out. Although Zoe had told him how their first evening had gone Matt wasn't absolutely sure there wasn't more to them meeting other than just chance. He was beginning to remember a few more things but his recollection of that fateful evening was a complete blur at the moment. It was very frustrating.

That evening Matt went on another wander around the wards, looking for anyone else with a black flashing figure one over their head. He still wasn't absolutely sure how long they had left to live, but was happy that it meant that they would die fairly soon. He gauged weeks as oppose to months, but it was really all guesswork. "It might actually be just days," he thought to himself as he scrutinised the wards.

I've Got Your Number

It was in a ward at the far end of the third floor where Matt found his next case study. It was man who looked to be in his late fifties who was called Stanley. Matt tried to engage Stanley in conversation as he checked and rechecked his black flashing number. He tried desperately to befriend the man, but he was much harder work than Eric had been. Matt felt that Stanley was suspicious of him by his reactions but he persevered, and talked to him until he felt Stanley had had enough.

"I'll come and see you tomorrow, Stan," Matt called as he waved from down the ward. Matt had learnt that Stanley had come into hospital with chest pains, and that the doctors were trying to identify the problem but Stanley had no thoughts that he was about to die. Matt of course more or less knew he was going to die, and fairly soon. He didn't know exactly when, but he was certain it would happen. Matt found this situation a bit difficult to deal with at first. Eric had almost seen his death coming, but Stanley saw nothing but himself getting better. Matt thought about telling him otherwise, but then thought better of it.

Matt returned and visited Stanley the next day, and once again tried to get to know him better but he came up against the same defence. In fact, Stanley started to get a little aggressive towards Matt, but that didn't put Matt off. He decided that perhaps the next day he would try another strategy. He was too late. Stanley died during the night. Matt took all of this in and began to adjust his thinking about the flashing black number meaning that someone had weeks to live. He was now beginning to think that it meant they had only days left.

Chapter 10
Orange Red Purple Black

As time went on Zoe's visits to the hospital became shorter, but they were still regular. Matt had got used to her chatting to him about all sorts of nonsense and he would try and picture many of the things that she told him about in the hope that it would help him bring back those last memories he was trying to recapture. He considered where he was. Not physically, in the hospital, but whereabouts in his life. He at least knew his name and where he was supposed to live. He was keen to leave the hospital and visit his flat to see if he had properly remembered it. The doctor had told him that he was well on the road to recovery but needed the last few things to fall into place properly before they were happy to let him go home. The fact that he lived alone was a real setback but he would just have to go with it for now.

Matt also carried on wandering around the hospital. He had now discovered where the lift was, so he could venture into more wards than he had been able to previously. Many of the people in the hospital, especially in the wards where Matt was looking, had the number one over their heads. It was almost like a meeting place for the dying to come along and get some peace in their last days. Matt had pretty much worked out that orange was the usual colour for all the numbers, but through noting the different patients he began to work out that orange changed to red which in turn became to purple and eventually turned to black. Matt also now knew that when the black number one started to flash it meant time was almost up.

It was also becoming evident to Matt just how differently the colours changed from one person to another. In some it would probably take months to change from orange to purple, but then in others it took merely hours. Matt found himself in a ward on the second floor where there were six beds occupied by women of different ages. Two of them already had flashing black number ones, whilst most of the others had solid number ones, either red, purple or black. However, there was one woman who had an orange sixteen over her head. As the two women with flashing black ones seemed unable to communicate in any sort of way Matt found himself talking to the woman with the orange sixteen.

"It's good of you to come around and try and chat to some of us," the woman told Matt. "I'm Elsie, what's your name?"
"Oh, I'm Matt."
"And you're in a wheelchair, so you're not very well either, are you?" Elsie thought Matt was very good coming to try and talk to everyone.
"Yes, I was in a car accident."
"Oh that's terrible. Have you broken anything?"
"A few bones here and there but I'll be okay."
"Yes you probably will. I have a heart problem and

don't expect to live much longer." Elsie said very casually. Matt looked at her strangely as she continued. "I mean, you look at everyone here, and they all know it's their last few days so I'm assuming I will be going the same way."

"Don't be silly, you've got years yet," Matt said in a very positive way. It sounded fantastically true, as if Matt was able to decide whether or not Elsie was going to die. Elsie smiled at the encouragement in Matt's words. Matt, of course, was beginning to believe himself that he knew that she wasn't going to die for another sixteen years.
"You're just saying that. I've heard some of the nurses saying the same to others who die the next day."

"No, honest Elsie. For instance, that woman over there in bed three," Matt pointed to a bed where a woman lay with her flashing black number, which he had seen for at least a couple of days already. "She's not for this world much longer I'm afraid, I can see it. But you, you've got at least another fifteen or sixteen years left to go and enjoy yourself yet." Matt spoke as confidently as he could, hoping that what he was saying would be the sort of thing that Elsie would want to hear but she remained silent, deep in thought.

The silence continued for a few more seconds until it was suddenly broken by a familiar voice to Matt's ears.

"And what do you think you're doing down on this ward, Matt?" It was Nurse Simpson. Matt turned his wheelchair around to see the lovely Janet with her orange number twenty-nine intact over her head.

"Hello, Janet."

"I take it you're on your mercy missions again. We've all been hearing about them, Matt," Janet told him. "Now let's leave Elsie and get you back to your room," Janet said as she pushed him back up to the third floor.

It was unclear exactly what the spark was, but from that day Elsie found herself well on the road to recovery. She had visits from her family, who were quite amazed at what a remarkable change had come over her, and even the doctors were impressed with how much she improved. Elsie confided in her daughter that this young man had come along and told her that she was going to be alright, and it was as if he had healed her. Elsie certainly thought Matt had some magic sort of powers even if her daughter wasn't as convinced.

Elsie's recovery was in fact so good that the hospital allowed her to be discharged just a couple of days after Matt's visit. All of Elsie's family had by now heard about this young man with the healing words. They also managed to find out where Matt was, and Elsie, her daughter and son-in-law all made their way to Room 375 to find him.

Many of the hospital staff had also heard about Matt and his mercy missions, as Janet called them, but they were less than impressed with what he was doing. There were concerns that he would tell a family that their loved one would live and then if they died, the hospital would have to deal with the fallout. Behind the scenes there were many discussions about Matt and what to do about him.

As yet there had not been any incidents that the hospital feared, which medical management staff were thankful for. They guessed that their luck wouldn't last, but in the meantime there were some happy people. Elsie's family were really the first to feel indebted to Matt, and the whole family appeared in room 375 to see Matt. Well, three of them at least. "This is the young man I've been telling you about, Jane," Elsie said to her daughter as she stretched out her arm to introduce Matt. Jane held out her hand for Matt to shake.
"Thank you for helping my mum through."

Jane didn't want to say too much as she was still uncertain as to exactly what Matt had actually done, but then she didn't want to appear ungrateful either. Matt shook her hand and that of her husband too.
"Oh, it was nothing," Matt replied, shrugging his shoulders to play it all down. He didn't really fully understand what all the fuss was about anyway, as all he had done was tell Elsie that she wasn't going to die yet, and he thought this quite a simple statement

to make.

"We've bought you a little present, I hope you like it," Jane said sheepishly as she presented Matt with a cute little cuddly bear sporting the words 'Thank you'. Matt took the bear and smiled at Jane and then Elsie.
"Thank you, I'll treasure it," he said, lying.
"You're a lovely young man," Elsie added as she gave him a hug. The three then all stood looking at Matt, uncertain as to what to do next. All were slightly embarrassed.

After the fuss was finished, and Elsie's family had made their way out, Matt picked up the bear again and looked at it. He thought how silly it was that someone had bought him a gift simply for reading what was just on top of someone's head. It did start him thinking though. I wonder if others might also reward me for telling them they aren't going to die, he thought.

Matt's was recovering well, and he soon found himself able to walk around the hospital with the aid of a stick. He felt more in a position to go and visit other patients in other wards. The doctors also said that they felt he was really able to be discharged, but suggested that he move in with his girlfriend. Matt wasn't keen and resisted the idea, being a little uncertain as to what he really felt about Zoe, but it was likely to be his best chance of getting discharged and back into the outside world, so he agreed. He was still trying hard to rediscover who he was, and new bits of his childhood kept coming back to him, but he needed to know more of who he was today. He knew his name, his date of birth and all those silly little things that most people take for granted. He knew his address, even if he couldn't definitely remember what his flat was like. Matt just wanted to try and remember Zoe better, and that evening they met.

Whilst spending time in the hospital, Matt made friends with another couple of patients who were flashing black. Both were men. One was named Dan whilst the other was Steve, and both were in their sixties. Dan was quite an ordinary bloke and had a tumour that was not responding to treatment properly. He chatted about things with Matt, but knew he was dying. He talked about the fact that his wife had left him and that his son's daughter, his grand-daughter, was the person he lived for. Dan found Matt an easy listener and he confessed some of the mistakes he had made during his life. Matt listened and almost acted as a priest giving absolution, but in truth none of it really interested him.

Steve was a different matter. He didn't ever envisage that he was going to die, even though he knew he was in a bad way. Steve was extremely positive about being in hospital and only saw it as a place that would make him better. Matt spent a fair bit of time chatting to Steve and found out that he had a family, most of whom were coming to visit him. Matt also found out that he was quite a successful businessman. Like many successful men he also had secrets. Again Matt found it amazing that these people in hospital all seemed to want to confess to someone the things they had done during their lives that they wanted to make amends for. Steve was no different.

Steve's big regret was that in his early days of setting up his business he practically ruined his first partner in order to put himself on the road to success. Steve told Matt that he knew he was a ruthless man in his early days, and in fact not a nice person at all. Matt chatted to Steve about it all, and paid attention to what he was saying. Matt allowed Steve to open up whilst he listened.

"I really feel for the guy now as he's unemployed, and on really hard times," Steve told Matt. Matt started to think that this was a bit like he sort of felt about himself. He didn't know for sure, but felt that he was possibly suffering some really hard times. He couldn't quite put his finger on it, but it all seemed to ring with a strange familiar resonance.

"So you know where this bloke is, then?"

"Yes, he's still around. And what's worse, he still says hello when he sees me and I feel responsible for having put him in that position."

"Surely it's not all your fault?" Matt replied. "Don't

kick your arse over it." Matt tried to sound reassuring. "It takes two, and he should have fought back a bit."
"I walked all over him, he was such an easy mark." Steve said, "When I get out of here I'm going to try and put things right." He nodded affirmatively as he said it.

The conversation showed just how positive Steve was about it. Matt didn't want to upset him, but thought to himself, "Little do you know mate that you're probably not going to get out of here". Matt continued to nod and agree with Steve as he talked about what he had done and his plans for what he would do when he got out. To Matt's surprise, Steve had some other secrets that he felt he could share with his new found friend, and he told him where he had a few hundred pounds stashed in case of emergencies, and that this would be the money he would use to try and put things right. Steve talked about how he had always put a little bit away in case of sudden emergencies, but then said there wasn't a lot of money in the stash, which Matt thought sounded like he was trying to play it down. Matt played it cool and never mentioned it again. Steve was talking about his plans, but Matt was making plans of his own.

Chapter 11
Don't you know who you are?

As the sun began to shine through the window blind, things in the hospital started at their normal early hour. It was in fact only just a quarter past six in the morning, and Matt rubbed his eyes and yawned as the noises disturbed his sleep. He found it hard to wake up. The quiet of the night shift had passed, and nursing staff starting their day shifts were already busying themselves with their duties. The blinds in Matt's room were opened with gusto as a nurse made her usual wake up call. "Time to wake up, Mr. Briswell!" she said loudly, as she checked charts and monitors. Matt drifted back to sleep and into a dream.

He hadn't really dreamt much, if at all, whilst he had been in hospital, but this morning he was living a life in a small flat in London, and everything seemed so real. The dream moved to Zoe sitting at a table in a bar somewhere and then the two of them were walking along the street chatting. No proper conversation was heard but Matt knew he was talking to Zoe.

The nurse gave Matt a shake to try and wake him, and the dream came to an end. He found himself back in his hospital bed and the words of the nurse repeating in his ears, "Come on, time to get up." Matt slowly opened his eyes and remembered where

162

he was. He knew exactly where he was. It was a weird feeling though, as suddenly he also remembered exactly who he was. Not just because he had been told his name, he really remembered it. "Matt Briswell," he said to himself. "Matthew Ellington Briswell, that's who I am! Matt Briswell" he continued repeating in his head. Without even thinking about it, Matt could remember who he was, his mother, his shit life, and even exactly where he lived. Matt wasn't quite sure if he was just recalling the flat in his dream or not, but he was able to confirm his address and imagine how to get into the flat and everything about it. He remembered that mainly he would climb the fire escape, and it made him laugh with relief recalling the sound the stairs made as he ran up or down them. He was pretty sure he could remember almost everything. Matt smiled to himself. He felt happy.

Suddenly, Matt wondered if the numbers could see over people's heads had all been a dream. Perhaps he was now properly awake and the numbers would be a thing of the past, but very soon a nurse walked by his open door, and he could see that she had an orange thirty-four over her head. The numbers were still visible. Matt wasn't quite sure how to feel about this. In one way he was pleased that he was still able to see the numbers, as he was beginning to get used to them and felt he would miss them if he couldn't see them. In another way though it still meant that he was different to everybody else or so he assumed.

Matt pondered over the weird way brains worked. How was it that one day he could remember hardly anything about who he was and what he did, then the next he could remember everything. "I must tell the nurse," he said to himself, "and the doctor." Matt thought excitedly: "Wow! Yeah, and I'll be able to tell Zoe as well." It wasn't long before a nurse came back into Matt's room. "Nurse!" Matt spoke quickly, but then realised this was a nurse he hadn't met before. She had an orange forty-one above her head. "What is it, Matt?" The nurse knew all about Mr. Briswell.

"You probably don't know what I'm in here for..." Matt started to say before the nurse interrupted him.

"Oh, don't worry, I know all about you, Mr. Briswell."

"Oh, right." This made Matt pause briefly. "Anyway, I think my memory has come back."

"That's good, Mr. Briswell."

"Yes, I mean all of it."

Matt wasn't sure if the nurse had understood what he was trying to tell her. "You may need to tell a doctor, nurse." The nurse turned towards Matt and grabbed his wrist and felt for a pulse. She looked at her watch and briefly looked at Matt with a smile. She then nodded with approval.

"Yes, we'll let the doctor know and he'll come and see you soon, but you need some breakfast." The nurse helped Matt sit up properly and smoothed down the bed sheets and blanket before leaving his room.

When the nurse reported Matt's message to the senior nursing staff and then to the doctor, hospital staff rang Zoe and asked her if she could come in to see Matt as soon as possible. Zoe was told that this was all good news, and she was able to get time off, so duly obliged and by ten thirty was in Room 375. The senior nurse had already prompted Zoe as to what would happen, as she and the nurse both entered Matt's room.

"Matt, you remember your name now?" Zoe said excitedly.

"Yes, it sort of came to me this morning. My name is Matthew Ellington Briswell."

"Ellington!"

"Yes. I seem to recall my mum telling me that her dad was a big Duke Ellington fan, so I got lumbered with it as my middle name."

"It's not that bad," Zoe sniggered.

"I never ever met my grandparents."

"Didn't you?" Zoe replied with a sad tone to her voice. "Neither set?"

"Well, no, because my father was an immigrant."

"Oh, right." Zoe paused to think before continuing. "Where did he come from, then?"

"I don't really know. Some Eastern European country." Matt was quite matter of fact about it all. "My mother never got on with her parents either so I never saw them."

"Never!"

"No, never, as far as I can remember. I know my mum came from West Baden in Indiana in the United

165

States. She told me a little bit about her childhood but it wasn't a happy one, and she was pleased to leave home."

"It all sounds rather sad, Matt," said Zoe wiping a tear from her cheek.

"Well the other thing is, I think I can remember exactly where I live."

"That's great."

"Yes, not just because you've told me my address but I can tell you how to get there and everything." Matt was very relieved and found that lots of things were all coming back to him. Silly little things, but it was obvious that his brain was beginning to function properly again.

The conversation was interrupted as a doctor came in. He looked into Matt's eyes through some sort of scope and then got him to follow his finger left and right. Then he checked the charts before turning to Matt.

"Well, Mr. Briswell, you will need to come back and have yourself checked over again in a couple of days but as long as you take it relatively easy I don't see why you can't go back home."

"That's fantastic, Doctor," Matt said as he beamed a massive smile. "Thanks!"

"I just need you to sign some forms that the nurse will bring along in a few moments, but then you can go." The doctor turned and gave the nurse some instructions before she scooted off. He then turned to Zoe. "You need to look after this young man for a couple of weeks, but he's well on the way to a full recovery."

"Okay, Doctor, I will."

"He's a bit of a miracle man all round," the doctor gave a half laugh. He then nodded a little bit and showed an astonished expression on his face. "Yes, Matt, a miracle man," he repeated slowly.

The doctor left them to get things ready for Matt's departure. "It'll be great to get back to normality, Zoe."

"Do you know what normality is, Matt?"

"Yes, I think so." The conversation continued whilst they packed a bag that Zoe had brought to the hospital for Matt to use. She helped him with his forms, and then his packing.

"Just before we go, Zoe, I want to call on another patient."

"Yes, okay." Zoe knew that Matt had made lots of acquaintances whilst he had been in hospital, not that she approved of how closely he had become involved with some of them.

Matt left Zoe to make her way down to the café bar near the hospital entrance, whilst he went off to see Steve. Steve's bed was empty and Matt made some enquiries with the nursing staff about what had happened to him. He wasn't surprised to find out that Steve had passed away. In fact, Matt was expecting it to be the case. His next task was to use his charm with the nurses and with a little bit of charm and a few well-placed lies, saying that he wanted to send his condolences to Steve's family, Matt managed to find out his address. With this information safely tucked away, Matt rejoined Zoe and they set off back to Matt's flat.

After getting Matt safely back to his flat, Zoe agreed to allow him some time on his own to settle back in and try and get his bearings back.

"I'll only leave you for a couple of hours," Zoe told him.

"It's okay Zoe, you have things you need to do as well, I'm sure."

"Work have given me the day off to look after you, so that's what I'm going to do."

They hugged and kissed before Zoe departed.

"I'll be back this evening, then."

When she returned, Matt had tidied the place up a bit, Zoe concluded from what she could see. It was quite a homely little flat, small, but homely. Matt gave Zoe a hug and a kiss which he enjoyed. He looked at her again, and began to realise what it was he had seen in her a couple of weeks ago. She still had the bright shining orange forty-three over her head, which was quite distracting, but he was able to ignore it long enough to look at her facial features a bit more. He found it strange, if he was honest, because she wasn't really the sort of woman he would normally pick up, but he was fairly confident that he wasn't in much of a position to actually choose, so decided he should simply be happy that he had a girlfriend.

That evening's conversation was a bit difficult, as neither really knew what to say, and neither had that much money. Zoe suggested they might go for a walk but Matt didn't feel that it would be easy for him to walk far, even if he had a stick. Perhaps in a couple of days he would be able to do a bit more, but for now he just needed rest. With the fact that there wasn't a lot to talk about it wasn't long before Matt raised the subject of the numbers. At first Zoe tried to engage with the conversation and understand what Matt was talking about, but as he went on she got more and more dismissive of the whole subject.

"So you honestly cannot see the numbers like I can?"

"No, I cannot see any numbers," Zoe shook her head and smirked a little, unsure as to whether Matt was just trying to pull her leg or be funny.

"But they are there over everyone's head."

Matt tried to convince Zoe but she wasn't really prepared to listen. "There's a number over your head."

She still wasn't listening.

"It's a number forty-three."

"Yes, you've said before." Zoe hoped that was all Matt was going to say about the bloody numbers and eventually he did stop.

Zoe changed the subject, and talked about various places in and around London just to see if Matt had

169

regained his full memory. Matt passed her test without making too many mistakes, and in fact more things were coming back to him as he remembered the regular walk he would make to the newspaper stand. They talked about what they did with their days, and Matt had pretty much got the idea in his head that he was unemployed. "Well I spend most of my days sitting around here except for when I have to go and sign on so I get my benefit payment."

"Oh, right!" Zoe replied with an automatic response. "In fact perhaps I should contact them, as otherwise my benefits won't come in."

They looked around his flat to see if they could find an official document that showed he was unemployed, but they found very little.

"Actually, I've just remembered you said you had got a new job when we first met," Zoe told him.

"A new job!" Matt sounded impressed. "Did I say what sort of job?"

"No, I think you had only just started." Zoe concluded. "But I don't actually know."

They continued to search the flat, Matt moving around the place to help look. Suddenly he felt in the pockets of his trousers. He found a screwed up piece of paper with an address on it that he quickly realised was Steve's. "I must keep that safe," he thought to himself, and instinctively moved into his bedroom to hide the scrap of paper under a book on his bedside cabinet. To his surprise under the book was a sort of diary.

"Zoe, I think I've found something," Matt shouted out. Zoe came into his bedroom.

"What have you found, then?"

"It's my interview diary. It was under this book." Matt showed her the little diary. He opened the diary and tucked inside was a job search activity sheet with one line of writing on it. The diary also contained writing that mentioned the Job Centre in Leytonstone, and Matt began to recollect the place. A vision of a woman sat behind a desk then flashed into his mind. It was Sonja. Matt started to get aroused at the thought of her but then remembered he was with Zoe.

"That's brilliant. Do they tell you where you've got your new job?" Zoe asked more in hope than anything else. Matt looked at the last few pages of the diary.

"No. Nothing." He was a bit disappointed. "I'll have to go and visit them again and see if they can tell me."

Matt kissed Zoe goodbye before she made her way back to her own flat via the subway.

"I'm at work tomorrow, but I'll be round in the evening and perhaps we can go for a drink?" Zoe wanted to get Matt out of his flat, as she didn't think it was really good for him being cooped up.

"Okay, I haven't got much money but perhaps just a couple of drinks."

"Look, I'll pay for a taxi. We don't have to go far, just somewhere out," Zoe suggested to Matt.

"Yes, that'd be nice," Matt concluded as Zoe put on her coat. They hugged and kissed, and Zoe left the flat. Matt watched her walk to the end of the corridor before waving to her and blowing her a kiss. He then shut his flat door and sat himself down on his bed. His mind turned to his job, and he thought back to his visits at the unemployment agencies, when it all came back to him about who he was working for. He remembered that Sonja had put the job aside for him, and he then remembered going to the offices of FedEx and chatting to the bloke behind the counter. It was all coming back.

The next morning Matt got himself ready and made his way to the FedEx offices. It wasn't the easiest or quickest of journeys but Matt was determined. More was coming back to him as he slowly made his way there. It was a courier job and he remembered thinking about buying Sonja a bunch of flowers out of his first wage packet when he got it, to thank her. He then recalled that he hadn't actually started work, but then didn't really think that was his fault. Matt arrived at the counter and the same man was there.

"Can I have your ticket?"

"No, I've not come to collect."

"Oh." The man looked up and noticed Matt. He gave him a look as if he knew who he was. "Have you come to complain, then?"

"No, I've come about the job."

"What job?"

"My job. The one you gave me a few weeks ago."

Matt stood his ground. The man stared at him and the appeared to suddenly remember where he had seen him before.

"You never turned up mate, that job's gone."

"But I was knocked down by a car, and I've been in hospital for the last couple of weeks." The man wasn't interested.

"I don't care," he replied. Matt looked at him and noticed that he had an orange twelve over his head. Matt continued to insist that they had no right to give his job away but the man just kept saying he wasn't interested. He got rather angry with Matt's persistence, and Matt could see the rage rising inside him. He turned red as he angrily told Matt what he thought, and Matt began to argue, when all of a sudden the orange twelve above his head turned into eleven. Matt stood there in silence, almost aghast at what he had just seen. Matt saw that the geezer had just taken a year off his own life. It was a bit of a shock to start with, and Matt stopped arguing immediately, leaving quietly, and slowly made his way back to his flat, looking at all the orange numbers as he did so. Occasionally he would see a very low number, but he didn't see any red numbers, or purple or black for that matter.

Matt then started to think about what he used to do before he went into hospital, before he had got a job. "What on earth did I do with myself all day?" he said out loud to himself. The thought of wasting all day around his flat wasn't great, when Mikey and Mop

173

suddenly came to mind. Matt got depressed at the thought of what he'd been like, but decided that with his new found talent, things were going to change, and his life was going to get much better.

The evening seemed to take a while coming, but Zoe arrived as promised and ordered a taxi to take them out to a local pub. They had a couple of drinks but the conversation was a struggle with Matt seemingly more interested in others in the bar than Zoe. They went out again the following evening, and sat in a nearby park, but their dates weren't that inspiring. Due to neither of them having much money, the next few evenings were spent watching the television in Matt's flat. Matt seemed okay with it, and though these weren't the most exciting dates Zoe had ever been on, she was reasonably happy with life and how things were.

Matt found life quite slow and boring, but looking at the numbers was interesting. He wanted to try and talk to one or two people he saw, but Zoe wouldn't let him. Matt couldn't get the numbers out of his head, but it was more serious things like food, drink and bills that were keeping him awake at night. He still had no job, and although he was able to claim some sickness benefit, this was almost nothing, and did very little to lift Matt out of his recent slump towards poverty. Matt then got the thought in his head that he would be a lot better off if he had a car. "True," he thought to himself, "I don't really need one, but how good it would be if I had one." That thought stayed with him for a while.

As Matt was pondering over his situation he suddenly remembered Steve, and more particularly the stash that he had told Matt about. Matt found the scrap of paper with Steve's address on it under the book in his bedroom, unfolded it, and looked at it hard whilst thinking. He considered the fact that there might be a couple of hundred quid sat in Steve's shed that nobody knew about. "I need to liberate that money," he thought to himself, "and I need to do it sooner rather than later before anyone else comes across it." A plan was beginning to evolve.

It was obvious even to Matt that he was not fully fit yet, but his body had responded rather well to his treatment and he was now able to walk much better without his stick. He also felt he would have no problem climbing over a fence or gate, so he decided that he needed to go have a look at where Steve lived, and case the joint a bit. He made his way to the house and by walking around the area identified what he imagined was the alley behind the yard. Counting along the gates, he picked on what he thought was the right one, and pulled himself up to look over. He quickly saw that the yard had a shed that looked close to how Steve described it, and an old bike that Steve had also told Matt about. He was sure that he had got the right place. Matt realised it was too light to do anything now but he noted that the shed was padlocked, and made sure that there were no obvious traps he might encounter, before making his way back home.

That evening Matt went back to Steve's house and rang the front doorbell, but nobody answered. Matt guessed that most of Steve's family would still be away, as again Steve had told him that his wife Shirley had taken the kids to her mother's. Under cover of darkness, Matt climbed over the gate and into the back yard. He looked around and noted that there were probably half a dozen windows that had a view of the back yard, and knew that if any one saw him they would call the cops. No lights seemed to be coming on in Steve's house which was just how Matt wanted it. Mikey and Mop had often shown Matt how to deal with padlocks, and he pulled out a small jemmy from his inside pocket which within seconds had removed the lock. There was a rather loud creaking noise, Matt thought, as he opened the shed door, but he stepped inside and closed the door behind him before hiding the forced lock amongst the contents.

Matt looked through the small window in the shed to see if any lights had gone on because of the noise of the door opening, nd was relieved to find that nobody seemed to have heard anything. He swiftly looked around the shed for what he hoped would be an obvious box full of money.

Matt was lucky. Steve was a very organised person, and most of the things in the shed were neatly stacked. He had already concluded that the cash box, or whatever it was in, would be in a hiding place somewhere, and he just had to find where. Matt searched all the typical places before noticing a hidden shelf under the work bench where there was a small metal box. Matt tried to open the box, but it was locked. This was a bit of a set-back, however Matt was convinced that this was what he had come to find. He sighed. He then noticed a light go on in an upstairs window next door. He stood absolutely still and watched to see if anyone was looking out, but the curtains were drawn and nobody seemed to have noticed him at all. Matt quickly left the shed and climbed back over the gate clutching his prize. He jumped down on the other side with a bit of a fall and pain reverberated around his ribs. He grimaced and doubled over with pain. "Ow!" he cried, as silently as possible. Matt felt his pockets to ensure he had kept hold of his jemmy. All was good. The pain began to recede slightly and Matt took a few deep breaths before he walked briskly down the alleyway and back towards his flat.

As Matt returned to his flat he felt a rush of adrenalin come over him. He placed his prize on his kitchen table. He could feel his heart beating faster. It was strange, he had not felt like this all the way back, but perhaps the pain and the need to be constantly on the lookout, had taken his mind off it all. He wasn't proud of what he had done, nor keen to repeat his actions of this evening, but he knew there would be some money in the tin and he needed it badly. He also told himself that nobody else would have found it if he hadn't taken it, and used this as an excuse for what he had done. He had seen his mother steal money when he was a child and sort of grew up with the ethos of needs must, even as he knew deep down it was wrong.

All he needed now was to get into the bloody thing and see how much was in there. He remembered Steve saying that it would be a start towards helping his business partner, so hoped that there might be a few hundred quid in there. Again Mikey and Mop had shown Matt how to open locked cash boxes before, so with a screwdriver and hammer he soon forced it open.

Inside were a number of bank notes rolled in different bundles and immediately Matt saw that some of them looked like they were twenties. In fact, many of them were twenties. Matt tried to count how much there was as he unrolled the first of four bundles. It looked like at least five or six hundred. His heart beat even faster. He counted the first roll. It came to exactly a thousand pounds. "Wow!" he exclaimed, both excited and pleased. The next two bundles were again a thousand pounds each, and the last lot of notes amounted to eight hundred and ninety-five. Matt had got himself just under four thousand quid. He needed to sit down. It had been a tiring evening.

Chapter 12
Years left

Matt didn't have a good night's sleep. He tossed and turned and woke a number of times during the night, still thinking over what he had done the previous evening. It was really the first time he had ever done such a thing without Mikey or Mop being involved. "It was wrong," he thought to himself, but the thought that he now had nearly four thousand pounds in cash was a fantastic thing to take on board. He went over in his mind what chance there was that anyone else would actually have found the tin. Matt was able to convince himself that this belonged to nobody, and that nobody else would miss it. Nobody apart from Steve and himself even knew it existed, so the family wouldn't miss it. Matt was beginning to get a headache. It was still early but he decided it was no good, he needed to get up.

After rummaging around in his bathroom cabinet, Matt found an ancient packet of paracetamol which he popped out into his hand. "God knows how old they are," Matt said out loud, "but they'll do," he continued. He downed them with a couple of swigs of tap water. He had a shower and slung on some clothes before sitting down in his small lounge. The cash box was still there on the table. Matt looked at it. He knew he had to dispose of the tin. He also knew he had to keep his money well out of Zoe's way. He would have to think of a story about how he came by it as well. It could easily be a debt paid back that he'd loaned Mikey, he thought. Zoe didn't know how much money he might have had in the past. Yes, that would be his story, Matt decided.

Despite his new found wealth, Matt realised that he couldn't sit around all day doing nothing. He would have to go back to the Job Centre or try and find a job somewhere like before. He also needed to check his bank account although guessed he wouldn't have been paid anything having missed some weeks of appointments. First though, he would invest some of his cash in buying new clothes. He also thought it would be a good idea to actually try and visit a few businesses to see if they were taking on any new staff. Talk to them face to face, rather than wait for them to advertise. Matt decided that a more proactive approach was needed to solve his unemployment problem. This was a new Matt, he thought. There were a number of businesses around that would regularly take on new workers, so Matt set off on his walk around the area. He called in to a nearby factory that often advertised for casual staff. It was called Beales. Without any fears, Matt walked into the office and up to the counter. There was an older woman sat behind a desk typing as he walked in. She looked up at him and smiled, and stopped what she was doing, but remained in her seat. "Can I help you?" she asked.

"I'm just enquiring to see if you have any casual vacancies?" Matt said, as he looked at the woman.

She had an orange seventeen above her head, and looked as if she could be in her late fifties.

"Sorry, sir, none at the moment, but we will probably be looking for some extra bodies in a couple of weeks. Can I take a mobile number so we can call you?" The woman grabbed a pencil and paper as Matt gave her his number.

It was the same story at the next few places he visited. It was hard to keep going, but Matt was determined to find a job, and the weather was good, so he carried on. As he walked around the streets he couldn't help looking at people's numbers, and very quickly he got distracted from his original intention and concentrated on the numbers.

Nearly all the numbers he could see were coloured orange, and this was the norm, but if anyone had a red or purple number above their heads, Matt would immediately follow and watch them. He also looked out for anyone with an orange number one, as they probably had less than a year left to live. He was fascinated by it all. When the opportunity arose, he would actually try and chat to these people and find out more about them. He became quite an accomplished communicator and listener, and he was surprised to find that many of them had absolutely no idea that they were dying, and in fact some weren't even ill. Matt had begun to realise that of course it was impossible for him to determine exactly how they would die. Some might have a terminal illness like cancer, but for others it could be a more sudden death with no obvious indications leading up to it. Matt just knew what they didn't, that they were going to die soon.

He was also surprised to find that many of the people he stopped and chatted to were very happy to have someone talk to them, ask about them, and take an interest in their lives. Many were lonely. A lot of them either had no family or had family that had moved far away. Matt's charm gave them some long desired friendship, and they were only too willing to give Matt the time of day and have a cup of coffee with him. He brought them some small pleasure with his friendship. Matt's recent experiences of trying to get a job and some money in the usual way led him to the conclusion that he was never going to get rich quick that way. He knew he had a sort of skill when it came to communicating and he would listen to all of his new found friends talk about their lives, and as and when the opportunity arose, he would try and encourage the friendship a bit more, especially with those he thought might have a bit of spare cash. He was also beginning to find it easy to ask these new friends that had money if he could borrow some from them. He would always start with a low amount and make sure he paid it back quite quickly.

One such friend was Brad. Matt had managed to chat to him now on a few occasions. Brad was in his sixties and suffering from various problems like arthritis and rheumatism, but he was a nice guy and Matt managed to get him to talk about his life. He had his own property in Barkingside and it sounded as though he might have had a bit of money too. Brad's number one had already turned red so Matt knew he was getting nearer to death. Brad was keen to meet up with Matt most days and liked getting the tube to Leyton to visit some of the places he had worked in his lifetime. Chatting about these days with Matt was just great, and it made Brad happy.

"Hey, perhaps tomorrow I should travel to Barkingside and you could show me some of the places you know there," Matt suggested. The two of them discussed the plan and the visit was agreed.

The next day Matt met up with Brad in Barkingside. They met in a park where Brad used to play as a child. Matt knew how to be patient and friendly, but he also knew what his goal was and eventually got invited back to Brad's house for a coffee before he returned home. Brad's house was full of old things which Matt instantly decided were mainly rubbish, but Brad talked about his family and his interests in collecting books and paintings which sounded a lot more interesting. Brad mentioned that he had some really interesting old books in his sitting room and wanted to show Matt, who of course sounded very keen and happily went along with the idea. Matt knew nothing about books but from the way they were stored he immediately noticed some old volumes in a glass cabinet which Brad told him were all first editions and possibly worth a little bit, but not as much as his painting.

"It's an original Edouard Cortes," Brad told Matt, who had absolutely no idea what he was talking about. Brad showed him the painting which was stored away in a cupboard. It was a picture of some people with a horse-drawn carriage, and not very interesting at all as far as Matt was concerned. At least it wasn't as a painting to look at, but he'd made a mental note of the artist's name.

Brad also had some old coins, and he spent a couple of hours showing Matt his collection, whilst chatting about his family who had nearly all moved abroad. Matt picked up one of the books from the cabinet. It was One Flew Over the Cuckoo's Nest by Ken Kesey, which Matt had sort of heard of.

"This was the film that Jack Nicholson was in, wasn't it?" Matt asked.

"Yes that's right. That book was published in the early sixties."

"I've never seen the film, but I heard it's good."

"Not as good as the book, though. You could borrow it if you wanted to read it?" Brad offered the book to Matt.

"Not at the moment, I'm a bit too busy to find much time to read," Matt replied. Almost immediately he realised that if he could borrow the book when Brad's number was flashing, then his chances of ever having to give it back were pretty non-existent. "Hey, if you don't mind when I get some time I'd love to read it, please." Matt tried to resurrect the situation. Brad nodded. The two chatted for about another forty-five minutes before Matt offered his apologies for leaving, explaining that he had other engagements to be going to. Brad had enjoyed the company and was satisfied with how the day had gone.

Matt had arranged to meet up with Zoe. His plan was to take her out for a real slap-up meal, which he was able to do now he had some proper money. He had gone out and bought himself a suit and a new shirt for the occasion. Perhaps it was a bit showy, he thought. Matt didn't see it just as showing off though, more like rewarding Zoe for her help whilst he was in hospital. He told her to expect a surprise, but didn't tell her anything about where they were going that evening. It all started well. Zoe was hopeful that Matt might now start to get back to being that lovely fellow she had fallen in love with. Matt on the other hand just wanted to get Zoe into bed.

"So, where are we going then?" Zoe asked.

"Oh, you'll just have to wait and see."

They started off by walking to a local bar for a couple of drinks, but even during this short walk, there were signs of problems ahead. As they walked there, Matt was obviously distracted, looking at everyone as they went about their lives, and Zoe found it rather annoying. She would be chatting to him, but noticed that he was really not listening.

"What are you looking at?" Zoe found her patience

at an end.

"Just people!" Matt knew Zoe didn't believe what he could see so he didn't fully explain.

"What people?"

"Oh nobody in particular, just everyone." Matt felt that Zoe needed more of an answer than he was able to give. The only fuller explanation he could give her was to tell her that he was looking at their numbers, so he tried to change the subject a bit and pointed to a rather large man sitting at the far end of the bar. "Just look at that blimp down the end there."

"That's rude, Matt." Zoe replied angrily. "I don't like it when people comment on other people's bodies, especially when they're a bit fat." She tutted as she slapped Matt's wrist. Matt was happy. He had changed the subject and managed to get around the numbers issue.

The two of them spent half an hour in the bar trying to make small talk. It was a little bit awkward, but they got through it. Matt looked at his watch and decided that it was time to leave. He took Zoe to a really smart restaurant. Matt had never eaten at such a classy place before, but was determined not to look out of place.

"Can you afford this?" Zoe asked. She had noticed that Matt seemed to have a bit more money than usual, but still thought tonight was going to be far too expensive for them.

"Of course I can."

Matt managed to chat with Zoe over dinner, although

every now and then he couldn't help himself staring at her orange forty-three, and for a while Zoe felt that perhaps things might be getting back to normal. It didn't last though, as Matt spotted a couple in the restaurant where the man was obviously a lot older than his companion.

"Look at those two," Matt said to Zoe. Zoe took a quick glance and saw who Matt was referring to.

"Oh, right. She's a bit of a gold digger, isn't she?" Zoe giggled as she said it.

"Well perhaps I should tell her that she's only got three years to wait."

"What do you mean?"

"Her old man will be dead in three years."

"Oh Matt, stop it." Zoe's giggling turned to a grunt of annoyance. "You're not still on about these bloody numbers again, are you?"

"You don't believe me, but they are there."

"That's all you ever think about nowadays, and you never pay attention to anything I'm talking to you about." Zoe was close to tears again. Matt tried to think of how to make Zoe feel better.

"Don't get upset, you've got a long life ahead of you," Matt said as he began to point to her numbers, before quickly lowering his arm.

"I don't want to know."

"Well spare a thought for those like him over there who only has three years to live." Matt was getting a bit anxious about the fact that the night wasn't going as perfectly as he'd imagined it would, and his voice was a bit louder than it should have been. A

188

few people at other tables turned to Matt as he said it. Then almost as one they turned and looked at the old man who Matt was talking about. This was enough for Zoe, and she got up to leave.

"Don't go, Zoe," Matt pleaded.

"You've embarrassed me. We need to get out of here." Zoe walked towards the exit as a number of the other diners watched. Matt paid the bill and joined her outside.

They made their way back home with Zoe a little calmer than she had been. Matt managed to put his arm around her shoulders and he tried to talk her round to coming back to his flat or allowing him to go back to hers but unsuccessfully.

"Look I'm sorry, I didn't mean to say it out so loud."

"But just for one day, or one evening, I needed you to be normal."

"I am normal!" Matt exclaimed.

"No you're not. You see weird things." As Zoe replied, it shut Matt up instantly. He couldn't really argue with her logic. After a long pause, he said that in order to make it up to her he would take her to the cinema. Matt thought this might be somewhere he could concentrate on Zoe a bit more. Zoe said nothing as she left him, to enter her apartment block. It hadn't been the fantastic night both had hoped for. Matt also came to the conclusion that if he'd been able to pick Zoe up in a car then he might have had more luck. "Yes, a car," he said to himself, as he walked back to his flat. "That's what I need, a car."

189

The next day Matt knew he would have to go and visit his employment agency again and tell them what had happened to him. He wasn't actually getting any benefit income paid into his account at the moment. This wasn't such a great problem due to his new found wealth, but Matt wasn't sure if this was because they thought he had a job, or the fact that he hadn't been in recently. Whatever the reason, Matt wanted to make sure he did things properly, and sensibly thought that he needed to do something to sign back on. It wouldn't do to just live on the money he had taken. The authorities would want to know why he wasn't signing in.

Matt found his paperwork for the Job Centre and he made his way there without any further delay. Within half an hour Matt was in their office looking at the notice board again which advertised some jobs and it began to come back to him, the endless hours he spent trying to find work and getting absolutely nowhere. He looked around at the others who were also there. Various ages, various nationalities! Various numbers! Matt tried to see if there were any reds or purples but everyone had an orange number.

After being spoken to by one of the security men, he was seen by a young man who took a few personal details and then looked at a computer screen and asked a number of questions. Matt explained what had happened, and the young man entered the details onto the computer. After about ten minutes of questions and answers the man arranged for Matt to return at three o'clock for another interview. Matt had very little else to do so spent the rest of the morning and early afternoon walking and sitting around just watching people and their numbers.

At three o'clock on the dot, Matt returned to the Job Centre. They seemed much better organised than he remembered but some things weren't properly coming back to him. As Matt sat waiting, he noticed people at the three interview desks and in particular a brown haired woman. Matt couldn't help but stare at her lovely dark-stockinged legs as she sat there in her smart skirt. He looked at her face and recognised her as Sonja. He recalled some of their previous meetings. This was good, as Matt was still uncertain as to whether or not his memory had fully recovered, but he knew he'd met her before.

"Mr. Briswell, please?" Sonja called out, asking for her next customer. Matt went over and sat down. He focussed on her name which was printed on a badge pinned to her breast. It read Mrs Sonja Wright. Matt felt a sort of warmth from her. It was almost as if she was a real part of his old life, and Matt gave her a warm comfortable smile as he got ready for the interview. "So, you're jobless again Mr. Briswell?" Sonja opened the conversation with a question.

"Well, yes but I had a car accident."

"What sort of accident?" Sonja read some of the notes newly entered on Matt's record but it didn't give much away.

"I was in a coma for a week or so, and failed to turn up for my first day of work."

"Yes, the company have confirmed that they gave you the job, I see. Oh, and we are now taking some money off you each week to pay a court fine. Not the best of situations is it Mr. Briswell, we need to see if we can get you another job."

"Call me Matt, if you like."

"Thank you, but Mr. Briswell will do fine."

The conversation continued for about fifteen minutes, during which Matt checked out Ms Wright closely. She avoided eye contact throughout. It was actually quite a normal situation for Sonja, and she knew Matthew Briswell of old so was quite impressed that he had, on this occasion at least, managed to spend almost ten or fifteen minutes without actually trying to chat her up. She was in fact amazed that he was able to apparently concentrate on getting on with the business of looking for a job. It didn't last though.

"Those ear-rings really suit you," Matt said, as he looked at the little studs that Sonja wore. Matt was really impressed by Mrs Wright, and thought to himself that she was really attractive, and someone he would like to know better. Sonja didn't respond to the remarks, but fought a little smile which Matt noticed. "What a hot lady you are, I must say," Matt continued as Sonja wrote further notes.

"Thank you, Mr. Briswell, I'm well used to your

flattery, but as you should know by now it does you no good," Sonja replied. Matt was stopped in his tracks by her remark and taken by surprise a little. He watched Sonja's mouth as she talked. The actual words took a little longer to be heard. Matt thought about Zoe and then thought about the fact he could now afford to take a real woman out, and he knew that Sonja was the woman he would love to be able to take out.

"I think we've met before, haven't we?" Matt said what he was thinking.

"Yes Mr Briswell, we have met before and I've heard most of your best chat up lines as well."

This left Matt lost for words temporarily.

"Well, with someone as foxy as you I'm going to have to try a lot harder."

Matt looked to see if Sonja would show some sort of indication of blushing, but he was disappointed. Sonja wanted to look at him and see exactly what this Mr Briswell looked like, but she was extremely professional and knew better. She was not supposed to fraternise with any claimants and certainly not with anyone who was on her list of clientele. She kept her eyes firmly fixed on her reports.

"Mr Briswell, you would be better off spending your energy trying to find a job." She dared to give him a stern look as she blinked slowly and lifted her gaze from her file. "And then actually try and turn up for it when you do get one."

She smirked a little as she said it.

"I'll get a job. You'll be impressed," Matt replied as Mrs. Wright indicated that their interview was over by closing the file and laying it on her desk.

A further appointment was arranged for the following week, and Matt was dismissed. He looked back at Ms Wright as she sat scribbling, hoping to catch her eye, but she never looked up. Matt noticed that she had an orange fifty-one over her head, and judged that she was probably at least in her mid-thirties, so felt she must be quite fit in more ways than one. This thought stayed with Matt as he made his way out of the agency. He was also thinking over his previous failed evening with Zoe, and wondering how he could make a better impression with the women in his life as he looked at the local ads in a shop window. 'American car for Sale' caught Matt's attention immediately. As he read a bit more it described the car as a yellow Mustang and straightaway Matt could picture himself driving such a vehicle. The price was shown as £12,000 but Matt couldn't help wondering just how nice a car this might be. He also thought that he had already managed to earn nearly £5,000 this week through his new found gift, so with a little luck he could probably get more if he put his mind to it. Matt dialled the telephone number on the advert and arranged to view the Mustang. He was excited at the thought of owning such a car.

Chapter 13
Gerald is a red 1

Matt was having what he would now consider to be quite a normal day. He walked around pretty much aimlessly, looking at people, following some, watching others and chatting to those he could, but only those of special interest to him. It was a very different Matt to the one of only a few months ago. He had found a new inner confidence, and was now happy to start conversations himself as well as respond to others and if the right person just briefly caught his eye, instead of either turning away from them or completely blanking them he would now do everything he could to turn that glimpse into the start of a new friendship. Yes, it was a very different Matt indeed and he vaguely knew a lot of different people nowadays. One such chap was a man in his twenties called Gerald. Matt didn't know much more about him other than his name, and that he worked in a sports store, but he had a red number one and so Matt was very interested in getting to know him better.

Over the last couple of weeks Matt had already chatted to Gerald a couple of times, and hoped that he'd made a good impression on him, so was pleased when Gerald greeted him like they were lifelong friends.

"Hey, Matt, how are you doing?" They gave each other a high five.

"Not bad, my man, not bad." Matt beamed a big

smile in Gerald's direction as he replied. Matt was pleased to see him again. "Hey, I wondered what you were doing this evening, as I'm out for a drink and just wondered if you wanted to join me?" This was the first time Matt had offered Gerald such an invitation.

"Er, a drink?" Gerald replied, a bit lost for words. The friendship was going well and he was quite honoured at the invitation.

"No problem if you're otherwise engaged," Matt quickly added, slightly concerned. He wondered if it might have been a bit too soon to suggest such a thing. There was no instant reply from Gerald. "I mean it's not important," Matt added, a little concerned that he had put Gerald on the spot.

"Yeah, man, I finish work at six. We can go to one of the bars around here if you fancy. Nice to have a beer before getting off home." Gerald was happy with the idea and a plan seemed to have been made. Gerald then thought to himself that he might have accepted the offer a bit too quickly. "What sort of time do you finish work?" he asked Matt.

"Well…" Matt began, but couldn't quite find the words he needed to explain his situation, so instead gave a shaky hand movement as if he was unsure. "To be honest I don't have a normal finishing time, but six would be spot on tonight," Matt answered. Both were happy with their arrangement.

Gerald met Matt at six that evening as agreed, walking over to the same bench where he had left

196

Matt sitting that morning. As he approached the bench Matt stood up and patted Gerald on the shoulder as a greeting before they made their way to a nearby bar.

"Two beers," Matt ordered as both he and Gerald stood at the bar and looked around to see who else was in. There were a few workers in their various groups, including some very smartly dressed women. "Matt, she's fit," Gerald indicated a young woman on the other side of the bar. Matt saw exactly who Gerald was referring to. She had an orange number over her head so Matt had no real further interest.

"Yeah, she is. Don't let me stop you if you want to chat her up."

"No, that's fine, she can wait."

Matt and Gerald had a few beers as Matt started conversation after conversation to get Gerald to talk a bit more about himself. "So you work in a sports shop?" Matt asked.

"Yes, it's not a very big place."

"So, which one is it?"

"You probably know it. It's JD Sports on the High Road in Ilford," Gerald answered glibly.

"Are you into sports then, man?"

"Well, I used to be!" It was another throwaway remark from Gerald as if he had lots to say but didn't really want to waste any of Matt's time telling him. Matt continued to pry.

"Did you play sports?"

"Yes, in my schooldays I was a bit of a cricketer."

Gerald frowned. "I was asked to sign professionally for Essex when I was sixteen."

"That's awesome, man!"

"Yeah, but I didn't, and as I got older I lost that edge, and I finished up a bit of a has-been."

"Oh, I can't believe that you're a has-been," Matt poured on the praise. "You could probably hit a few sixes now given the chance."

"Maybe, but it takes a lot more than just skill to succeed," Gerald replied rather gloomily. He rubbed his chin with his fingers and huffed. He was obviously annoyed at his inability to make the grade. "But I suppose I enjoy my life which I wouldn't have if I'd gone pro." Gerald tried to sound sincere. Matt had noticed that a few others in the bar nodded in Gerald's direction as if they knew him so guessed he was fairly well known to them. Matt continued to chat to him and through the conversation eventually found out that Gerald had his own house near to Gants Hill, and had a reasonable amount of money that he had inherited through his parents. Matt's eyes lit up as he heard Gerald trying to talk down just exactly how much he had. As far as Matt was concerned, everything was going well. All he had to do now to put his plan into action was to try to work out what Gerald's desires were.

As they chatted Matt also noticed that there were more hardened drinkers in the bar, and most of them had low orange numbers. Quite often those numbers dropped towards the latter part of an evening as they drank more.

"There are a few of us alkies in here this evening," Matt said as he looked along the bar. Gerald laughed as he downed the rest of his beer and ordered another. "Yeah, this is where they seem to be."

Gerald ordered a double scotch to go with his next beer. Matt thought to himself that it was a strange thing to actually watch people gradually kill themselves as they sat at the bar. Gerald knocked back his double scotch as his number turned from red to purple. "Wow!" said Matt to himself. Time was running out fast for Gerald.

Through their numerous conversations, Matt had worked out that cricket was Gerald's weakness, and he suggested they go to an Essex match. He gave Gerald some bullshit about the fact that he had always wanted to get to a game but would appreciate someone who knew the finer points going with him to explain what was going on. Gerald was really up for the idea, and had some plans for making a real day of it. He told Matt he still had some contacts, and could probably get VIP tickets, so that side of things should be left to him. Matt told him that this wasn't going to be a day where Gerald paid for everything, so continued with the idea that they would make a whole day of it. Matt said he would pay for a few beers and a proper English breakfast before the match, and engineered an invitation to Gerald's house the following evening to set out what they were going to do. Matt had got his foot in the door, and from there it was going to be a simple job of borrowing or stealing whatever he could. "All in all, a good evening's work," Matt thought to himself as he made his way back to his little flat.

Chatting to his new friends was now normal for Matt, and he was beginning to get good at extracting information from them about their status and wealth. He had borrowing money down to a fine art as well with various excuses and stories as to why he would need it. As before though, he would always make sure he paid it back quickly to gain even more of their confidence, but he always knew when the right time was to borrow big. Occasionally Matt would pick a real loser with no money, no assets, no nothing and quite routinely would identify them and then drop them as soon as he could.

Also as part of his current routine, Matt met up with Brad regularly, and occasionally called round to see him at his home in Barkingside. Brad was particularly pleased to have Matt come and visit him on days when his arthritis was playing up, which meant it was very painful to walk about. More often Brad was finding it harder to catch the tube or get out of the house so was glad to have a friend he could talk to without having to leave his home.

Today was one of those days. Matt had caught the underground and called in to see Brad.
"Hey, Brad, how are the knees today?" Matt gave

his now accustomed smile as Brad opened the front door.

"Playing up again Matt, come on in." Brad took a step back and invited Matt into the big lounge of his home. They talked about Brad's family and the fact that they now lived quite a distance away from him, so if he was ever to be ill, fall over or have any problems there wasn't anyone who to call on.

"Look, you need to have my number." Matt got his mobile phone out ready to read the number off of it. "I could then get to you in an emergency." Matt fired off his number so Brad could write it down. "And let me have your number so I know who's calling," said Matt, laughing a little as he said it, "you know how it is, I have so many women calling me I need to know if I should actually answer the call." They both laughed. Matt thought he was on a bit of a roll so pushed his luck a little bit more. "Perhaps I ought to have a spare key to your door as it makes sense just in case you had a fall I could then get into help you." Matt laid it on thick.

"Yes, well, that might be an idea but my neighbours would be able to get in if I was in trouble." Brad reassured him.

"Oh, you have a spare key hidden away somewhere?"

"Well, sort of." Brad wasn't sure how to answer.

"That's good." Matt made it sound like he was pleased that Brad had made other contingency plans that didn't include him. There was a bit of a pause before Matt continued. "Of course if I was the only one you could get hold of it would help if I knew where the key was too." Matt made it sound like a bit of an afterthought. In the end Brad told him about the spare key he already had hidden away in the garden, and thanked Matt for having such consideration for him in case of any problems.

Matt had noticed that Brad's number was beginning to turn to purple so time was running out faster than even Matt had assumed. Matt had also spent a lot of time trying to get Brad to tell him what his biggest wish was in life. He had asked him the question a number of times and got various answers from "Seeing my family," and "Saving the world from starvation" before Matt finally tuned in on the fact that Brad had always wanted to go to New York. They talked for ages about what the city was like and what films Brad could remember that were shot in New York and eventually Matt found his opportunity.

"Why don't you sell one or two of your things that you can't take with you when you die, and give yourself a nice break in the city of your dreams?" Matt made it sound like such a great holiday. Brad's mouth was watering. His eyes were ablaze with excitement. He could imagine Times Square and the yellow cabs and really wanted to go.
"But how much would a holiday like that cost me, Matt?"
"If you were going to do it in style, probably two or

three thousand!"

"That's a lot!"

"Yes it is, but you've got it so why not spend it on yourself. Book a ticket for a first class flight, a flash hotel and go for all the works." Matt laid it on thick. "That painting you keep locked up, that might well pay for it all, you know."

"But I wouldn't want to sell my prize possession, I was going to pass it on to my grandsons." Brad shook his head at the thought of parting with the painting. "No, I don't think I could do that." Matt thought about another line of attack.

"But you have plenty of other things that you can pass on to your grandsons. Many things that they will appreciate rather than a painting that they'll only sell themselves anyway." Matt was in top form at the moment. "You deserve some holiday time so let's get it sorted." Brad moved his head from side to side as he thought hard about what Matt was suggesting.

"I wouldn't know how to sell it anyway," Brad confided.

"Don't worry about that, I can do it for you." Matt had his plan in action.

Part of the plan involved getting Brad to be confident enough to allow Matt to take the painting into a dealer's shop. He thought of various ways in which this could be done before coming to the conclusion that there was nothing for it but to get the use of a car. Matt had spoken to the owner of the Mustang a couple of days before and felt that he could probably take the car out for a spin if he paid him some money. In fact, he even thought he would be able to persuade him to loan him the car. It wouldn't be easy, but Matt was convinced he could do it, so that was another part of the Brad plan he had to put into action.

Over the next few visits, the plan was laid out and expanded upon a little bit more each time. Matt said that he would guess that Brad could expect at least four or five thousand pounds for the painting if a dealer could verify it was genuine, but this would mean leaving it with the dealer for a while. Brad became reluctant. Matt wasn't going to give up that easily, and tried to convince him again. "Look, next time I come over I'll drive, and we can take it to a dealer together so you don't lose sight of it." Matt sounded very positive.

Brad was thoughtful, but seemed to agree. "Hey, if you get a few thousand for it perhaps you'll give me something for the fuel!" Matt tried to sound funny as he dropped in this last comment.

"Oh, don't be silly." Brad felt slightly ashamed that Matt had had to ask such a thing.

"You can have a percentage of what the painting sold for as you'll be doing most of the work." Brad told him immediately.

"We'll see."

This part of the plan was organised and on the day that Matt took Brad and his painting to the dealer, he had managed to borrow the Mustang. Brad was suitably impressed. They drove to a dealer in the city and whilst Brad sat in the car Matt went into the shop and chatted about the painting. Brad could see them discussing things, and both looking at the painting. Matt appeared to be making enquiries exactly as he had said he would, but he returned to the car carrying the painting with him. He placed it in the back of the car and told Brad that "we just have a couple of problems to sort out."

"Firstly, they've got to have the painting in order to test it for originality, but unfortunately, I've said that the painting was mine and the dealer wanted some sort of bill of ownership or bill of sale to prove it."

"Oh, that's blown it then, no New York for me." Brad was a bit downhearted.

"No not really, I think we could find a way round this." Matt told Brad he had an idea.

When they got back to Brad's house, the full plan was explained to him. Brad would have to sign a backdated bill of sale to Matt so that he could give it to the dealer. Matt knew that Brad wouldn't just do that so he continued, explaining that so that Brad kept ownership of the painting, Matt would sign another document explaining that the painting was in fact still owned by Brad, and that the bill of sale was only a temporary arrangement. It seemed complicated but eventually, Brad began to see where Matt was coming from. Matt explained that Brad would then hold on to this second document until he had got the money from the sale, at which time it could be destroyed, but until Brad was happy that he'd got all the money for the painting he had that as his insurance. It took a bit of persuading but Brad agreed, signed the documents and Matt took the painting away with him.

On the way home that afternoon Matt had to keep turning around to look at the valuable painting sitting in the back of the Mustang. "What a life I'm living!" he thought. It was hard to believe just how easily he had been able to convince someone to part with such items. He could also see that both would finish up being his, in time. Matt shook his head in some disbelief as to how life had changed.

Chapter 14
Old friends

Matt thought long and hard about how his relationship with Zoe was going, and it didn't make good thinking. They weren't meeting up every evening any more. On weekdays Zoe needed to get to bed early, as she was always up for work the next day, so their dates were mainly confined to weekends. He'd taken her out to the park, but things didn't go well there. He had taken her to a number of pubs and bars, but again he was easily distracted. He'd even taken her to a fancy restaurant and he still kept looking at other people so he decided that it was time that he and Zoe did something a bit different for a change.

"Ah, yes," Matt said out loud, as he remembered that Zoe had often talked about wanting to go to the cinema. He nodded to himself as he decided that was what they should do this evening. Matt didn't actually tell Zoe until he called at her flat that evening, but she seemed keen to go and looked up the listings in her weekly free paper. She picked a film she hoped they would both like and they made their way to the cinema. Everything seemed okay to start with. They exchanged general chit-chat as they made their way to the cinema, and Zoe hoped that this evening would be a turning point in their relationship. Matt worked hard keeping his focus on Zoe and whatever she was saying, and all was going well, but Matt hadn't bargained on the darkness of the cinema causing him a problem.

They sat down in the dark theatre, and gradually more people arrived and sat around them. Each one had their bright glowing number, which made looking at the screen almost impossible for Matt. It wasn't that bad as he and Zoe shared some popcorn through the trailers, but when the main attraction started and Zoe snuggled down holding Matt's arm and tried to concentrate on the film, he found watching the screen very difficult indeed. He kept moving his head to the left and right to avoid the glare of numbers and in order to get a good view of the film, but eventually he lost the storyline and gave up. He closed his eyes to bring himself some relief, but Zoe noticed and nudged him to make him watch again. Matt found it all very frustrating and by the end of the film, all he wanted to do was go back home. He thought of an excuse he could use. "I've got a real stinker of a headache coming on, so can we just go back home?"

"Matt, I'm sorry to hear that." Zoe wiped his forehead as they left the cinema. "I'll have a look in my bag and see if I've got any tablets." She rummaged around but without success. "How about we grab a quick bite to eat?"
"I'm just not that hungry, Zoe." The two walked arm in arm without saying much until Zoe broke the silence.

"I was surprised to see Morgan Freeman in the film weren't you?"

"What part was he, then?"

"You know, the old man who saved the dog."

"What dog?"

"The black and white dog," Zoe said giving Matt a long hard stare. "You did watch the film, didn't you?"

"Look, I couldn't really see the film properly," Matt thought about explaining.

"How come?" Zoe said in a surprised tone. Matt didn't really answer. "You didn't want to go to the pictures at all, did you?"

"Yes, I did," Matt replied honestly, but Zoe didn't look as if she believed him.

They were nearer to Zoe's flat so stopped there first, but by the time they got there, Matt had made his excuses for the evening and left her. It was a bit of a naff Friday evening for both of them. He knew that things weren't going well between the two of them, and indeed realised that he would be quite happy if they weren't actually seeing each other but he didn't have the courage to just end it with her. Zoe was still trying to find the Matt she had first fallen in love with and wasn't ready to give up on him quite yet. She used the accident and the coma as an excuse for him, but hoped that if she could just find the inner man again then they could move on to the next stage.

Over the next few weeks Matt and Zoe went out a few times, but Matt's obsession with looking at everyone and seeing their numbers remained. Zoe was just getting completely sick of the whole deal. Her patience was really being tested and although she was convinced that somewhere deep down there was still a beautiful Matt just waiting to return, she had very much got to her wit's end with it all. Zoe's friend Ruth got a lot of earache about it, too. Most Monday mornings at work Zoe would come to her depressed, and by Friday Ruth had built her back up, only to see her fall again the next weekend. Ruth had decided that some intervention was required if the situation was ever going to be resolved.

There was a knock on Matt's front door. He ignored it to begin with as many of the local kids would play knock and run but there was another knock. Matt wondered who it might be as he wasn't expecting anyone.

"Hello," he said opening the door and seeing a young woman stood there.

"Hi, are you Matt?" Ruth asked. Matt thought this was a nice surprise, a nice looking female calling at his door and one who knew his name.

"Yes, this is Matt. Who are you?"

"I'm Ruth, Zoe's friend." Matt's enthusiasm sunk. "I wonder what this is about?" Matt thought to himself, fearing the worst.

"Do you mind if I come in for a moment and have a quick chat with you?"

"By all means, come on in," Matt shrugged his shoulders as he opened the door wider and allowed Ruth in.

Ruth immediately looked at what Matt's flat was like. Nothing to great but clean enough, she thought. "Can I get you a drink at all?" Matt indicated he meant alcohol.

"No thanks, I won't be staying long," Ruth replied.

"Oh, okay. What did you want then?"

"I want to ask you what you think of Zoe."

"What I think of Zoe?" Matt exclaimed in a rather high-pitched voice. "We're going out together, so do I love her, is that what you mean?"

"*Do* you love her?" Ruth emphasised the 'do' in her question.

"Is it really any business of yours?" Matt was slightly pissed off at the interrogation.

"She's my best friend, and she's so confused. She doesn't know whether you want to be with her or not, and she's getting depressed over it."

"Of course I want to be with her," Matt was beginning to feel annoyed. "Anyway she should be here talking about this, not you." There was a long period of silence.

The silence began to get a bit awkward with Ruth waiting for Matt to give a proper answer to her question, and Matt waiting for Ruth to say something else. It seemed like neither was going to ever say anything ever again when there was another knock on Matt's door. Both Matt and Ruth sighed with relief. Matt went to the door and opened it and stood there was a woman he had met up with a few times, called Beverley.

"Oh, hi, Bev, how are you?" Matt and the woman kissed cheeks and hugged briefly before Beverley entered the flat. Ruth saw that they had kissed but had guessed that the woman was in her forties, so didn't really get alarmed by it. She briefly wondered what another woman was doing visiting her best friend's so called boyfriend but didn't think Matt was actually seeing another woman. Beverley immediately looked over in Ruth's direction.

"I'm fine, Matt. Oh, hello, I'm Bev, you are...?" Beverley put out a hand towards Ruth.
"Er...oh, hello." Ruth quickly touched hands but said nothing else. Beverley waited briefly to see if Ruth was going to say more but as nothing was forthcoming, and Matt seemed okay with things, she got on with what she had come for. There was a slight embarrassment on Matt's part.
"This is Ruth," Matt introduced her to Bev.
"Matt I've just really called round to thank you." Beverley said, as she sat down in one of Matt's easy chairs.

Matt looked at Bev, and in particular the red number one that was shining above her head. Matt had chatted to Bev quite a bit now and knew she was only just forty-seven, and as far as he could tell wasn't ill, but he knew what she didn't, that she had less than a year to live. In fact, by Matt's calculations it was probably nearer to seven or eight months as he had seen her for a while now with her red coloured number.

"Oh, it's nothing Bev, you know it was just easy to sort out." Matt was conscious of the fact that Ruth was listening to their conversation. "Are you happy for me to discuss the item in front of someone you don't know?" Matt looked over at Ruth.

"If you think it's okay, no skin off my nose," Beverley replied, still curious to find out who this other woman was.

"In that case, yes, they have given me a receipt for the vase if you want to see it, and they'll ring me as soon as they have a proper valuation for it."

"Oh, Matt, that's great. You keep hold of the receipt for now but when they give you a valuation, what happens then?"

"They will also offer the price they are prepared to pay for it."

"What, and we just accept it?"

"No, I think we should try and get a second valuation just in case they are trying to rip you off, as the vase is pretty valuable."

"That's great." Bev jumped up to her feet as she said it. She then walked over and gave Matt a big kiss on the lips as she hugged him. "I can see you're busy so I'll be on my way, but I won't forget what you're doing, you darling."

Beverley said goodbye to Ruth and then made her way out of the flat.

"So, who the hell was that?" Ruth asked as soon as the door was shut.

"Oh, that's an old friend of mine called Bev."

"She seemed quite a close friend."

"Not really, just a grateful acquaintance, I suppose."

Matt knew that Bev was quite fond of him. He also knew that she was an attractive woman who he could probably quite easily sleep with, but he was far more interested in her money. "She wants to go on a trip to Australia to see her grand-daughter and I'm helping her raise some money to finance it, that's all." Matt started explaining. After telling Ruth the first bit of the story he stopped thinking that he wasn't quite sure why he felt he had to explain anything let alone to this woman.

"Oh, right, so you're not going out with her then?" Ruth didn't actually think he was but wasn't absolutely sure what to make of Matt. She didn't really know him.

"Of course not!" Matt replied with a forced laugh as if to indicate that the suggestion was ridiculous.

As if the visit of Beverley wasn't enough there was yet another visitor to Matt's flat as there was a knock on the door again. This time Matt answered it and there was a man stood there.

"Doug, come in, my man." Matt was pleased to see a man this time as Ruth was beginning to get too

214

inquisitive.

"Matt, sorry to bug you, but I need to know what you're doing about the car?"

"Hey, yeah, the car." Matt led Doug into the room and introduced him to Ruth. "This is Ruth, my girlfriend's best friend." Doug shook hands with Ruth. "This is Doug, a mate of mine." Matt looked again at Doug and the black number one over his head. Matt knew he didn't have long left. "So Doug, the car!" Matt led Doug into the kitchen as he was talking.

"Yes I just want to know what you're intending to do?"

"Well you know I want it but I'm just trying to free up some of my assets at the moment so that I have the cash to pay you in one lump sum."

"So when will that be, and will it be the full £12,000?" Doug needed the money but didn't want Matt to know this.

"Yes, it will be the full £12,000, but I just need a few weeks to get it together. How about in the meantime I pay you £500 to use the car and I still pay you the £12,000 on top when I get it?" Matt suggested. He sensed that Doug was desperate but he couldn't tell how desperate.

"Is that £500 a week?"

"How much dough do you want from me? I was thinking more like £500 a month."

"No, that's not enough. If you made it a week, then you might have yourself a deal and you can just take it off the price as well." Doug tried to work out if that amount would get him out of his current gambling debt this week.

Whilst all this was going on Ruth manoeuvred herself nearer to the kitchen so she could hear what was being said and although she couldn't pick up every word she began to get an idea as to what was going on.

"Look, I'll pay you £800 now if that will help, but I'm not sure I can get £500 each week." Matt tried to work out how much money he had in the flat.

"Yeah, okay." Doug immediately agreed hearing that he was going to get £800 straightaway. He also knew that the car was probably only worth about £10,000 and even less if he went to a trader to sell it so was pleased to think he would be getting enough eventually to clear all his debts.

"So I'll get you some money now and then I'll pay you another £500 next month until I can get the cash to buy the whole thing outright." Matt felt he had a deal.

"Yes, but I need some money now."

"That's okay, I'll go and get it." Matt went off to his bedroom where he had some money stashed and counted out £800 which he placed on his bed. He then counted out a further £200 and put that in his back pocket before returning the rest of the cash. When he returned to the kitchen, Doug seemed nervous. "Look, I have the cash now," Matt showed Doug the £800. "There is just one thing though, I have been stopped a couple of times by the cops, and

I need the registration document to take into the police to show that I have the right to drive it and haven't stolen it from you."

"You give me the cash now, and I'll drop the document off tomorrow but I want it back as soon as you've taken it in."

"Okay, man, don't get crazy." Matt looked at Doug and wondered if he would bring the document he wanted. "Hey look, I will get some more cash for you tomorrow when you come round."

"Okay." Doug sort of agreed. Matt saw him to the door and briefly shook his hand. He hoped that Doug would keep to his word and bring the registration document tomorrow.

When Doug had gone Ruth was back to give Matt some grief.

"So can we get back to Zoe?"

"Yes, I love her." Matt tried to sound genuine. "We've had some problems but we can sort those out and I want us to be together." Matt laid it on as thick as he could, and eventually Ruth seemed happy that at least Matt was trying to make Zoe happy. She left him with a warning though that she would not forgive him if he upset her anymore.

After Ruth had left Matt immediately went back to his money stash. It was now starting to diminish a bit and he needed to see if he could get some more money from somewhere. He returned the £200 back to the box and worked out where he could get some more money from. It quickly came to him that he could try and borrow some more money off his DJ friend, Dave. "He's always good for a quick loan," Matt thought to himself. That evening Matt went to the little pub-cum-club, Bella, and did his usual, taking leftover beers from tables here and there, making it look as if he had bought a drink, whilst he chatted to the DJ. Things were always slow at the start and Matt chatted with Dave for a good hour before saying he had to try and meet a girl in another bar.

"Bring her back here and let me play you some proper music," Dave said.

"Yeah, of course," Matt answered then he felt around his trouser pockets "Damn, I've left my wallet at home." Matt felt around again, shaking his head. "Dave, lend us a couple of notes so I can just buy my girl a drink and I'll get it back to you when come back." The DJ shook his head in a knowing way, and handed a twenty to Matt. He knew full well he was unlikely to ever see it again, but he looked forward to meeting Matt's new girlfriend later during the evening. Matt didn't return.

Matt made his way out of Bella wondering where he could go next to get a drink, but took a few moments to consider his life. He kept coming back to the point that he now had so many different friends, that there was always someone he could go and chat to and borrow some money from. He knew it wouldn't take too much effort to raise some more cash, but he needed to visit people quickly to do it in the time he had. Matt had more friends now than he ever had before, but when he seriously thought about it he realised that most of them were much older than him. This was, of course, because he would befriend those with only a year or so to live and hence they were mainly older people and quite regularly dying. This also brought about other problems for Matt, as he was often told by some of these friends that he was being written into their wills. This was all fair enough, but Matt realised that if he ever met any of his new friend's family before they died, it would look better if he attended the funeral. It just made it appear that he had been a friend much longer than he really had, so that when the will was read it didn't come as too great a surprise when they found out that Matt was being left a family heirloom or valuable masterpiece.

Tomorrow was another one of those funerals that Matt felt he should attend. The person involved was an old man named Byron who Matt had actually grown to like a lot during their meetings. Byron was in his seventies, but in fairly good health, so although Matt wasn't surprised at all, many of Byron's relatives were shocked when he passed away quietly in his sleep one night. During the occasions that the two of them got together Matt had got to know one of Byron's best friends but had never actually met any of his relatives. Matt decided that although he would make a point of speaking to Thomas he would try and speak as little as possible to any of the family, but try and make sure he was noticed. Even if by nobody else, he would make sure Byron's friend Thomas saw him there. Assuming he turned up of course, although Matt was certain he would.

Morning soon arrived, and the sun shone very brightly through the trees in the cemetery. As was usual at these things, there were less than a dozen people at the funeral and Matt calmly waited for the obvious relations to go into the chapel before entering and sitting down in one of the pews at the back. There was an only son with his wife and children, and what looked like a sister of Byron's. Matt knew of the son from his chats with Byron. Matt also knew that his name was Spencer or Spence and that Byron hadn't actually seen him for over a year. Matt also looked around for Thomas, and spotted him, also sat towards the back of the chapel. The service was short and the coffin taken to the grave fairly quickly. Matt nodded briefly to Spencer as the family followed the coffin out of the chapel. There was a quiet conversation between Spencer and his wife.

"Who's that?" The woman indicated with her eyes that she was talking about Matt but didn't actually look at him.

"I don't know," Spencer replied. "Surely it isn't that Matthew Briswell guy from the will. He's so young,

for God's sake."
"No, I reckon that it'll be the chap sat at the back here." The woman indicated in Thomas's direction.
"No, I've met him before, his name is Thomas something," Spencer advised.

After the family had passed by there were only Thomas and Matt left in the chapel. Matt hated these moments. The family would all be waiting outside and everyone had to say something to the next of kin as they left the chapel. Matt expected it to be the son, but was happy to see that Byron's sister seemed to have taken on the responsibility. Thomas looked at Matt with a nod.
"I'm glad you could make it, young man, as Byron liked you," Thomas said quietly as they got nearer to Byron's sister. Thomas spoke to her first, before Matt made some simple but appropriate comment. She replied with the usual polite 'Thank you' before Matt and Thomas moved away to the side and stood apart from the rest of the party. Matt could feel the stare of the son looking at him almost constantly. Matt also looked around at the numbers above everybody's heads and they were all orange. In fact, all except the sister were in double figures. Matt looked at the number sixteen above Thomas' head, which he was surprised to see.

As the burial progressed, Matt stood away from the rest of them. He didn't want to be seen much more as he'd achieved his goal of being noticed and that was enough. Unfortunately, as the son was regularly looking at him he didn't feel that he could slip away yet, but when the chance came he would certainly take it. As soon as the burial was over, the son and his wife started to make their way from the grave side in Matt's direction. Matt stood a bit further back, hoping that they would just carry on past, but the son had other ideas and he approached Matt. He was okay to start off with.

"Morning, thank you for coming to my father's funeral."

"Please don't mention it, it's a sad day." Matt hoped he had said as little, but as much, as he needed to.

"I'm afraid I don't actually know who you are though?" Spencer's tone had changed.

"I was a friend of your father."

"Oh right. Are you Matthew?"

"Well I'm called Matt but I suppose that's me." Matt guessed what was coming next.

"How long have you known my dad?"

"Not too long, about a year or so perhaps."

"So how did you get written into his will?" Spencer's voice was aggressive. His wife pulled back on Spencer's arm, interrupting the conversation.

"Spence dear, let's not worry about that now." She pulled him away to encourage him to carry on walking but Spencer wanted one last word.

"I don't know who you are, but I'll contest your inclusion." The son was happy that he had said it, and then did as his wife asked and started to move on. Matt had been through this once before and knew that at the right time he would remind Spencer that he had not visited his father for almost a year before he died.

Matt allowed the others to leave the cemetery through the main gates as he departed by another gate. He decided to take a slow walk home and found himself in an area of the city that he didn't know too well. There were kids playing football and others throwing a frisbee but Matt's immediate attention was drawn to three youths who were standing around a car. They all had flashing black ones above their heads, though they seemed decent enough. However, as Matt approached they took up more aggressive stances. Matt decided to try and avoid eye contact, but one of the youths called out to him.

"Hey, you. Geezer, are you lost?" There was a brief silence as Matt looked up at them.

"No, I'm fine." Matt noticed that they had a bottle of what looked like vodka, and had obviously been drinking. "You all be careful if you're going to drive that car."

"What's it to you? Are you a Pig?" One of the lads replied. He stood up as if to confront Matt, but Matt kept moving.

"Nothing, I'm just saying the roads can be dangerous, but nothing else." Matt moved a bit quicker and got far enough away from the youths to consider himself safe from any further confrontation.

He guessed that they might be half pissed and happy to show off so he wanted to diffuse any possible situation before it started. Despite moving away, he listened as much as he could to what was being said. "Hey bro, perhaps you shouldn't swig no more if we're cruising, man," one of the youths spoke out. The others just laughed at him and started to push him around a little whilst mimicking what he had just said.

"Shouldn't swig no more," one mocked.

"You don't think I can drive properly, man?" asked the one with the bottle of vodka as he swigged down some more of the spirit and coughed as he shouted. It was said so that not only could all the boys hear him, but also Matt.

"Yeah, you stay in the park whilst we cruise for the laydeez," another of them joked.

The first youth walked around trying to get things back on track, but the vodka drinker just downed more of the spirit, and got into the car.

"Leave the young one here, bros. We're cruising!" The car engine started. Matt watched as the three got into the car, but pushed the other one out of the way. Matt found the whole scene fascinating as the car did a couple of spins in the road. He saw the two boys half poke their heads out of the side windows whistling and shouting. Their flashing numbers could clearly be seen. They finished the vodka and then threw it in the direction of the lad standing in the road as the car did another spin, and sped off down the road. As the car skidded around a corner and roared off, the one left behind stood and stared after them. Matt watched him as his flashing black number one became a solid number. It then turned from black to purple almost immediately, and then to red. Matt was amazed as within seconds the red number over his head changed to orange, and then increased to sixty-four.

'Wow!' Matt said as he shook his head. "I think I might have just saved somebody's life."

Matt called round to see Brad again that evening. Although it was late and getting dark Brad was very pleased to see him. "I was a bit worried that I would never see you again, nor my painting."

"Don't be a dunce, Brad," Matt consoled him. "I'm a friend, I'm trying to help you."

"Yeah, I know but still it's a lot of money and you never know what people might do these days."

"Look, I'm sorry. I can go and get the painting back tomorrow if you want me to, and we'll forget all about that trip." Matt looked to see how Brad would react to him saying that. Brad moved his head side to side a bit but was obviously still keen to go west. Matt also noted Brad's number change to purple.

"I'm not saying that, I'm just a little concerned, you know."

"Yes, I understand. What can I do to put your mind at rest?"

"Well, what is the name of the place where they are

doing the valuation?" Brad wanted just a little bit more convincing.

"Oh, it's called La Freze or something like that. Look, I'll call in there again tomorrow and get their card."

"Yes, that would be good then I can ring them to confirm what the valuation is."

"That might work." Matt didn't really want him doing it though, so thought of a reason to put him off. "But don't forget it'll take a few weeks for them to check the originality and we don't want to harass them yet, do we?"

"No, I suppose not. San Francisco, eh?" Brad looked up to the sky, obviously dreaming about his holiday.

It was only a short visit and very soon Matt left Brad thinking about New York as he made his way back home. He laughed a little to himself at the thought that Brad would never get out of his home, let alone to New York. He took a brief moment to consider exactly what the situation was, and to confirm that he was well in control of things. He knew Brad had only weeks left, and even if he was trying to buy a ticket to New York he would never go on that trip. That wasn't his doing, Matt concluded. The painting was as good as his. As Matt made his way through the streets towards Barkingside, a man in a dark coat lurked in the shadows of an alley watching his every move. He could see what had been happening with Brad and he wasn't happy with Matt at all.

Byron's funeral had come to an end, and the few family members that had gathered to give him a send-off congregated at a local restaurant. Spencer had pondered for a while over his annoyance that this Matthew Briswell was included in his father's will, and without consulting his wife he went to the police in order to try and relieve his pain a bit. Spencer was adamant that some foul play had taken place. Detective Sergeant Joe Clarke took the details almost automatically. As soon as he heard what the complaint was about he switched off knowing that there was no offence they would be interested in following up, but hoped he satisfied Spencer's insistence that someone would indeed look into the matter.

Chapter 15
Need to check on Brad

Matt and Zoe went out a few more times but none of their evenings were that brilliant. On each date Matt would somehow find a way of bringing the conversation around to illnesses or dying and Zoe was just plain sick of it. She still didn't believe that Matt could see these bloody numbers that he kept referring to, and most evenings this would end with an argument. Usually it was over something to do with death or dying. Matt tried to show Zoe that he still loved her, but he wouldn't listen when she started to complain about the number of elderly people he was mixing with. He didn't see it as a problem, and tried his hardest to convince Zoe that she shouldn't worry about what he was doing, but it all fell on deaf ears.

Their arguments became quite regular and to be honest, Matt was sometimes quite relieved to be on his own without Zoe. He was beginning to weigh up exactly how he felt about the relationship. He fancied her a lot, and thought he sort of loved her, but he wanted to continue with his new lifestyle. It was a bit of a relief to him when Zoe decided that they should perhaps cool things a bit and have some space. Zoe wasn't sure how she felt about Matt either, and Matt was just so intrigued by all the new aspects of his life. New things had really only begun since he had been able to see the numbers, and he found it all rather exciting. He tried to calculate how many new friends he had made and was surprised that it was currently more than ten. He would of course target those who had black or purple numbers and see if they had anything of value that he could get from them before they died, and he was beginning to get quite good at it.

There were of course also a number of women Matt befriended. Many were depressed for some reason or another, but there were also a couple of women who weren't that old and still good looking enough to arouse him sexually. Not that this was his reason for getting to know them. His main aim was of course to borrow or take money or things of value from them, so that he would end up owning whatever he had when they died, but occasionally because he showed a lot of interest in these people it led to much closer relationships and with women, more physical relationships. He pondered again over what his future might be, and although he was now fairly solvent he knew he was never going to become a millionaire overnight. He realised however that he was beginning to acquire quite a bit of money one way or another. He was also still getting some benefit income which all added to his wealth.

There was one particular woman he had a great friendship with, called Polly. As far as age was concerned, she fitted perfectly into his new group of friends, but although she was in her sixties she was still extremely attractive, Matt thought. He was in fact very impressed with how fit she was, and he knew she went to the gym regularly in order to keep her body trim. He found it hard to believe her age, let alone knowing how long she had left to live, and on many of their meetings he seemed to get on better with her than he did with Zoe, or anyone else nearer to his own age. He had got to know Polly very well, and found out a lot about her past. She had been married a couple of times before, and each time to rich husbands, but she was obsessed by the fact that she was beginning to lose her looks. Matt disagreed with her and told her so. She was extremely flattered to find a twenty-five-year-old man taking an interest in her, and in return she regularly bought him smart clothes, expensive jewellery and top of the range toiletries, all things that she wanted her man to have.

Matt was quick to take advantage of this situation, and he would often tell her that he had some business idea that needed financial support. He managed to persuade her to take some forward dated cheques of his in return for immediate cash injection. Polly was convinced that she would get the money back, and wanted to keep her new found toy-boy around, so the whole idea seemed just right for her.

Because Zoe was not around it was possible for Matt and Polly to have a brief but amorous relationship, with him spending more time at her place. He had convinced her that she should give him his own key, and he would surprise her every now and then, naked in bed waiting for her when she returned from the gym. Polly was really happy with Matt and thought she was the happiest she had ever been in her life. Occasionally Matt would also make use of his time in her place to check out her valuables.

There were a couple of bronze statuettes that Matt tried to value, but if he was honest he had no idea how much they might be worth. He thought he would bide his time, and even if he didn't manage to get them back to his flat he was probably already four or five grand better off because of Polly anyway. There was no real love lost when Polly died of a heart attack one morning whilst at the gym, and Matt wasn't particularly surprised when he was eventually told. It was something he was just getting used to as an everyday event in his life.

The morning was bright again and Matt got out of bed and started getting dressed and ready for the day. He had another interview at the Job Centre and he was fairly certain that he would meet the luscious Mrs Wright again, so he put on one of his new shirts, a tie and some aftershave, just for luck. As Matt waited for his turn at the agency, he kept his eye on Mrs Wright, watching lustfully as she uncrossed and crossed her fantastic long legs as she sat behind the desk. Matt just wanted to go over there and kiss her, but he was prepared to work at it.

"Hello, Mrs Wright, or may I call you Sonja?"

"Mrs Wright will be sufficient, Mr. Briswell," she replied, catching a hint of his aftershave. It was a very nice scent, and she allowed herself a brief look at him. She noticed immediately that he was very smartly dressed for a change. She had only intended to confirm that it was indeed the Mr. Briswell she had been expecting, but his new look kept her gaze lingering rather longer than she was professionally happy with. Matt winked as she looked at him, but Sonja just looked away. She was quietly impressed, though.

The interview went along its normal course, with Sonja telling Matt that he had to get some job interviews every week and bring in evidence of them when he had his next appointment in two weeks' time. Matt dropped in a few chat-up lines, trying to get some reaction from Mrs Wright, but it never seemed to work. The short interview came to a close and as Matt stood up Sonja spoke. "Thank you Mr. Briswell, I'll see you in two weeks' time. The aftershave is nice, by the way." Despite not wanting to give him any indication that she was taken by his new look, she couldn't help her voice becoming softer than she would normally use when speaking to clients. Sonja was annoyed with herself. She cursed under her breath knowing that she mustn't mix business with pleasure.

During the next couple of weeks, Matt visited Brad a few times ensuring he could locate the spare key if he needed to, and he told Brad that the originality testing and subsequent valuation was going on longer than expected. He said he was hoping for some confirmation as to the auction date. The painting was of course safely tucked away in Matt's flat. Brad's number had now turned black, and on Matt's penultimate visit had begun to flash. Brad did seem to be struggling a bit, but the thought of getting to New York kept him going. Matt could see he was becoming weaker, but the flashing number over his head said it all. Matt also got the idea of driving over to Brad's but parking his car away from the house, and then walking from there. It was just so on the last occasion that he visited and found he couldn't get anyone to answer the door. He used the spare key to let himself in, and immediately saw that Brad had collapsed and died in the hallway.

There was no light shining above his head so Matt knew for certain that he had gone. He knew he had to act quickly, and he knew what he wanted. There were some coins that Brad had left in a drawer, some books that Matt had also got his eye on. Brad had also stashed some cash away in a biscuit tin, but more importantly Matt wanted the document he had signed stating that the painting was still Brad's. It took him ten minutes to gather these things which he placed in an old plastic bag, before locking the place up again and returning the key to its hiding place.

Despite having got to know him very well, and

having seen him just after he had died, Matt felt no true compassion for Brad at all, even though he had grown to like him a lot. It was all part of a day's work for Matt, and he strolled casually back to where he had parked his car. Matt had known that Brad was going to die fairly soon, and when it did happen he just accepted it. This was how he was with all the new people he met.

When Matt returned to his flat he made a couple of calls on his mobile to Brad's as if he was trying to ring him. Matt had learned that he might sometimes be questioned by the police regarding his interest in the deceased, and he wanted to make it look as if a death was as much a surprise to him as it was anyone else. The next day he made another call to Brad before ringing a neighbour and telling them that he had been unable to get hold of Brad for a couple of days, and could they perhaps just knock on his door to make sure he was alright. Almost as if Matt had written the script, the neighbour called round to Brad's, couldn't get any answer, so later that evening they used the hidden key and found Brad dead on the hallway floor. From then on, it was over to the police and emergency services.

Whilst all this was going on, Matt had decided to have a drink at the White Hart. After all it was his local and he hadn't been in there for a while. Jed was behind the bar as usual. Matt currently owed him about twenty quid by way of a bar bill, so Jed was surprised to see him.

"Hey, Matt, you come to pay off your bar bill?" Jed wiped the bar down where Matt sat, and held out his palm waiting for some money. Matt searched around his pockets and pulled out a five-pound note.

"Will this cover it and get me a beer?"

"Nope!" Jed replied, just standing there.

"Well, I need a beer, but you can have the change." Jed moved his head as if he was deciding whether or not to serve Matt and then he pulled out a beer mat from under the bar and opened a bottle.

"You still owe nearly twenty." Jed grabbed the note from the bar as he served the drink. Matt sipped his beer thinking about how well he was now doing. He felt around in his other pockets, and checked that he still had the cash on him he knew he had. He counted it quickly whilst Jed was out of sight and there was over £100 in total.

Chapter 16
What was his number?

Matt was settling in to his new way of life pretty well now, and he was getting used to being visited by the various friends or relatives of his new friends who had recently died. Matt was always surprised at how many times his name was linked to them, despite all his efforts to remain relatively anonymous. Fortunately, he also remembered, from the conversations with those he had befriended, the names of those relations who had let them down, by not visiting enough or sometimes at all. Matt knew that with people's busy lives, it wasn't easy to visit older relations regularly, but if any angry family gave him problems, he was usually capable of turning the argument back on them.

There was a knock on Matt's door. When he opened it, there was a well-built tallish man standing in the hall. He was wearing a big overcoat and was very well dressed, and he stood calmly as Matt looked at him. It was unusual to find someone as composed as this at his door, as usually they would be agitated and stressed but this man was very different.

"Can I help you?" Matt asked, as he looked at the man. It wasn't immediately obvious, but after a few moments Matt got the strange feeling that he had met this man before though he couldn't quite put a name to him, or even a relative's name. Matt looked at the number above his head and saw it was an extremely vivid orange colour. It was much brighter than many he had seen.

"Hello, Matthew," the man replied, as if they were old friends.

"Hello." Matt wasn't quite sure what the situation was, but continued assuming that this man was a friend or relative of someone he had known.

"May I come in?"

"Er, yes." Matt moved out of the way and allowed the stranger to enter. Normally, he would have wanted to know exactly what anyone's business was before he let them in, but for some reason this time he simply just agreed with the man's request.

"Can I help you?" Matt asked again, but the man simply looked around as if he was trying to find something. Matt thought that there might have been a number of items he had procured that this person might be looking for.

"You're doing quite well for yourself, Mr. Briswell," the man said. It was a strange statement to make, and Matt was a bit confused by it.

"I'm doing okay. Sorry, I don't know who you are," Matt replied.

"Well, perhaps you should." Matt's reply seemed to have slightly annoyed his visitor, and his response was more barbed than his previous comments. Matt looked again at the man as he turned towards Matt, but he still couldn't imagine where he had seen him before. The guy then continued to look around, walking into Matt's bedroom as he did so.

"Are you from the police?" Matt tried again to make the man identify himself, but he received no reply, just a severe eye to eye stare, which seemed to look right through him.

It was hard to believe, but Matt had been feeling almost helpless as the man continued his inspection of the apartment. After a few moments, however, Matt regained some of his composure and decided he needed to get rid of this person. He suddenly became aware that were he to try and throw the man out of his flat, it wouldn't be as easy a task as it might have been with many of the relatives who had paid a visit before. This man looked fit and strong, and Matt concluded that if it did end in a fight he probably wouldn't come out on top.

"I didn't catch your name," Matt tried again to find out who the man was.
"My name is Luther," the man said slowly as he turned to stare at Matt. His stare was most intimidating, and Matt felt that the situation could quickly turn into something aggressive. He looked around and spotted a bronze statue he had forgotten about tucked on a low shelf. He decided he would make his way over there, so if things got nasty he could use it as a weapon. Matt also noticed that his Cortes painting was still on show, as well as a valuable vase he had acquired, and the more he looked, the more he noticed just how many of his acquisitions were evident. Matt took a step closer to

the bookshelf.

"I'm sorry Luther," he said, "but I'm unable to recall exactly how you might think you know me."

"Is that so?" replied his guest.

"Er, yes." Matt felt tense and unable to move, but forced himself to reach behind him and grab the bronze statue, but failed to touch it.

"I've seen enough!" The man's voice was almost a bellow as he spoke. Matt tried to glance back to check exactly where the statue was, but the shelf seemed to be empty. He wanted to turn away to see where it actually was, but the guy was in his face before he could locate it.

"You're taking a lot of things that should really have become the property of others." Again the man's voice was loud, and Matt had nothing to say as he glared back into his eyes. His number was as bright as ever, and Matt looked at it again. It was forty-five, which was not what he thought it had said when the man was first at the door, but he couldn't really remember.

The man then moved swiftly to the front door and Matt turned to pick up the bronze piece, which was exactly where he had imagined it was. As he grabbed the heavy item, he heard the door opening, and as he turned back the man had already left his apartment. Matt's heart was racing, and he could feel sweat on his forehead, although the whole incident had probably lasted less than three minutes. He sat down on his sofa, panting with fear, still holding the bronze statue. He tried to work out what had just happened. The relief flowed through him. He felt as if he had got himself out of a very dangerous situation, but when he looked back over what had actually happened, there wasn't really anything that he could put his finger on to explain why he had felt how he did. It took a few more moments before he was back to normal.

Luther made his way from Matt's flat, quickly disappeared down an alley opposite, and within seconds was out of sight. He was annoyed that Matt was abusing his new found abilities, and hoped this visit might serve as an awakening. Acting merely as a watcher, he could only hope that Matt would use his power for good, but couldn't really tell him so as it would make his own position very awkward. He would just have to come back a bit sooner than planned to make sure everything was okay. Luther had two or three humans he was keeping an eye on at the moment and he would have his work cut out, but he knew he had to make sure things didn't get out of hand.

Brad's next of kin had been contacted with the news of his death, and within a couple of days his nephew was in London trying to sort things out. Brad had two children, a son and a daughter, but his daughter had died tragically in her teens and Brad's son never really managed to grow up normally. He had a couple of children of his own, but he was in a relationship fuelled with alcohol and it was doomed to fail. In Brad's last ten or so years he had no idea where his son Lacey was living. The grandchildren had made occasional contact but nothing regular, so it was Brad's brother's boy, his nephew Jim, who was the closest relative.

Jim had spoken to Brad a couple of times in the past few years, and received a letter from him a couple of years ago, which was about the extent of the contact. Jim was aware though that Brad had one last wish, which was that his most valuable possession, a painting, was to be given to his grandsons, who had not had a very happy upbringing. Jim had a letter which said that this would make up for what Lacey had been unable to do for them. Jim had never seen the painting but knew vaguely what it looked like as his uncle had described it to him once. He did know that it was by some French artist. When he discovered it wasn't in the house, he went to the police.

As far as the police were concerned, nothing appeared to be missing from the house and there were no signs of a break-in. Nobody really knew what Brad had, so it seemed to them that everything was there. Matt had been careful not to be greedy in what he took. Jim was adamant though that this painting should be in the house somewhere, and he thought from what little he'd been told that it was worth a bit. The police listed all obvious valuables in the house, but they also knew from their original report that a neighbour had used the spare key to find his uncle.

Jim wanted the police to ask the neighbour if he knew where the painting was. The police had no suspicions about the neighbour, but they asked, and weren't surprised to hear that he knew nothing about it. The police had been let willingly into the neighbour's house, and had been able to give the place a once over, but there was nothing to be seen of the painting. During that interview the name of another visitor did come up. He was called Matt, and the neighbour told them that he was a nice young man whose company Brad enjoyed. The neighbour had no idea of Matt's surname or address, and no reason to suspect him, so the police enquiry came to nothing.

Jim, however, wasn't convinced that the neighbour was completely innocent, and was a bit perturbed by the fact that he had gained entry to his uncle's house without having to break in. He read over the police report, then he searched for the letter he had received from his uncle which contained the artist's name. It wasn't where Jim thought it might be and he wondered if he might have thrown it away, so he looked up a few painters in case any of them rang a bell, but none did. He felt that if the police weren't going to search for the painting then it was up to him.

Chapter 17
They all die

Matt was meeting and making friends with all manner of people now. One such was another woman in her early fifties, who was called Courtney. Matt remembered when he first spotted her, walking slowly through a park, with her red number standing out like a sore thumb. He remembered how, almost without thinking, he created a situation where he could start talking to her, by sitting down beside her on the bench that she stopped at. Matt did this sort of thing automatically now and had casually begun chatting to her.

Courtney was quite lonely, but was also used to men trying to chat her up, so wasn't immediately taken in by Matt. In fact, she ignored him to begin with, but a lot of the men she usually attracted were older and were often looking for a cheap night's company, and she was pleased that a younger man was happy to pass the time of day with her. That first talk in the park started badly, but the two of them got along, and their conversation lasted nearly two hours. By the end of it she was willing to think of Matt as a new friend, and maybe even contemplate their relationship going further. She had been won over as far as immediate acquaintance was concerned. Courtney found something a little bit different about Matt, he would ask questions, try and find out something about her, and she liked that.

The friendship quickly developed, and Matt offered to walk Courtney back to wherever she was going that afternoon, but she refused. This was somewhat out of character for her, as she craved the company, but she saw something different about this friendship with Matt and turned down his offer, but without hesitation took his mobile number and promised she would call him. They arranged to meet at the same park bench the next day, and from this second meeting a rather interesting relationship began. Matt wasn't too bothered about a physical relationship but Courtney longed for some male company on a more permanent basis, and Matt was happy to oblige. Before long they were sleeping regularly in the same bed, and discussing how they could live together in the future.

Courtney was extremely flattered that Matt had met her several times, was still apparently interested in talking to her rather than just getting her into bed, and she was determined that she would keep him as long as she could. She wasn't sure what she could do to keep him interested, but she let him know that she had money and that she was keen to spend it on him. This, of course, was music to Matt's ears. He had of course noticed that the number over Courtney's head was turning purple, so he pushed the idea of them living together. She had told him that she would like to live in a house again, which she hadn't done since she was a child. Matt was good at identifying people's dreams or ambitions, and when he recognised Courtney's dream of wanting to move from a flat, he shaped it into the two of them buying a house together. Matt had no intention of giving up his apartment, but the talk of doing so was enough for Courtney to put most of her money into the plan. Being typically opportunist, Matt also managed to borrow money and by the time Courtney died of a heart attack he was indebted to her to the tune of about eight thousand pounds. He had told her the money was being put aside for a down payment on their home, but of course this never materialised.

Courtney's death was strange. Even though Matt expected it imminently, it all came as a bit of a shock, even to him. It was a weird feeling for him, because although they were lovers, he had felt no real sexual attraction towards her. It was almost as if she had become an elder sister to him, or perhaps a surrogate mother. His own mother had told him so very little about her life or childhood, and having Courtney open up to him about her early life had touched him. He was fond of her, and missed her when she went. On the day of her death Courtney was making her way back home from work, and suffered a heart attack on the tube. She was rushed to hospital, but she died very quickly. Matt didn't find out for a couple of days, and when he did he spent hours imagining the pain she might have gone through as she died which saddened him even more. They had arranged to meet up that evening and Matt was quite put out when Courtney didn't call, but this wasn't unusual and he didn't actually know that she had passed away until the following day when he called at her home. A neighbour gave him the news. It wasn't a shock, exactly, but he shed a tear having enjoyed her company over the previous weeks. Matt actually felt some loss.

Courtney had only one remaining family member, her younger brother Ray. He had constantly tried to talk his sister out of moving in with such a young man as Matt. They had never met whilst Courtney was alive, and Ray wasn't aware that Matt had attended Courtney's funeral, but he knew of him, and when it was revealed that his sister's estate was quite depleted he could only think of one person who might have his sister's money. That was this Matt, or whatever his real name was. Ray knew a little bit about his sister's affairs, and was distraught that she had possibly been fleeced by this young man. He wasn't able to pinpoint actual amounts that might have been taken, but after some consideration he decided to make a formal complaint about the whole situation to the police.

A DS Morrison spoke to Ray about his complaint and he named someone called Matt as the perpetrator of the crime but he was unable to give them any more details about him or indeed what the crime was. For their part, the police said they would investigate, to identify whether funds had been taken from Courtney's account, but in truth they did very little except file the complaint. The report wasn't even filed under Courtney's name but under his own, Raymond Patterson, as if he was the victim rather than Courtney.

This all happened without Matt's knowledge, while he was busy trying to borrow money from a more permanent source. He was working on his old DJ friend, Dave, trying to persuade him that he needed a larger sum of money to buy into a deal that would bring them both profit. Matt had some idea of how to invest his money in a scheme that would bring a good return, but the minimum investment amount was much higher than he could afford, or at least he didn't have that much to spare at the moment. The DJ was used to giving Matt twenty pounds every now and then, but Matt was now suggesting he borrowed a couple of thousand pounds and from Matt's past record Dave was reluctant to part with that amount of money. Not that he couldn't afford it, but he just knew it would be the last he would ever see of it.

There was a lot of discussion over how long Matt would need the money for, and what assurances he would give the DJ that the money would bring a return. Matt told him that he hoped to almost double whatever he was prepared to lend him, and eventually Dave gave in and stupidly lent him five hundred pounds with a signed note from Matt as a receipt. Matt said that it may take a couple of months but that he would be pleased he lent it to him. Matt counted out the money in front of both of them to confirm it was all there before they shook hands on it.

Brad's nephew Jim called in for an update of his enquiry, but was told by the police that they had no evidence of theft. Jim still wasn't convinced. He had spoken to Brad on the phone a while before his death, and the painting for his grandsons had been mentioned during their conversation, so Jim was sure that the painting had been with him then. He thought that if Brad had been trying to sell it he would have said something. It had taken a while, but Jim now had access to his uncle's house, and as he began to sort through all the junk that had collected over his life he found the artist Edouard Cortes mentioned name in the paperwork. This indicated to Jim that the painting had existed, and he wanted to find out if his uncle had indeed sold it. He was convinced that when they last spoke, the painting was still in his possession, and that it was still his intention to pass it on to his grandchildren so was absolutely certain that he hadn't planned on selling. If he had, where had all the money gone? "Perhaps it wasn't worth as much as Brad imagined," Jim thought to himself. There was always the possibility that it was a fake.

Jim thought over the situation, and concluded that he wanted to make an effort to find out what had happened to the painting. He hired a private detective to enquire into the sale of any Edouard

Cortes paintings recently, and who had sold them. Jim still had a nagging suspicion that the neighbour might have it hidden in his house, but wanted to just make a few enquiries before accusing anyone. The private detective's instructions were straightforward. He was to see if he could easily identify any such paintings being sold in the last three months and report back. Jim wasn't going to spend too much time or money on it.

Matt, in the meantime, went for his next appointment at the Job Centre and again Sonja Wright was his interviewer. It was a fairly swift interview this time. "Mr. Briswell!" Sonja called out without looking up. Matt made his way over to her desk, admiring her shining brown hair.

"Hello, Mrs Wright, you are looking gorgeous today."
"Please sit down, Mr. Briswell." Sonja caught the scent of his aftershave and thought again that he smelt rather nice. She struggled for what seemed like minutes, fighting the urge to look at him and see what he was wearing. She knew it was wrong to engage with him on anything but a professional level but the desire was hard to fight. "Have you been for any interviews at all?"
"Yes, a couple." Matt handed her letters which demonstrated that he had been trying to find a job. Sonja looked at them and scribbled some notes down. "If you could just write down your number I

will call you," Matt said jokingly.

"I note that you are looking a lot smarter than you used to, Mr. Briswell, and I have to say that if you go to interviews dressed like that you stand a far better chance of getting employment."

"Ah, but dressed like this do I have any better chance of asking you out?" Matt couldn't resist the opportunity. Sonja started to look at him, and pushed her glasses back up the bridge of her nose towards her eyes as she sighed.

"It would make sense for you to concentrate on trying to get a job," she said. Sonja looked at him for a few seconds and briefly their eyes made contact. Matt thought she was so sexy but decided that the cheap lines that he had been using were not good enough for her. He would have to be a lot more sophisticated.

"Thank you, Mrs Wright. I will prove to you that I am worth all this effort."

When the interview came to its conclusion, Matt walked towards the exit imagining himself and Mrs Wright together in bed. His daydreaming hadn't lasted long when he recalled having such thoughts before. He wondered if he would ever find a woman as glamourous as Sonja, and he looked back towards where she was sitting. Sonja meanwhile was quietly impressed with the new smart looking Mr. Briswell, and had remembered a vacancy that perhaps she should put his way. She looked up and saw him looking her way, and although she didn't want to, she waved at him, trying to beckon him back to her desk. Matt saw the wave and was uncertain of exactly what it meant, but made his way back and sat down. "You forgot to give me your number, didn't you?" Matt smiled his best smile, knowing that it was another one of those old cheap lines, but was pleased to see that Mrs Wright actually seemed to find it funny. She smirked and then smiled at him, and sort of half laughed.

"No, it's not my number but I do have a number I think you should ring."

Sonja found the details of the job she had in mind. It was in the offices of an advertising agency, but didn't require too much in the way of qualifications or experience, so she thought that Mr Briswell might be able to convince them.

Matt was quietly pleased at how things were going with Mrs Wright but although he was now able to stop worrying about money for a while, he knew he would have to get some kind of job so it was less suspicious when he was spending a bit more. He made his way to the square near to Matalan and sat down to think how he could get a job. He didn't need anything that paid a lot, but wanted a job that also gave him some time to do the things he was now doing. Matt huffed as he sat down and thought. A voice broke his concentration.

"Hey, son, what's going down?" It was Bob. Matt was surprised to see that he had a number two over his head but then guessed as he didn't really know

Bob that well there was no way he would ever he able to tell just how healthy he was.

"Hey, Bill," replied Matt.

"It's Bob."

"Yeah, man, Bob. How are you?" Matt patted him on the back like a long lost friend.

"Still looking, just like you."

The two of them chatted and joked a bit about being out of work, and Matt managed to turn the conversation around to him taking out his new girl and how he would love to take her to just a small diner, but he had no money until his benefits came in later that week even though this was a lie. Bob lent him twenty quid.

The private detective made a few enquiries with art galleries and soon realised that anyone selling a genuine Cortes would be noticed immediately. Most dealers would be suspicious of anyone claiming that they had one, so would check its authenticity before listing or buying it. He went to a number of galleries getting the same story, until eventually he found someone who seemed to have a story to tell.

"Coincidentally, I had someone in a month or so ago, saying that he had a painting for sale that might be worth a bit but although he brought it in to the shop, I never saw it properly."

"Oh right," he replied, wondering why the dealer was telling him this. The guy continued, "No, he had a cover over it and although I thought he was going to show it to me he never did."

"Right, well, thank you," he said, ready to move on. The dealer spoke again.

"I wondered what sort of painting it might have been, and I noticed part of the signature in the bottom corner as the cover moved, and it was Cortes."

This made the detective's ears prick up.

"A Cortes painting then?" he asked.

"Well, like I said, I never actually got to see it, but the signature looked right. I guessed it was probably a fake though, the bloke never came back."

"Did he leave a name?" Pad and pencil were ready to write it down.

"No."

"Or any contact details?"

"No, nothing. As I said, he never really seemed that interested in letting me look at it."

"Ah, well. If he returns I would appreciate it if you could let me know, please?"

He handed the dealer a card. It was one shot in a million that the dealer would actually contact him but he was glad when the dealer took it and started to read it. "Once again, thank you for your time."

"Yes, okay," the dealer replied thoughtfully. "I did watch the man leave and noticed that he was driving a bright yellow American car. I think it might have been a Mustang, if that's any help. There can't be too many of those about."

As the dealer spoke, the detective scribbled frantically.

This visit had been most useful. There was an

indication that someone might be trying to sell a Cortes, and he now knew the man was probably driving a yellow Mustang. This was a useful piece of information and using his usual contacts it only took about three days to find out a bit more. He found out that there was a yellow American car in the area, that it was a Mustang but even more importantly where it was garaged, and with a few more enquiries he was able to find the name Matthew and a mobile number.

Matt went to the advertising office of Marsh & Pannel with the details that Mrs Wright had given him. Matt had to go, and needed some proof that he had been, but although it was a good job he wasn't sure he really had enough time to do it. After some brief discussion, Matt had found out that he would be working five and a half days a week for around fifteen hundred pounds a month. He weighed up what he thought he was likely to make from his present scams and decided he should try and flunk the interview.

It was difficult at first, as it seemed that they had almost been given instructions to employ him, but Matt tried really hard by answering a few questions rather badly and then not seeming interested in what the interviewer was trying to tell him. He was conscious of the fact that he needed to say the right things to make it appear that he was desperate for the job, but he tried to come over uninterested. Even so, it still seemed as if he was going to be offered the job until he looked at his watch several times as if he had somewhere else to be. This did the trick and in the end he was told that they didn't think he would be right for the vacancy.

Not wishing to miss an opportunity, Matt called in to the Job Centre and waited to briefly see Mrs Wright. Sonja had just finished her early afternoon interviews and had collected up her files to return them to the office. Matt saw an opportunity to speak to her, and managed to intercept her before she got to the office door.

"Mrs Wright, I'm glad I've caught you," Matt said, as Sonja turned to see who it was. She was surprised to find that it was Mr. Briswell, and a little embarrassed to be seen talking to him, but she wasn't one to be rude.

"Oh, hello Mr Briswell, how did your interview go?" Sonja asked. Matt was impressed that she had remembered.

"Well, I thought I'd done enough, but they said they didn't think I was right for the job."

"Oh, did they, that's a shame," Sonja replied. She tried to sound genuinely disappointed for him but was in fact quite annoyed, having written the letter of recommendation to the company. In fact, she was more shocked than disappointed.

"I will keep trying though," Matt said to her.

"Yes, do that, and I'm sure we'll find you a job somewhere," Sonja said vaguely as she looked at Mr. Briswell and realised that when smartened up, he was quite good looking.

"I just want to thank you for helping me out, and if you would ever allow me to take you out to dinner I would be most honoured." Matt put on his classiest voice and Sonja did blush a little.

"It's all part of my job, Mr. Briswell, and I would do the same for any of my clients," Sonja lied and then smiled at him again before walking into the office.

Matt felt that he might have made a bit more of the situation, and was annoyed that he hadn't been able to say nicer things to her. Sonja couldn't wait to get into the office and out of sight so she could cool herself down a bit. She hated to admit it but she was beginning to like Matt. She pondered on what he had just said to her and felt really good about it. A man more than ten years younger was doing everything he could to ask her out and she liked it. Having spent a couple of minutes considering the situation she concluded that in fact she did fancy him a bit, but as he was a client there was no way she would let it go any further. She just couldn't. It would be most unprofessional.

-

The private detective reported back to Jim and advised him of how close he thought he might be to finding the painting. Jim wasn't sure how confident he should be that this was his uncle's painting but he convinced him that he shouldn't drop it now, and after arranging further payment said he was convinced he would be able to find this Matthew, and would see if he had a painting of interest. It was a bit more than Jim wanted to pay but he did it anyway. The detective then made more enquiries, and was able to get the address to where the mobile phone was originally registered. It was at Flat 37, Bolan House, Riverley Close, Leyton. There was no name, but it was a start.

Chapter 18
It's over for Matt and Zoe

It had been almost four weeks now since Matt had even spoken to Zoe, and nearly two months since they had gone out anywhere together. Matt had to admit that his life had changed quite a bit in that time. He pondered over it as he somehow found himself drinking in Dysans Bar again after seeing various acquaintances about various matters. The place was open earlier than normal and Matt had sort of stumbled in, but at least he wasn't here to see Mikey although there was something about the place he just didn't like. He downed a couple of shots as he stood at the bar. This was the place where he had met Zoe, he thought, and recalled how he had had to steal some other punters' drinks just to survive back then. Matt called the barman over to order another shot, in the hope that it would be the same barman who had served him back then, but to be honest he couldn't really tell if it was or not. He pulled out a roll of notes from his back pocket, peeled off a couple of tenners, and laid them on the bar.

"Your bill only comes to eight thirty, mate," the barman said to Matt. Matt looked at him and decided he probably wasn't the same barman he had seen previously.

"Yeah you're right, a ten-pound tip is too much for you," Matt retrieved one of the notes. There were a few other people in there listening to their conversation, including a couple of women sat at the bar not too far from where Matt was stood. They were smartly dressed and seemed to be checking him out themselves. Matt had already made eye contact with one of the women, so he walked over to them rolling up the ten pound note on the way.

"The barman doesn't want his tenner tip, ladies." He slowly placed the rolled up note down the bra of the woman he had winked at. She watched as he did so and allowed him to push the note right down her cleavage. He left his hand on her breast for a second or two before winking at her again and leaving.

Matt decided he didn't want to go back home, so made his way to the next pub, and the one after, and the one after that, until around nine o'clock, and at least four pubs later he was beginning to be rather drunk. He was in a showing off mood, which was often the case when he was drunk, but he craved some female company. He decided he'd phone Zoe.
"Hello!"
"What you doing, honey?" Matt tried to sound sophisticated and sexy, but came across as exactly what he was, drunk.
"Hi, Matt," Zoe replied excitedly. She was surprised to hear Matt actually calling her, and she was pleased to hear from him.
"Do you fancy a bite to eat, or have you eaten already?"
"No I haven't eaten yet," Zoe lied. "What did you have in mind?"
"There's a Chinese restaurant not far from yours, we

259

could go there if you fancied it?"

"Okay," Zoe answered immediately, unable to hide her enthusiasm.

"I'll be round in about thirty minutes," said Matt as he concluded the call. He was initially surprised just how easy that had been, but then arrogance took over. "Ah, it would have been impossible for Zoe to resist me once she could hear that I am just so cool," he thought to himself. He was wrong of course, as although Zoe was keen to see Matt again she still held out hopes that it would be the old Matt who would be coming round.

It didn't take Matt more than twenty minutes to get to Zoe's. He pushed the button for her flat at the entrance and she buzzed him in. He'd been to her place a few times before, so he knew roughly where he was going. He knocked on her door confidently. Zoe opened the door and Matt thought she looked pretty good. She'd changed her hair colour and style, and looked slimmer than he remembered her. Zoe couldn't believe how much smarter Matt looked. He was in a designer suit and he just looked fantastic.

"Well hello, baby," Matt said, looking Zoe up and down. "You look gorgeous, babe."

"You don't look so bad yourself," Zoe replied and her spine chilled at the thought of finally finding the real Matt. "Come in." She opened the door wide to let Matt in. He walked in self-assuredly. Zoe had never seen him looking quite so confident and she just couldn't stop staring at his superb body in the smart suit. She had a sudden urge to apply more lipstick. "Hang on. I'll be ready in a moment." Zoe rushed to her bathroom.

As Zoe checked her face and hair in the bathroom mirror. She could feel her heart thumping in anticipation of what the night might bring. She hadn't felt like this about Matt since she first walked home with him that fateful night. She checked herself in the mirror just to make sure that her new dress was right. She quickly searched for her favourite lipstick and swiftly applied it, before brushing herself down and returning to Matt. Matt became the epitome of charm, giving Zoe another few compliments and then helping her on with her jacket.

They made their way to a decent Chinese restaurant and managed to get themselves a table without too much bother. The place was pretty busy, and Matt flashed his money around in the restaurant which Zoe wasn't completely happy about, but she had to admit he was great to be with again. Not quite the old Matt, but much better than the last Matt she had known. They spent a little time catching up with each other's lives, not that she had much to tell him. Matt on the other hand had lots to tell Zoe, in particular telling her about how his life was now full, meeting people, doing deals and selling things, and the fact that he was now rich enough not to worry anymore. Zoe lapped it all up with the wine and the food and before long they were back in her flat and her bed. It had been a fantastic night as far as Zoe was concerned.

It was three thirty in the morning by the time they started to relax. Matt had wanted to bed Zoe for ages, although he had never really wanted to enough to see it through to a conclusion, but she had looked so much prettier this evening that now there was no stopping him. Zoe hoped that this would be the start of a more meaningful relationship.

"I've got to be up at seven for work, I need to try and get some sleep, Matt."

"You don't need sleep," Matt joked, "when you've got me."

"Yeah okay, we could go again, but I think sleep would be better for me right now."

"Whatever you say, babes!" Matt sat up and turned round so he was half out of bed before turning back and stroking Zoe's shoulder. "If you're sure?" The two of them laughed and then hugged and kissed for another ten minutes or so before Matt finally agreed that perhaps he should let her get some sleep.

Zoe knew she would be a wreck the next day anyway, but some sleep would be better than none. "So, what are you doing tomorrow?" she asked Matt. "Me? A bit of this, a bit of that. You know it depends on who I see, really." Matt's answer didn't really tell Zoe a lot.

"Oh, right. What do you mean it depends on who you see?"

"If I see someone with a black number I try and chat to them."

"Not bloody numbers again."

"But babe, they are what get me through life, now."

"I don't want to hear about your numbers, Matt. What do you do workwise?"

"That is my work. I can tell people how much longer they have to live."

Zoe put her fingers in her ears as Matt spoke. Even if she didn't actually believe that Matt did what he said, she hated him saying it. "Anyway, babes, you don't have to worry, you've got forty-three years left."

"Don't say that! Don't say that!" Zoe half screamed. "I hate it! I hate it!" She started to cry and covered her face with her hands. Matt decided it was probably best to leave at this point. Zoe was obviously tired, and he could do with getting back to his own bed.

"Come and see me tomorrow evening, and we can go out for dinner again if you want."

Zoe wasn't really listening to him as she lay back down in bed with her hands over her ears. She was feeling very tired and just ignored what Matt was saying.

"I'll see myself out then," Matt said as he got dressed and left.

The next evening Zoe thought about what Matt had asked her and decided she would go and see him. She wanted to see if she could get to the bottom of exactly where he was getting all this cash he apparently now had. She had half listened to what he told her, but she still didn't really believe it, and she had got to know Matt well enough to believe that he was lying about how he was getting his money. She hoped he wasn't doing anything criminal, but she felt she had to try and find out. At seven she was outside his door and she was extremely pleased if not a little surprised to find Matt in. He gave her a big kiss as he let her in.

"Hello, babes, are you up for another night of passion?" Matt asked her as she walked in.

"Well, you'll have to wait and see," Zoe replied, a bit coyly. She noticed that Matt was smartly dressed again but in a different suit from yesterday. She looked around Matt's flat and he had obviously been busy buying clothes. "Wow!" she said, "you've really sorted things here."

"Would you like a drink?" Matt asked, pointing to a selection of bottles. Zoe was impressed that Matt had some alcohol and not just beers, let alone the choice that was available.

"Yes, I'll have a vodka but I don't want to get bombed like we did yesterday," Zoe replied. Matt duly poured her a drink and then opened up a beer for himself. "Cheers," he said, lifting his bottle. The two of them sat down on the old settee that Matt still had.

"So, what have you been doing today?" Zoe started

her interrogation.

"The usual babes, this and that," Matt replied.

"You've been kidding me haven't you, you must have a job somewhere," Zoe pleaded with him. "You must tell me what sort of job you've got that pays you this well."

"Yeah, I know, I'm really getting paid and seem to have deep pockets these days but I've told you what I do, you've just got to believe me." Matt's answer was plain.

There was a deathly silence for a moment. Matt took a swig of his beer, and then took Zoe's hands. Their eyes met and he held her vision. "Look Zoe, I know that what I do isn't what you might hope for, but I'm blessed with this vision and I feel that I have to use it." Matt took a deep breath and made sure Zoe was looking into his eyes. "What's more, it makes me money and I can keep us living in comfort."

"Er, I..." Zoe started to reply, but was interrupted.

"What I'm trying to say, Zoe, is that I would like you to live with me. We can probably afford to get another gaff in a few months' time, what do you say?" Zoe never really gave him an answer but Matt kept pouring on the charm and the alcohol, ordered in some food, and they spent the evening in his bed. Zoe was very happy when Matt wasn't talking about numbers, and she was able to imagine what the two of them could make of their relationship. She could see them with a couple of children, a boy and a girl of course, in their detached house with a garden, somewhere in Chigwell or Loughton. She dreamed of the future and hoped that Matt would eventually grow tired of thinking about people who were dying, and just get on with life whatever his job was. She was having such a good time that she decided to stay the night.

This was the first time that Zoe slept overnight at Matt's, and the morning arrived late for both of them. Matt wasn't up early, but was the first to rise and start getting washed and dressed. Zoe was still slightly hungover and took her time to come round.

"Are you going out?" Zoe asked Matt as she watched him dress.

"You just have a lie-in, babes, and before you know it I'll be back."

"Where are you going, then?"

"Don't you worry yourself with facts," said Matt walking over to Zoe. He kissed her, then lifted the sheet and smacked her naked bum, perhaps a bit harder than she expected.

"Ouch!" Zoe exclaimed, as she looked up at Matt

"Don't complain, I know you love it," Matt said, before kissing her again and leaving the flat.

Matt was always doing something for somebody, and today he had a rather important errand to deal with. In many ways he was always helping people out, but Matt knew that as long as he took his time and stalled for a couple of months, his errands would never actually come to fruition. It was how Matt made his money, and today was just one of those tasks he was doing for a friend. He had befriended a chap by the name of Garth, who Matt calculated had only weeks to live. During their discussions, Matt had learnt that he wanted to book a holiday of a lifetime for himself and his wife, but he wanted it to be kept secret from her until everything was organised. Matt had of course offered to be the run-around, and to get everything sorted for him. Unlike many of his other friends, Garth lived with someone who was not going to die, well at least not quite yet, so this job needed special attention. It was all about the holiday.

The trip was to be a week in Paris and then a fortnight's cruise around the Mediterranean. Garth had been saving money for years, and had managed to put away quite a bit without his wife knowing. This was his holiday money. Matt did ask himself if this was one task he shouldn't get involved with, but he knew that the money was away somewhere safe where Garth's family would never be able to find it, and even when he died, the money would just go unclaimed. Matt had decided that if anyone was going to have the money, it was going to be him. After chatting about his plans, Matt had made some enquiries through a travel agent and found the most expensive holiday Garth could afford. It had already been mentioned that he was expecting it to cost around £4,000, so Matt knew how much he could spend, or at least appear to spend.

The two of them had arranged to meet up and the plan was that Matt would visit a travel agent on his own in case Garth's wife or anyone else he knew might see him and start asking questions. First though, they stopped off for a full English breakfast.

"Hiya, Garth, any problems getting away earlier this morning?"

"No, my wife was getting ready for work, and I just left about twenty minutes earlier than usual. She has no idea."

"Okay, let's have breakfast." Matt picked up a menu and the two of them chose their food whilst they chatted. "I've had a word with a girlfriend of mine."

"Oh right, what about?" Garth wondered what was coming next.

"Well, she's in the travel business and she's prepared to do me a deal."

"Oh, okay." He wasn't sure if Matt meant for him or himself.

"I've mentioned Paris, and a cruise, and there is a holiday package costing around £4,500 - £5,000 that is just superb."

"But that's just a little bit too much for me."

"Whoa, don't fret my man, due to my gentle persuasion she's happy to sell it to me at staff discount for £3,500. That'll give you nearly a grand spending money."

"Hey, that sounds good. Let's get there and get it booked!" Garth was excited now.

"Well, that's the problem. If she finds out that I'm doing this for someone other than me, then she won't play ball, but I can put it in your name because she only knows me as Matt, she doesn't know my full name. Booking won't be a problem, but I have to do it on my own."

"Oh, what a bummer!"

"Anyway, as we discussed you don't want anyone seeing you in a travel agency, do you?"

"No, you're right there, Matt, I'd forgotten that. It needs to be a secret."

"Right, give me the cash and I'll put a deposit down, then bring you back the forms to show you what I've booked. Then all you have to do is give me the money for the rest when you're happy."

"Sounds simple enough." Garth was convinced and he handed £500 to Matt.

Matt of course didn't have any such friend. He was just good at spinning a yarn and on this occasion had come to an arrangement with a travel agent. It hadn't been easy convincing them, but he promised that he would pay them the full price of the holiday once it was all agreed but that it could only be on deposit at the moment as his client wasn't absolutely sure if he wanted that exact holiday or not. The agents weren't totally happy about this but got Matt to agree that if the holiday wasn't actually booked within thirty days then they would claim the £500 as an administration fee. Matt was happy with that and the holiday planning went ahead.

While Matt was out with Garth arranging the deal, Zoe decided that his flat needed a good going over. Although she was impressed that it was now full of nice clothes and new things, it needed some tidying, and she set about sorting some of Matt's clothes and putting them into his wardrobe. She picked up some rubbish from around the place, and tidied up the bedroom as well.

Matt was gone for about three hours.

"Hi, Zoe," he shouted as he unlocked the door. "Zoe, where are you?" Matt waited for a reply but none was forthcoming. He then saw Zoe coming out of the bedroom and she didn't look happy. Matt assumed she was annoyed that he had had to go out. "I'm sorry babes, but I just had this business to do."

"What sort of business?" Zoe's voice also indicated that she wasn't happy.

"I had to go and pay for a holiday for a friend."

"What friend?"

"Nobody you'd know," Matt tried to play the whole thing down.

"So why did you have to go and pay for it?"

"It's a long story but he needed someone to book this holiday so his wife wouldn't find out." Matt hoped this would be enough but he was wrong.

"So he's having an affair?"

"No, not at all, it's a bit of a snow job really. He's not even going to go on the holiday."

"What are you talking about?" Zoe gave him a stare that said she was really pissed off with him. He tried to charm her a little.

"Hey, it's okay. I do these sorts of deals all the time."
"I don't care about your deals," Zoe's tone had changed.
"Oh!"
"Whose is this?" Zoe held up a stocking that she had found under Matt's bed. Matt gulped before replying.
"Oh that. If you must know it belongs to a woman I used to know called Courtney."
"And who's Courtney?"
"She's nobody."
"If she's been taking her stockings off or even sleeping with you she must have been somebody," said Zoe, getting angry but trying not to show it.
"She was just someone I knew, but she's dead now."
"Dead!" Zoe got even angrier.
"Look, she meant nothing to me, I promise, she was always going to die and I just got to know her." Matt looked at Zoe hoping that this would explain everything. It certainly shut her up, but she wasn't happy and Matt watched as the orange forty-three over her head changed to a forty-two. Zoe didn't really know what to say and blurted out "This is something to do with those bloody numbers again, isn't it?" before picking up her coat and making her way hurriedly to the door. Zoe turned swiftly and looked at Matt. "You're an absolute bastard, do you know that?" She slammed the front door hard as she left.

As Zoe left Matt's flat, a tall dark man was walking along the corridor and he watched intently as an upset Zoe stormed out of the building. Luther had heard most of what had been said and was not impressed.

Zoe was exhausted. She was angry with Matt, and was surprised to find how much energy it took out of her. She needed solace, and knew exactly who to go to for it. She rang Ruth immediately.

"Hi Ruth."

"Hey Zoe, you alright?" Ruth could hear immediately that Zoe was almost crying.

"No, it's Matt again."

"What's he done now?"

"It's the usual. He makes some really strange friends that I don't like."

"What do you mean, you don't like?"

"Oh, I don't know. They are all old, and not the sort of people I think he should be mixing with all the time"

"Is it all the time, Zoe?"

"Well I don't know, it seems to be, oh yeah, and I found a stocking in his bedroom which he says belongs to one of these old women who just needed to change at his."

"Oh, that's not good." Ruth was a bit worried on hearing this. "Hey, let's get a film and watch it whilst eating pizza this evening, what do you say?"

"That would be good, but what about Frankie?" Zoe didn't really want to spend the evening with Ruth and her husband.

"Oh, he's out playing five-a-side or something with the lads from work until nine or ten. He'll be out of the way."

Zoe thought Ruth's plan was just what she needed, and the arrangement was confirmed for that evening. They discussed what sort of film they would like to watch and then what sort of wine they wanted to drink. It was all planned.

A couple of days later Garth met Matt again, and they chatted over the final points of the holiday. Matt handed over a receipt for £500 and then got him to pay another £1,000 whilst arranging for the final payment to be made in another couple of days. Matt was able to give him a breakdown for everything he had spent so far, which at the moment was only about £500 so he was expecting to collect another £3,000. The meeting went as planned, and immediately Matt went to the travel agents and arranged for them to issue an itinerary for the holiday. There was the usual discussion stating that Matt's client was still not sure if this was exactly what he wanted to buy, and wanted to maintain the option of cancelling, but understood he would lose his £500 if this was the case. Matt showed Garth a detailed itinerary for the flights, hotel and cruise, so that he knew what was being booked, but Matt explained that he had arranged for all the paperwork to be delivered to his own house. They didn't want his wife to find anything in the house that might give away the surprise, so as arranged Matt held on to the forms.

Garth was so pleased with what Matt had done for him that he paid him a £100 tip which Matt accepted willingly. It seemed a strange arrangement, but Garth felt it was the only way he could manage to book a holiday without his wife finding out. Matt, on the other hand, had talked him into waiting a couple of months before setting off on holiday by which time Matt knew Garth would be dead. This would just leave Matt to cancel the holiday, pay the cancellation fee and pocket the rest. All in all, it seemed quite a tidy deal.

It was time again for Matt to visit the Job Centre and because he still hadn't officially found himself a job, it meant another interview with Sonja. Matt thought these interviews were boring and a waste of time generally, but he looked forward to his meetings with the sexy Mrs Wright. He had come to the conclusion that she would rebuff all his flirty comments, and treated it a bit like a game to see if he could interrupt her cool regimented routine, or even better, make her blush. She wasn't easy to throw off balance, but he enjoyed the attempts. This time though, he was dressed in a suit as well as a shirt and tie, and looked more like Sonja's boss than her client.

"Well Mr. Briswell, you are looking very smart today, do you have a job interview to go to?"

"No, not today, I'm just dressed up to impress you."

"Oh, well, there was no need," Sonja lied. She liked how he looked and was quite impressed by him today. Matt had also come to the conclusion that Mrs Wright was probably happily married, and it didn't matter how much he flirted with her or chatted her up, she was never going to agree to go out with him, and in fact this made him much more relaxed in front of her.

"Oh that's a shame, and I went to some lengths as well."

The short interview went through its normal course with Sonja giving the usual advice, but the conclusion was always that Matt just had to keep trying with the interviews and something would eventually come his way. Matt realised that the interview was coming to an end, so just thought of a few chat up lines he could try out before he went.

"Well, it all seems like it is back to square one for me then," he said.

"Yes, I'm afraid so Mr. Briswell,"

"However, I do have to keep saying thank you for your advice and help again Mrs. Wright, or can I call you Sonja?"

"I call you Mr Briswell, so to be polite you should call me Mrs Wright, I'm afraid. And don't thank me for the advice, it's what I tell everyone."

"But you seem to have given me lots of help, and I'm sure if we were to have dinner perhaps one evening at a restaurant of your choice, we could perhaps discuss whether there were any other options open to me."

It was one of his best lines, Matt thought, and in fact Mrs Wright wasn't as quick to fend off his chat. She looked up at him and caught his eye.

"I don't think that would be a very good idea, Mr. Briswell." Sonja smiled and Matt winked back at her.

"I thought you might say that."

After Matt had gone, Sonja thought back over what had been said during the interview as she made her usual notes, but the words 'a restaurant of your choice' kept repeating in her head. Sonja had been married but she and her husband were separated and living apart. Most of the office knew what the situation was and there had been a couple of colleagues try and make a play for her but she had always thought she would regroup and give her marriage a little time before trying to make another go of it. Matt had really got her wondering if indeed she ought not to go out with someone else. The thought of it excited her and Matt was a good looking bloke. After all, it wasn't as if she was cheating on her husband. She knew that there was a danger going out with a claimant but guessed it would probably only be the once. She knew of others who had done the same. The more she thought about it, the more the words 'a restaurant of your choice' went around her head and the more she seriously considered it. There was always that nagging problem about Mr.

Briswell being a client, though. She had a plan to move him to another officer's workload if necessary.

Chapter 19
Did you ever love her?

Ray, Courtney's brother, had heard pretty much nothing from the police, and it was nearly two months now since his sister had passed away. As the only living relative he was eventually given access to all her papers, accounts and documents, and of course, access to her flat. It wasn't a duty he would enjoy, nor one he would take lightly, so he put aside a few days to try and get things sorted. There were numerous items that needed chucking out as well as some that could be sold, but Ray tried to look at each and every one of them.

He found her diary and decided to read it. He found entries relating to this guy Matt she had told him about. He was able to read some of her more personal thoughts about Matt, and it brought tears to Ray's eyes to see that she cared for him far more than he had realised. Every day almost she had made some sort of mention of Matt in her diary, of all the little things he did and said, and how he took a great interest in her, and it was clear that she enjoyed every minute of his company. There was also mention of the fact that they might be moving in to a house together which Ray had known nothing about, but it gave very little extra detail than that.

Ray also found Courtney's bank statements, and they showed that she had withdrawn a number of sums over her last weeks. Despite knowing this, there was no indication about what it was for, or indeed what she had done with it. He was in no doubt where it had gone. He was convinced that this Matt had most likely pocketed it, which seemed to upset him more than he would have liked it to. Was it greed? Was it jealousy? Perhaps it was the feeling that Matt had done more for his sister in a few weeks than he himself had ever done. He didn't know why it annoyed him but it did, and he wanted to know exactly what had happened to the money. After all, there was a good few thousand pounds unaccounted for.

Ray looked around and found Matt's details written in his sister's address book. He thought about what he could do, but he wasn't prepared to confront this man with his accusations, so he decided to go back and see the detective he had already spoken to, to see if they had made any progress.

Without a moment's further consideration, Ray made his way to the police station, and marched up to the public counter. Without any niceties he immediately barked his order to the uniformed officer stood behind it. "I need to see Detective Sergeant Morrison," Ray said, reading from a scrap of paper he held in his hand. He was pointed to a seat, and he waited there for a few minutes watching the comings and goings of The Met's finest. There were many in uniform, but also a lot more in plain clothes than he had expected there to be. One such officer, who Ray recognised instantly as DS Morrison, opened the door at the end of the counter.

"Mr Patterson?"

The unshaven detective stood at the half-open door, and called in Ray's direction. Ray stood up and followed the detective back behind the counter to a small room tucked away out of sight, so they could have some sort of privacy for their conversation.

"So, have you managed to find anything out at all about my sister's money?"

"Well, it's like this," the detective opened up the thin file, and fingered the two sheets of paper and witness statement that were within, scratching his head as he did so, "I'm afraid, Mr. Patterson, we have almost nothing to go on."

"Have you spoken to this bloke Matt to see what he's got to say for himself?"

"We haven't been able to identify who Matt is, and if we had it wouldn't be a case of just calling on him and asking him. You've been watching too many movies."

"But I have his address."

Ray removed a piece of paper from his jacket pocket as the detective took a move back in his chair and his eyebrows lifted. "I found this in my sister's address book with the name Matt, so I know it's his." Bob Morrison took the paper with the address on, and looked at it, while rubbing his unshaven chin as he thought. "I'll check it out."

The conversation was at an end as far as the detective was concerned. He advised Ray to try and forget what he thought might have happened to his sister's money, and just get on with life. This was good advice and he was trying to help the man. Bob knew that even if this Matt had taken his sister's money there was very little chance of him actually admitting any crime or giving it back or the police being able to recover anything. He had seen this sort of situation too many times before.

After Ray had left the station Detective Morrison got on with his other reports. There were lots of real crimes being committed around East London and many with some actual evidence and a chance of the police getting a prosecution so these were his priority.

As he closed his final file for the day and placed it in his out-tray ready for filing, he saw the piece of paper on his desk with the address on it. Flat 37, Bolan House, Riverley Close. Bob picked up the piece of paper and looked at it a bit more closely, going over in his mind what Mr. Patterson had told him. He tried to look at this from as many angles as he could, but he still couldn't see any need for the police to get involved. He looked up the address and found a Matthew Ellington Briswell living there. In turn, he looked up Matthew Briswell to see if he had any sort of criminal record. It showed a couple of entries, mainly suspected of handling stolen goods, and a possible intelligence association with Michael Brewster, a well-known drug dealer, but nothing serious. In fact, to be honest, there was very little known about Matthew Briswell as far as the police were concerned.

It was in fact a sheer coincidence that the next day, Detective Morrison found himself in the vicinity of Riverley Close. The address was still in his mind, so he took a drive around the area and eyed up the flats where this Mr. Briswell lived. There was nothing particularly unusual about the building from the outside, except it was coloured green in a lot of places, but the entrance seemed normal enough. It was one of those typical high rise London block of flats that had seen better days. Bob parked up opposite and gave the building a good look.

He still wasn't sure why he was doing this but he decided to just knock on the man's door and see what he had to say. The detective knew to use the Tradesman's button to get into these sorts of buildings and he quickly found his way to Flat 37. Matt heard the knock on the door and guessing it was probably a neighbour asking to borrow something, he opened it, to find a casual but smartly dressed man stood there. Matt didn't recognise what flat this man came from, but was happy to engage with a neighbour.

"Yeah, man, what's doing?"

"Are you Mr. Briswell?"   The detective asked politely.

"Who's asking?"   Matt replied.   He was a bit surprised with the way the man asked him who he was.   The detective removed his badge from his jacket pocket, folded it back and showed it to Matt.

"Oh, you're the police. Yes, that's my name, what's the beef?"

"Can I come in, or do you want me to tell all your neighbours?"   Morrison wanted to make this as simple as possible as well as quick, and it suited him to go inside rather than talk in the corridor. Matt stepped back and allowed him in. The detective sat down and took out a sheet of paper with some hurriedly written notes on it.

"Do you know a Courtney Thomas?"

Matt paused before answering.

"I knew a Courtney, but never knew her surname."

"You say knew?"

"Yes, she died a couple of months ago."

"And how old was Courtney?"

"Ah, I would say in her early fifties perhaps. Might have been late forties."

"And exactly how did you know Mrs Thomas?"

"Well, we sort of met and became friends."

"How long were you friends?"

"For a few months."

Matt was quite relaxed, and happy to be as honest as

he could be because he knew he had nothing to hide that the police would want to know about. Detective Mannerheim was happy that he had established that this was the guy who had been seeing Ray Patterson's sister but wasn't quite sure how he was going to put the next question to him. As he scribbled a couple of notes the detective pondered.

"Did she ever give you any money?" he asked.

Initially Matt gave no response to this question, but had a quizzical expression on his face.

"Money?" Matt shrugged his shoulders, hoping to give an innocent reaction to the question. "Did she ever give me any money?" he repeated, as if he was totally shocked at the thought.

"Well, she did buy me some clothes and things, but I wouldn't call that giving me money."

At this point there was another knock on the door and Matt opened it. It was Zoe. "Come in, Zoe."

She stepped into the flat ready to chat to Matt, when she realised there was a man already in the room already.

"I didn't realise you had company, I'll come back later." Zoe turned to leave, but Matt stopped her.

"No, it's not a problem. I don't think the officer here has much more to say." Matt replied.

Bob stood up from his chair knowing that the situation had more or less reached its conclusion.

"Her brother is accusing you of stealing his sister's money." The detective looked at his paper again. "Courtney's money."

"Stealing her cash, that's a bit much." Matt looked at Zoe to see how she was reacting to what had just been said. "She never even gave me any money."

"Matt isn't a thief, officer." Zoe wanted to help Matt, even though she wasn't sure herself that it was the right thing to do.

"Okay, that's good enough for me." Bob folded up his sheet of paper and left the flat.

"Well, that was a bit of a bummer," Matt said, as the detective went. "Thanks, Zoe, for telling them I'm an honest guy."

"But you're not, are you?"

"What do you mean?"

"Well, this Courtney I take it, is the woman whose stocking I found."

Zoe had really only called round in case Matt had thought about what he had done, and might possibly have changed, but she was beginning to realise he was never going to change.

"Er, well, yes."

"And that was the woman the police were enquiring about?" Zoe didn't wait for an answer as she knew it was anyway. Matt just looked dumbstruck. "I take it you've been having an affair with this woman?"

"Zoe, don't say that, you've got completely the wrong idea. I just got on well with her. We were friends and she…" Matt wasn't quite sure how to finish this sentence.

"Do you love her?" Zoe spoke through tears.

"She's dead, Zoe."

"Did you ever love her?" she asked again, in anguish. She was tearful and getting a bit loud, as she wasn't quite sure what Matt was trying to explain to her, and in fact never got an answer to her question.

Zoe automatically assumed that Matt had been more closely connected to Courtney than he would admit. Matt tried to explain that he was only interested in her for her money. Zoe was getting more emotional and confused and actually thought his last answer was even worse than anything he had said before. There was a silence as the two of them had run out of energy arguing about the subject. Zoe shed some tears before leaving the flat. Nothing else was said as she picked up her belongings and left. Matt stood and watched her, not knowing what to say. He was as fed up with it all as Zoe was.

Zoe decided it was time to confide in Ruth again, but this time she went to see her in person, even though her husband was at home. Zoe did her best not to cry whilst telling Ruth all about the police visiting Matt, and the fact that they thought he might have stolen money from this woman. Ruth wasn't absolutely sure which woman Zoe was talking about, but The Stocking Woman was how Zoe described her, then Ruth knew. She managed to keep Zoe calm, but told her that she felt that it was about time that someone had a serious talk with Matt, and that Zoe should think a bit more about exactly where this relationship was going. Repeatedly she asked Zoe if she really loved Matt, and the reply was positive if not convincing. Ruth didn't want her best friend being taken advantage of.

Whilst Bob Morrison was visiting Matt, the name of Briswell came up back at the station. Detective Sergeant Clarke was chatting to Detective Constable Perry about all the crap they had to deal with, and mentioned that he even had to take a report the other day about a guy who had managed to get his name in someone's will. The two of them laughed at the thought of the time these reports wasted, but when Joe mentioned that the guy's name was something a bit funny, like Brimstone or Brimswell, Jay-Lynne Perry's ears pricked up a bit.

"Was it Briswell?" She asked.

"Yes, that sounds familiar. I'll have to try and find the report."

"Let me have a look at it when you find it, Joe."

The conversation moved on and they got on with the more important chores of the day.

After returning to the station DS Morrison looked at the actual evidence against Matthew Briswell in relation to the accusation of stealing or acquiring funds illegally from Courtney Thomas. That was the offence being considered, and whichever way he looked at it, even though he had a gut feeling that Matt was a wrong 'un, there was nothing that he saw that he could follow up to make any sort of case to investigate further. Bob shut the brown folder and closed the case.

Matt had lots of things going around in his head, but for some reason the main subject that came to mind was the fact that he needed to make sure the Mustang was ok, and it needed cleaning and checking over. He didn't want to use it too much at the moment, even though he had the registration document, but it came in handy when he wanted to impress someone, particularly the women in his life. There was no argument at all. It needed to be looked after. He made his way to the garage where he kept the car, and looked around to make sure that nobody was watching him before he unlocked the doors and drove the Mustang out. It purred. It was quite an old car but still, it purred.

 Matt couldn't explain it, but there was a feeling when he was driving it that he didn't feel when he was doing anything else. It wasn't power. It wasn't wealth. It was just that all was right with the world. Matt loved the feeling, but he knew he had to be careful not to break any laws, or bring himself any problems by attracting attention, so he drove carefully, but not too slowly. He went to the car wash and arranged for them to valet the car in and out, and check over the oil and other necessities. He'd done it once before and knew they were okay with this.

Not too far away from the car, but far enough away

from the water spray, Matt stood by the car wash and watched as four young men got to grips with cleaning his car, but he was surprised when a man walking by stopped and chatted to him.

"It's a lovely car, isn't it?" The man nodded towards the Mustang. Matt wasn't keen to talk but felt he had no option.

"Yes, it's great."

"Are you the owner?"

"Yes," Matt replied, insulted.

"Sorry, I didn't mean anything by it, it's just that I knew Doug and this used to be his," the man replied, without any gesture.

"Oh, right." Matt wasn't sure if he should say anything to explain, but then thought better of it. He then realised that the guy had said knew, and not know.

"You said you knew Doug?"

"Yes, he was an old work colleague."

"Ah, but now you've lost touch?" Matt felt a bit happier about this situation.

"Well, sort of, but I have heard about the unfortunate event."

The man spoke casually, as if Matt would know exactly what he was talking about. Matt didn't.

"I mean that Doug died, by the way."

Matt looked surprised even though he knew this would be coming.

"He died?" Matt couldn't help but try and find out a bit more.

"Yes, it was quite sudden I'm told. Shame, he was a

289

nice geezer."

The man decided that he could no longer hang around and chat. "Sorry to bother you," he said, then went on his way. Matt wasn't sure whether to smile, laugh or cry.

Chapter 20
Things are going wrong

There was always a regular discussion amongst the Force about the state of the Earth. Today was no different. Grand Counsellor Solon convened a meeting and declared it open for discussion, although The Force didn't actually speak. They conversed by thought transfer. It was a far more efficient method of communication. There were actually a number of individuals who were being discussed. Matt was one of the early topics today and he was becoming a bit of a headache for the Force. It had been identified that because of his actions, a number of people were getting upset, depressed, and in some cases considering suicide. The Force knew all this because they had watched over humans for millennia and they could sense when things weren't right. Humans may not think that something sounds like very much to worry about, but when it leads to an imbalance, that causes alarm within The Force.

Before the discussion had even started, some of The Force had already decided they wanted Matt to be finished. Counsellor Frode particularly was in favour of this, while others who were a little bit more forgiving were prepared to give Matt more time to adjust to his new powers, and begin to use them in a good way. The full extent of these powers, and exactly the best way to use them, had to be left to Matt to work out, as it was forbidden for anyone from

291

above to actually descend and tell him.

Matt was initially chosen to have an injection of good fortune some while ago. The Force was aware that Matt's parents had not found it easy to bring him up, and that his father deserted the family when he was quite young. The Force had tried to direct some help to his mother but eviction, alcohol and drug addiction were all that followed. The Force also knew how well Matt had coped with his mother's addiction and prostitution through his early teenage years, but it was hoped that his new life would prevail when he left her behind and moved into his own place. It had been agreed that all he needed was some proper female interest to turn his life around. It hadn't quite worked out as The Force had planned.

One of the Force took it upon themselves to investigate some of the people who had been caused heartache or pain because of Matt. This particular entity in the Force was very much of the mind that Matt should be stopped as soon as possible. There was Brad's nephew Jim who was being caused pain, Doug's family wondering what happened to his car, Maureen's family, Garth's family, Courtney Thomas' brother Ray who was stressing about how Matt had stolen her money, Beverley's family, Steve's family, Polly's family, not to mention the problems he was causing Zoe Winfield with whom they thought they had organised the perfect match. It was just too much misery.

Angel Luther was permitted to have his say, and tried to put in a good word for Matt, suggesting that perhaps it was he, Luther, who had been at fault, for not keeping a close enough eye on how things were developing. It was fine for an Angel directly involved with the subject to put their own views to the Force, but it was the Force who would finally decide what action would be taken. Some of the Force were keen to allow Luther another chance, and Luther was happy to take on the task, but all agreed things couldn't be allowed to continue like this for much longer. For now, Luther was given the opportunity to try to get Matt back on track, but was under no apprehension that time was short and action had to be quick, before things really got out of hand.

The immediate future was decided, and Grand Counsellor Solon declared the action to be taken, but the next days and weeks would be very closely monitored by the Force and they would observe the situation on a regular basis and decide further changes where necessary. This was a regular part of their everyday task, to order changes that would make things right. It went on all the time. Over the centuries they had dealt with these problems and sometimes far worse, and generally in the end the Force would return things to an acceptable level fairly quickly. They also agreed that they would try and put other plans in place to influence Matt, and they even considered removing his new powers, but after some discussion agreed that it was not possible to take this action. The situation needed rectifying but it wouldn't be easy.

Chapter 21
Luther visits

There was a sharp knock on Matt's door. He casually stood up, and walked over to the entrance, and as he opened it, saw there was a man standing outside. It wasn't anyone Matt immediately recognised.

"Hi," said Matt.

"Mr. Briswell?" asked the man, interrogatively.

"Yes."

"I just wondered if I could chat to you about an old friend of mine."

The man's voice was calm and soothing, and Matt felt happy to allow him into his flat, to see exactly who it was he was going to complain about.

"Come in!" Matt directed the man in with a nod of his head. As the stranger stepped inside, he seemed to grow a few inches taller, and from seeming quite a normal size in the corridor, he now appeared to be a towering bulk of a man.

"So, who exactly do you want to talk about?" Matt asked.

"Joe Martinez died a couple of weeks ago, did you know him?"

The man started off the conversation in a very polite manner.

"Er…Joe Martins. No, I don't think so." Matt felt a bit awkward as he lied.

"I think you did, Mr. Briswell, let me help you."

The man undid his big overcoat, and sat down on Matt's settee.

"Joe Martinez, not Martins, was a nice old man who worked on the subway, does that help?"

"Martinez," Matt shook his head. "No, I don't think so," he continued to lie.

"Joe used to meet you in the park most weeks, when you would allow him to buy you a burger, and chat with him about his life."

Matt shook his head as the man produced fact after fact, and he couldn't believe what he was hearing. He suddenly realised that this man knew a lot more about his relationship with Joe than he would have believed possible.

The conversation continued for another ten or fifteen minutes, and Matt mainly sat and listened as he was told things that he and Joe had talked about, almost word for word. Matt pretty much knew he had managed to get Joe to hand over almost all of his savings, but this man could state to the penny how much he had got out of him. As if this wasn't enough, the man then explained that Joe had had a son who was in great need of the money and that he should have been the recipient. Matt didn't reply, but began to feel slightly guilty - though not enough to consider admitting his guilt in taking the money. He remained silent. The man mentioned another couple of people from whom Matt had also taken money, which surprised him even more. He expected then to be threatened with the police, but there was no mention of any such action. The tall stranger made one final comment.

"I think you should consider how much sadness you are bringing to the lives of the many relatives of the deceased, and change your ways. You are being watched."

As if the man had delivered a rehearsed speech, and finished what he had come to say, he got up and buttoned his coat ready to leave. Matt stood there and watched in dumb amazement.

"I will think about what you have said, Mr - ?" Matt said, hoping the man would give him a name.

"My name is Luther," he replied, "and you already know who I am."

He departed from the flat, leaving Matt really confused. He hadn't noticed it when the man first arrived, or indeed whilst he was talking to him, but after he had gone there was a certain familiarity about him that Matt just couldn't put his finger on. It was as if they had met before but he just couldn't place where or when.

There were many people that Matt was now acquainted with, so it was inevitable that there would be the odd one or two still around that Matt would prefer not to bump into, and that afternoon he was unlucky enough to do just that. He was just walking along the street when he heard a shout behind him.

"Matt, hey, hang on a minute." The voice was quite familiar but Matt couldn't place exactly who it was until he turned around and saw Dave the DJ running over to him. "Shit!" Matt said to himself, quietly under his breath. "Hey, Dave, fancy meeting you!" Matt greeted him loudly.

"Yeah, it's unusual for us to see each other in the daylight."

"Do you live around here then?" Matt asked, hoping he might then know, and could avoid the area in the future.

"Yeah, I'm just down the next couple of streets." The DJ quickly changed the subject. "Where's my money, man, what's going on with the big deal?"

"It's safe." Matt made up an excuse. "It's all taken a bit longer than I first thought, but I'll double your investment for you, as long as you wait, and can be a little patient." Matt hoped this would be enough to appease Dave. "It was two hundred pounds you put in, wasn't it?"

"Five hundred. And I have it in writing."

"Yes, five hundred. Sorry, there are a few investors, I couldn't raise the cash alone that I needed to bring this deal off. I'm taking all the heat and putting all the work into it, you lot just get rich off of my deals."

Matt tried to make it sound like he was doing the DJ a favour, but he knew he would have to pay him back sooner rather than later. Things would all sort themselves out given time, and once the fuss had died down and he was able to sell the Mustang, then he would be able to pay him back so he wasn't too worried. Dave meanwhile had concluded that he might not ever see his money again, but that there was nothing he could do about it, and he let the matter rest there.

Because Matt had only really just got back on to unemployment benefit properly and there were a number of queries regarding his case, he was being scheduled for more regular interviews at the Job Centre. As far as Matt was concerned, this was a lot of wasted time which he could be better spending chatting to people. Unfortunately, he was legally obliged to attend these interviews, so he just got on with it. They always asked the same sort of questions, and wanted the same proof, but Matt much preferred chatting up Mrs Wright. Today was no different.

"Hello, Mrs Wright, not had too much luck on the job front again I'm afraid."
"Sorry to hear that, Mr. Briswell." Sonja looked at Matt, and again noticed just how smartly dressed and presentable he was. "I don't think it will be too long before you do get something, though."
Sonja perused her notes in the file, and was annoyed that her efforts had not landed this man a job yet.
"Anyway, if I got a job I wouldn't be able to come and see you anymore, and that would be a real shame." Matt flashed a smile in Sonja's direction and she gave him a knowing look over the top of her glasses.
"You are trying to get a job, aren't you?"
"Well yes, sort of." Matt wasn't quite sure how to

answer this.

"Now listen, Matt," Sonja started, looking again at the file. "If I thought you weren't trying, I could stop your benefits right now." Matt wasn't sure if Mrs Wright was serious or not, and totally missed the fact that she had called him Matt.

"I'm trying to get a job, but I would much prefer to take you out for a meal." Matt looked at her to see if he was able to embarrass her, but she remained calm. "And why would you think that I would even consider such a thought?" Sonja was already imagining the evening and struggled to keep her composure.

"Yes, you've got a point there." Matt paused briefly. "I'll up the stakes a bit then, Sonja." Matt just threw in her first name to see if she would allow it, and to his surprise she sat there waiting for him to complete his sentence. Matt nodded in pleasure as he continued: "If I pick you up in my Mustang then would you agree to have dinner with me?" Matt smiled with total smugness. Sonja looked at Matt again in disbelief.

"You haven't got a car like that if you're visiting this office!"

"I tell you, I have. You think I'm lying, but you'll never know for sure, will you?"

"Can you prove that you have a Mustang?" Sonja was intrigued as well as excited. Matt looked around for a scrap piece of paper and then gently took the pen from Sonja's fingers in a slow but mildly erotic way. Sonja wanted to bring this whole interview to a close but was just amazed at what was being said. She wondered how Matt was going to prove he had a car anywhere like he was saying. Matt tore off a small piece of paper and scribbled something on it then folded it in two before handing first the paper then the pen to Sonja.

"I know you don't take compliments here at the office, but Sonja, may I say you are just a fox from the Pleasure Dome." Neither Matt nor Sonja had a clue what that meant but it sounded okay. "Here's my mobile number. Let me know where and when you want me to pick you up, and my Mustang will be at your command."

Sonja was a bit gobsmacked as well as extremely excited. Her heart was pounding and she could feel it. She was beginning to believe that Matt really did have a decent car. Matt continued, "But if I pick you up we're going to dinner so be ready." Matt smiled as he stood up expecting Mrs. Wright to just bin the piece of paper but she opened it and took a quick peek and then held it tightly in her hand. "If you're serious, ring me Sonja." Matt blew her a kiss as he smiled at her. Sonja didn't know what to say.

"Okay, Matt, I might ring you," she said, almost without thinking.

The evening was going to be a relatively busy one for Matt, as he was getting ready to go out and see another dying friend. He was only half dressed when he was interrupted by a confident sharp knock on the door. Matt opened it to find a casually dressed man standing outside, another stranger he didn't recognise. Matt assumed he was a relative, perhaps of Courtney's, who had come to complain, and he was ready to see the man off, but instead, gave him a chance to explain his visit.

"Hi, are you Matthew?" The private detective asked very confidently.

"Yes, who are you?"

"I believe you own a Mustang?" The detective looked at a piece of paper on a clip board, as if it was an official report.

"Yes, but who are you?" Matt was intrigued and a little worried in case it was someone who knew Doug and that was going to make his ownership of the Mustang a pain.

"Oh, I'm from an agency that chases up unpaid fines, and there are a couple outstanding on your vehicle. Perhaps I can come in and discuss the situation."

Matt wasn't keen, and in fact wanted to be going out, but he thought if he could just sort this out quickly it would be for the best, so he allowed the man to come in.

"How did you trace the car to me, then?" Matt was a little puzzled.

"Er…eh…" the detective tried to sound a bit dumb.

"I don't actually know how they get the information, I've just been told to come to see you at this address, and see if I can get you to pay some of your fines off."

"So, where was this offence anyway, and when?" Matt thought he would just test the waters to see if in fact it was his offence, or Doug's.

"I haven't got an exact date but it's a parking offence in the borough of Waltham Forest." The detective took a chance that Matt had probably parked somewhere in the area at some time.

"Oh, Waltham Forest! That could be anywhere then? How much will the fine be?" Matt had given in and assumed that it must be his offence.

"I don't have that information; can you just get your fine letter?"

"Letter? I don't have a letter." Matt started to get annoyed. The detective scratched his head and looked at his clip board.

"Yes, they all say that."

"No, honestly, I've never had any letter, but then it's only recently registered in my name, so perhaps the records are old?"

"Okay, I'll report back to my office and will have to call back in a days' time or so." The detective wrote a few notes on the sheet but had already seen what he had hoped to see. There was a pause as Matt waited for the man to tell him what was going to happen next. "Right, I think that's all for now."

"Okay." Matt pointed towards the door.

"Oh, by the way, I see you have a painting down

there against the wall which you look like you might be selling, it looks like a nice painting. Is it for sale?" The detective pointed towards the half covered painting laid against the wall. Matt cursed as he saw what the man was pointing to.

"Oh, it might be for sale, but you won't be able to afford it I'm afraid."

"How do you know? It looks like an Edouard Cortes to me." The detective waited to see what sort of response this would bring.

"Yes, it's a Cortes, but do you know how much they sell for?" Matt wanted to sound flash but was also trying to get rid of the man. "They're worth at least three or four thousand pounds."

The detective had got what he wanted and left the flats.

Matt was pleased to get rid of the man, and in fact thought perhaps he should go out somewhere before there was anyone else knocking on his door, but he also wanted to think about getting rid of the painting. There were a number of items he could do with getting rid of, if he really thought about it. He tried to inventory all the things he had managed to acquire, and work out which he could get rid of soonest to start recouping some of the cash value. He wondered about using Mikey to fence the stuff, but then decided that since most of the goods weren't actually stolen, he could just take them to a pawn shop himself.

Chapter 22
I've had enough

Matt sat back and took stock of how far he had come in the last few months, and saw just how well he had done. He was a bit pissed off about still living in a small flat, but imagined that would change soon. He opened his wardrobe and looked at his clothes. Most of them were newly purchased in the last couple of months. He began to feel really good about who he now was, when he spotted the Mustang keys on the side. "Yes,'" he told himself in the bedroom mirror, "I'm a man who's made it," he continued smugly. "Women will be falling down in front of you, and begging you to take them to bed," he continued. He smiled in the small mirror and told himself, "I must be irresistible."

It reminded him that Zoe hadn't been around for a while, and he fancied getting her into bed again, totally ignoring that she had pretty much told him she couldn't stand him anymore. Matt then thought about Sonja, and concluded that she probably needed a bit more work before she succumbed to his manly charms. In conclusion, he decided he should ring Zoe and ask her round again. Matt called her but it went to a voice message. He didn't really want to leave a message, he preferred to talk in person, so he rang another couple of times but the result was always the same. On the fourth attempt he decided he had leave her a nice sexy message asking her to get in touch, to see if they could sort out their problems and get back to having some fun. Matt had decided that it would be inevitable that she would get back to him, so he guessed it was just a matter of time before he got a call back. Zoe didn't call. Not that day, not the next day, nor the day after that.

In the meantime, Courtney's brother Ray found himself struggling over some unpaid bills that he couldn't quite afford, and the thought of this Matt having taken what could have been his money, plus the fact that the cops were doing absolutely nothing about it, got the better of him. He decided that he needed to confront Matt himself. Ray searched for and found the details he had copied from his sister's address book and made his way over to Matt's address. He paced up and down outside the door for nearly five minutes before knocking. Ray didn't want to admit it, but he was feeling a little frightened. He had never liked confrontation, and was scared of violence, and also sensible enough to realise that he could be putting himself in danger, but he felt he had no other option.

The door opened, and Matt looked Ray up and down. "Yeah?" he said, as if to ask what he wanted. He wasn't quite sure who this guy was, but thought he looked vaguely familiar.
"Are you Matt?" Ray spoke rather timidly.
"Who are you?" There wasn't going to be any confirmation or denial at this stage.
"I'm Courtney's brother, and I think she knew you

before she died."

As he said the words, Ray suddenly realised that his approach was going to be one of sad sympathy in an effort to try and gain this bloke's trust. "Can I come in?"

"Certainly." Matt was surprised at how upset the man seemed, and felt he was close to tears. He was also pleased to confirm that he had met him before, and knew him to be Courtney's brother whom he had met briefly at the funeral. He sounded like he was in real pain and Matt wondered if he just wanted to talk about Courtney's life.

"My sister and I talked a bit before she died, and she talked about you a lot."

"Wow, is that so?" Matt was a bit surprised to hear this.

"I think she was really in love with you."

Matt wasn't quite sure how to answer that.

"In fact she said she had plans to try and buy a house with you."

Matt didn't want the brother to get the wrong idea. Matt was very fond of Courtney, and he needed to try and explain that to this brother, but he didn't want him to think that he had led Courtney down the path towards them sharing a house.

"Oh, I didn't know that!" Matt went on the defensive immediately.

"Well, that was what she told me."

"I did know your sister, and she and I were very good

307

friends, but she was nearly twice my age for God's sake."

"Yes, I thought that was how it was."

"Look, not that it's any of your business, but we had some fun times before she died, and I think I made her very happy."

"But you stole her money."

"What are you saying?"

"She had nearly nine thousand pounds taken from her bank account over the last two months of her life, and not a penny of it can be found, so you must have it." Ray clenched his fists and had to bite on his lip before taking a deep breath to try and calm down a bit.

"I'm a pretty rich man, so why would I need her money, YOU TOSSER?" Matt gave Ray a long hard stare as his voice became aggressive over the insult.

There was a tense brief silence, but almost as if it had been scheduled there was a knock on Matt's door. He got up immediately and answered it. He was expecting it to be that DS Morrison again, or perhaps more of Courtney's relatives, so he was quite surprised and very pleased when he found Zoe standing at the door.

"Come in." Matt stood back to allow her in. "I've got someone here at the moment, but he'll be going soon." Matt spoke loudly as much to tell Courtney's brother that he should leave, as well as let Zoe know what was going on. Ray wasn't in the mood to just leave things and indeed found something inside of him to attack this young woman who had just appeared.

"Oh, I suppose you're the floozy who spends all his ill-gotten gains are you?"

"Er, what?" Zoe was taken by surprise that a stranger should be so aggressive toward her as soon as she walked in.

"You'll probably say you know all about how he came by his money."

"I don't know who you are, but why don't you just clear off?" Zoe was quite shocked at herself at how angry she was. "Throwing accusations at me like that, someone you don't even know, you wanker!" She was getting really annoyed.

"This man stole money from my sister, and I want it back."

"Matt wouldn't steal from anyone, I'm sure, so what proof do you have?" Zoe was prepared to look at whatever evidence the stranger had, but he had nothing. She didn't even ask who this man's sister was but she had a pretty good idea. "I think you should get out now before I really lose my cool and call the police."

It was a strange moment, as if Ray had to wait a few seconds for Zoe's words to filter down into his brain, before realising that he might well be in a situation he would be better out of.

"Okay, I'm going," he said to Zoe, but then he turned and pointed at Matt, "but don't think you've heard the last of this." He walked towards the door and Matt made a show of shoving him through it before slamming it shut behind him. Matt assumed his charm had worked its magic on her and she had come round to fall into his arms, but he had to admit that she had arrived at just the right time. He wanted to thank her for her timely interception. "Zoe, my love," Matt started, but was instantly interrupted.

"Don't you give me that bloody 'my love' crap!" Zoe retorted, as her anger hadn't actually subsided. "Just who was that, and who was he talking about?" "Oh, he was the brother of that woman, you know." Matt shrugged off the question as if it was irrelevant to what was going on.

"What bloody woman?" Her voice got a little louder. As the row inside began to escalate, Zoe's voice could be overheard by Ray out in the corridor. He swiftly made his way back to Matt's door to try and listen. He couldn't hear every word, but he could easily get the gist of what they were arguing about, and when either of them shouted, it was possible to pick out what they were saying.
Back in the flat Matt tried to explain things. "You know, the one who died, but I'd got to know a bit. Who I told you about!" Zoe knew exactly who it was.

"The one who leaves her stockings all over the place you mean." Matt found her statement amusing, and did all he could to stifle a giggle. Fortunately, she

didn't notice, and continued. "And did you steal the money, or did she give it to you?" Zoe was initially going to wait for an answer, but as Matt seemed unwilling or unable to reply she continued. "In fact, I don't want to hear what you've got to say because it's obvious how you got it."
Zoe stopped for breath, briefly.

"You ring me as if everything has changed, but you're just one lying cheating bastard. I don't know you anymore and I hate you." She began to shed tears. She huffed and banged her fist on the table.
"Zoe, there's nothing wrong," Matt started, trying to explain, but was soon interrupted.
"I don't want to hear it, I told you, I don't like how you get this money. I'm so stupid thinking you might have changed," shouted Zoe. She turned away, and in a few steps had made the short distance to the door before stopping and turning back to Matt. "And don't ring me again, ever!"

Ray heard Zoe's words and had guessed she might be coming to the door, and abruptly took a few steps down the corridor so she wouldn't see him when the door opened. Fortunately, he had chosen to move along the corridor and over to the other side of the stairwell so he was more or less out of sight but he watched as she appeared from the flat, slammed the door shut and made her way to the stairs. He could see she was upset and crying, but he followed and called out to her on the stairs.

"Excuse me!" He didn't actually know what her name was, and Zoe ignored his call, so he ran down a bit and caught up with her. He tapped her on the shoulder. Zoe thought it was Matt and was ready to give him a real mouthful as she turned. She was stopped in her tracks and surprised to see it was the stranger who had been in Matt's flat.

"What do you want?"

"I heard you arguing with your boyfriend."

"And what business is it of yours?" These were Zoe's final words as she pushed Ray aside, and hurriedly made her way outside. Ray was now even more convinced that Matt had robbed his sister of the money.

As if arguing with Courtney's brother, and then Zoe, hadn't been enough for Matt, when he finally managed to sit down and try to absorb some of the morning's activity, his phone rang. Matt looked at the number and didn't recognise it. He thought twice about whether to answer it or not, but his curiosity was too much for him.

"Hi, Matt here!" Matt answered the phone in his usual way.

"Hello, I don't know if you'll know who this is, but I've been thinking about your offer."

The female voice on the other end was instantly recognisable.

"Oh, have you, Sonja?"

"Ah, you know it's me then?"

"Of course, I would know your voice till the day I die."

Matt couldn't believe that Sonja had actually rung him. Within moments he had forgotten everything that had just happened with Zoe and Ray.

"Well, I've given your offer some thought, and although I still don't believe that you actually have a Mustang I'm going to give you a chance to prove it."

"Sonja, you won't regret it."

"I'd better not."

Sonja didn't want to get her hopes up too high, and she didn't want to come across as easy. "And I'll be expecting a top restaurant meal," she added.

"Sonja, we'll have a great evening."

Matt's heart was in his mouth. The conversation after this was fairly brief, but Sonja had given Matt a chance to put his money where his mouth was. She arranged for him to pick her up from a spot in town that coming Friday evening. Matt had a smirk that almost covered his whole face and he really felt on top of the world.

Sonja's heart was beating fast. She could hardly believe that she had actually made the phone call but she had. There was still a big concern in her head about going out with one of her clients but she needed some male company and Matt was good looking, young, fit and more importantly, interested.

After leaving Matt's flat and calming down a bit, Zoe

considered all that had been said and all that had happened. She wasn't sure what to do. She needed to talk to someone, so she rang Ruth and told her what had happened at Matt's, with the brother of the dying woman, and their argument afterwards. Ruth knew just how to calm her friend down, and she got her to agree that Matt was not the right man for her. Zoe acknowledged that he had become someone very different to the one she had met that night, and that she was not really able to love him anymore. Ruth was very good at listening, and fairly good at reading people. She knew that Matt wasn't the right person for her friend, and without actually interfering she was determined to make sure that Zoe moved on to someone new.

Ray went and sat at a bus stop to cool down a bit. He wasn't sure if the visit to Matt had made any difference or not, but he was convinced that he was the sort of bloke who would fleece innocent women like his sister and then leave them high and dry. In some ways, he thought, it was a good job his sister died when she did, or else she might have lost everything. Ray then went over the argument he had heard between Matt and his girlfriend. The words seemed changed every time he tried to recall exactly what they had said, but he felt that the gist of it was that she knew Matt had stolen the money. He wished that she had said more to him afterwards, but perhaps she was afraid she might be implicated, and understandably said nothing.

314

The best course of action now for Ray was to go back to the police station and pass on what he had found out to Detective Sergeant Morrison. This time he only spoke to Ray in the foyer without actually taking any notes. In fact, Ray was warned not to take things into his own hands and risk being cautioned for harassment. He wasn't happy, but he had told the police what he had heard, and he would let them get on with it. Bob Morrison was beginning to find Mr. Patterson a real pain in the butt. There was no evidence against this Matt Briswell, and very little for the police to do. He went back to his desk and scribbled a couple of lines of notes, but then filed it away at the bottom of a very big pile of closed cases.

Matt made his way out for the evening. He had no plans to actually meet up with anyone tonight so had decided just to visit a couple of local pubs and see who was about when his mobile rang again. Matt answered it without checking who it was.

"Hi, Matt here."

"Matt, it's Mikey."

"Mikey, what's going down, mate?"

"I've got a little job for you for an easy twenty quid, what do you say?"

"No, can't do it my man, I'm too busy."

Matt was beginning to feel that Mikey was a thing of the past, and he didn't want to get involved in Mikey's petty crimes anymore.

"Oh, right, I can always get someone else if you're not up for it. Feeling a bit too flaky, perhaps?"

Mikey tried to goad Matt into helping, but Matt just wasn't interested.

"No, Mikey, those days are gone. I'm living the real life now. Hey, if you want a beer I'll buy you one, I'll be in the White Hart."

The call finished just as Matt got to the pub. He entered with a real confidence. Jed was behind the bar polishing glasses, and Matt knew just what he had to do. "Evening, Jed, how much do I owe you for my bar bill?" Jed walked back to the till and pulled out a folded sheet of paper.

"Twenty-two forty," he said.

Matt pulled out a twenty and a ten and placed them on the bar.

"Will this cover it?" Matt smiled.

"That certainly will." Jed picked up the notes and rang in the bill before returning with Matt's change.

"And I'll have a beer to celebrate."

Chapter 23
Maureen

Detective Constable Jay-Lynne Perry was probably one of the most experienced of the bunch currently working out of the Leytonstone station. She had been a police officer for nearly twenty-five years and a detective for at least fifteen of those but because she had taken time out to have children perhaps hadn't progressed up the ranks as much as she should have. It didn't worry her. She liked being a detective, and like the others at the station she would rather be out there arresting criminals than dealing with public complaints, but she was very switched on when it came to finding links between people, particularly criminals. She looked at the very thin file Joe Clarke had left on her desk. It was another of those trivial cases that never should have seen the light of day but as a member of the public had reported it, they had to allocate a case number.

Jay read through it briefly. It was a complaint by a Mr Spencer Cunningham that a Matthew Briswell was named in his father's will, and had been left a largish amount of money in it. Jay read Joe's brief notes that stated that he had seen a copy of the will, and it clearly stated that Mr Briswell was to be a beneficiary, so he couldn't see any way to take the complaint further. Jay read the few lines that he'd written, and could see that her colleague had pretty much nailed it. She was aware that deaths often brought about complaints from relatives who thought, without an ounce of justification, that someone else had done them out of an inheritance. It was just so common. Jay was thinking about a number of other complaints over the years, when suddenly the thought of a more recent case came to mind. She couldn't explain why the name suddenly seemed familiar, but she wanted to be sure and she searched through a number of recently closed files. She knew it was a thin file, and after five minutes searching she found it. She opened the file and read the report about the bizarre case - Mr Briswell at the Whipps Cross University Hospital had been talking to certain patients who all seemed to die a day or two later. Nobody had even been allocated the case, it was simply shut because there was nothing to investigate. Jay knew that it was likely to be a waste of time, but she felt she needed to investigate this Mr. Briswell a bit more.

Bob Morrison was hoping for a nice quiet day as he walked into the station. As usual the desk clerk was ready to press the release button whenever people arrived for work, and almost without looking up from his report, would automatically buzz in officers as they approached the door.

"Cheers, Col," Bob said as he pushed open the door, and made his way behind the counter. Colin knew exactly who each person was by their footsteps or voice.

"The Chief's been looking for you," he replied

looking at his watch. Bob knew he was supposed to have been on duty at nine, and was often a bit late but he knew ten minutes wasn't going to make the Chief want to see him about his time-keeping.

"What for, Col, do you know?" Bob asked, hoping for some sort of clue. Colin just shrugged his shoulders and shook his head without properly looking up. "You'll have to go and find out."

Bob didn't have to wait long, as within a couple of minutes the Chief was at his desk. "Bob..." the Chief paused before continuing.

"An old friend of mine has mentioned your name as the officer looking into suspicions surrounding the death of his niece."

"Oh, yes, Chief. What's her name?"

"Courtney something, I don't really know."

"I'm not actually dealing with any cases of murder involving women, are you sure it's me?"

"Well, he only mentioned your name, said his nephew had made the complaint."

"Do you know his name?"

"No, I don't. My friend is Paddy Patterson, we played golf together for years."

Bob interrupted the Chief before he went on any further.

"Did you say Patterson?"

"Yeah, Patterson. Does that ring a bell?" The Chief watched as his detective hurriedly searched through a pile of dead files, anxiously looking for one that he had hoped was buried and forgotten. "Does

Patterson ring a bell then, Bob?"

"Yes, I think I know the case."

After about three or four minutes of searching through various case files Bob found what he was looking for. He retrieved the file and the two of them went over the brief notes.

"As you can see, it's a simple case of hard cheese on the part of the brother as far as I'm concerned."

The Chief read through the report and ummed and ahhed here and there.

"Yes, I see," he said as he scratched his ear and then the side of his face.

They both agreed that there was very little to go on, and indeed this was pretty much just a case of sour grapes if the sister had spent all of her money on a young man instead of leaving it to the brother in her will.

"Okay, Bob, I tend to agree with you, but I've promised Paddy that we would make a full investigation, so just go over it again for me will you? I want a full job done on this, Bob. It shouldn't take you long."

"But Chief, what else can I do?" DS Morrison appealed.

"Give it all another good look for me and I need a full report on my desk by the end of next week. Every aspect detailed in full." There was a brief silence as the two men looked at each other. "I need to have something to tell him, that we have actually come to a conclusion that there is no case to answer, rather than just ignored it."

The Chief handed the file back to DS Morrison and walked away briskly.

Bob was annoyed, but knew that these sorts of things sometimes happened. Two of his colleagues had witnessed the whole thing, and started to give Bob some ribbing about it.

"Make sure you investigate it properly, Bob," one detective called out.

"I want a full job done on this case!" Another shouted, as they laughed.

"Okay, have your fun, one day you'll get a crap case like this, and it'll be my turn to take the piss."

Bob sat down and opened the folder again as one of the other police officers walked over to have a look.

"Who is this guy complaining about?"

"Oh, some young lad who was poking his older sister. It's nothing."

"No, what was his name again, it sounded rather familiar."

"Matthew Briswell. You heard of him Joe?"

There was a wait as the officer thought for a few seconds.

"No, it doesn't ring a bell but thought I'd heard the name. Sorry, you're on your own."

There was nothing for it, Bob would have to pay yet another visit to the home of Mr. Matthew Briswell. This time he concluded he would have to take more detailed notes, ask some more questions, and have enough information to put a report on the Chief's desk. He knew it was late, but he knocked on the flat door and Matt opened it. His face peered through the opening.

"Oh, it's you again." Matt's response wasn't the most pleasant and immediately put Bob in a bit of a mood. He huffed as he showed Matt his badge, and took a step as if to enter the flat, but Matt didn't open the door wide enough and so he had to stop.
"We can do this down the station if you really want me to arrest you," he suggested.

Matt reluctantly opened the door. DS Morrison gave Matt a quick look, since he was standing in just a pair of underpants. As soon as Bob walked into the flat, he could smell a mix of alcohol and cheap perfume. He noticed a low light on in the bedroom, but the door was almost shut so he couldn't see whether there was anyone else there. He guessed it might well have been the girlfriend that Ray Patterson had described, if in fact there was anyone. Regardless of that, there was no time to wait. Bob drew up a chair to the table and took out a note-book. It registered with Matt that this interview might take a bit longer than he had first thought.

"Excuse me, Officer, can I just put something else on?" "Please do."
Bob watched as Matt scurried to the bedroom door

and slithered in without opening the door very far. He heard the whispers of a conversation without being able to determine the words, but anyway this confirmed that there was someone else in the flat. Matt reappeared pulling on a jumper over some old jeans. He sat down and looked at the detective.

"I thought we'd finished our business the other day, Sergeant."
"So did I. And you call me Detective Sergeant."
"Oh, sorry, Detective Sergeant."
"I need some more details about how you knew Courtney Thomas."
Bob was checking his pen when he caught a glimpse of a half-naked body through the partly open bedroom door. It was clearly a woman's body, and she was obviously getting dressed. It distracted him momentarily.
"What do you want to know?"
"Eh?" Bob quickly got back to the matter in hand. "How did you meet?"

The interview had been going on for nearly fifteen or twenty minutes when an older woman appeared from the bedroom. She seemed to be wearing underwear but had a towel wrapped around her, giving the impression that she could have been totally naked.
"Matt, darling, I need to get going," the woman said, completely ignoring the police officer as she stood seductively with her forefinger on her bottom lip.
"Maureen, my love," Matt got up and turned

Maureen back to face the bedroom and pushed her toward the door. "Just hang on a moment longer, and I'll be back."

She turned her head and looked at Bob as she replied. "Don't be long, honey." She then went into the bedroom as Matt patted her shapely bottom. Bob couldn't take his eyes off the woman.

"Get your booty back in bed, let me finish the business I have here, and we'll get back to where we left off."

Matt spoke in his most charming voice and then kissed Maureen on the cheek before pulling the door closed.

Bob rubbed his mouth with his fingers as he watched the woman retreat back into the bedroom. He found her quite stunning, but guessed that she was probably older than he was, and he knew he was almost twenty years older than Matthew Briswell. This was not the girlfriend that Ray Patterson had described to him, and he wondered if this was another woman who was being fleeced.

"Excuse me, ma'am," Bob called. The woman opened the door and looked back at him. There was a feeling of suspense in the room.

"Sir!" The woman's voice was Marilyn-sexy.

"I'm Detective Sergeant Morrison, Metropolitan Police." Bob showed her his badge. "I just need to ask you for your name and details for my enquiries." Bob thought this request might well be met with some reluctance from the woman, and was ready with an excuse for wanting to know. There was a short pause while Maureen looked up to the ceiling as if in thought. She pursed her lips and looked back at Bob.

"Why, Officer, my name is Maureen O'Connell," said Maureen breathily, almost as if she was playing a part in a film, as she continued give him all her details, and told him how she knew Matt, without any reluctance at all. Matt just stood and admired her performance as the detective took down as much detail as he could. Matt winked at Maureen and then patted her bum as if she had been a really good girl. "Will that be all, Officer?" Maureen asked, as she returned to Matt's bedroom. She turned briefly and blew a little kiss before disappearing out of view completely. Bob had pretty much finished asking all the questions he had wanted to ask and within ten minutes he was on his way back to the station.

When he arrived back at the station, he perused his notes and got to work on his report for the Chief. The conclusion was no different, but at least he now had more detail to put into in. After about twenty minutes another detective walked into the office.

"Hi, Bob, you're working hard."
"Hello, Joe. Yes, I'm still on that case the Chief is bugging me about."
"What, that Briswell bloke?"

"Yes."

Joe walked over to Bob and placed a friendly hand on his shoulder.

"I thought I'd heard the name before. You ought to have a word with Jay. I think she's got something on this Briswell," Joe told him.

Bob looked at Joe, perplexed.

"You're pulling my pisser!"

"No, honest, she asked to look at one of my reports a couple of weeks ago, and I'm sure it was the same guy. If you don't believe me, fair enough, but you should just see what she has to say."

"Jay Perry?" Bob wanted confirmation.

"Yes. I'm pretty sure."

"Thanks, Joe."

Bob stopped typing. If DC Perry had something else of interest, he wanted to know about it before he finished his report. He checked the rota and saw that Jay was on duty but was currently out. He would just have to wait, but it would have to be this evening, he felt.

It was another couple of hours before DC Perry returned, and Bob was on to her almost as soon as she entered the station. "Jay, are you looking at some geezer called Briswell?"

Bob expected a smart remark to come back at him, but Jay wasn't laughing. She put her hands on her hips and thought for a moment.

"Yeah, maybe."

She waited to see what Bob was going to say next.

"The Chief has had me go and see him, and I have a report if you're interested?"

"Yeah, I'd like a look." DC Perry walked over toward Bob.

"It's nothing, though," Bob put his hand up in a sort of apologetic way, but also so that she didn't think Briswell was the criminal of the century.

"Does it involve anyone dying?" Jay asked.

The question seemed a bit strange to others overhearing the conversation, but Bob was taken aback at it and he looked at her, surprised.

"Well, in fact it does. Someone has complained that this Matt Briswell stole money from his sister who died."

"It fits a profile I'm working on. Let me have a quick look."

Bob gave Jay his report, and she read the whole thing twice. She occasionally scratched the back of her neck, but then slammed the file down on Bob's desk. "I think we need to go and see the Chief."

The two detectives discussed what Jay had read in his report and agreed that there were indications of possible foul play, but had to agree that it was a strange one. Detective Constable Perry wondered if this Briswell chap was actually killing off rich people but it didn't fully hold together. There was no evidence of anything other than natural causes. Despite the doubt, there was enough for Jay to want the Chief to see it. There was one last thing that DC

327

Perry asked Bob about.
"Who is Maureen O'Connell?"
"Who?"
"Maureen O'Connell. You've written her details down on a scrap of paper in the report."
"Oh, yes, she was in the flat with Mr. Briswell when I saw him. Seemed far too old for him, so I asked for her details. She might have been a bit of a cougar but you never know who's doing who."
"I'll check her out."

In the last week or so Matt had managed to sell a couple of his acquisitions and he made sure he was putting the money safely on a regular basis. He didn't want to use his bank account too much, nor open a new one, so he kept most of it as cash. He found little hideaways for his cash that even burglars who knew there was money in the apartment would have trouble finding. Mikey and Mop had taught him many tricks, and Matt was able to put them to good use. He had also seen his mother hiding drugs when he was younger and learnt some things from her.

Matt suddenly thought back to those last couple of years at home. Life was pretty awful, and dangerous, as his mother met with violent customers who were either there to sell drugs or use her for prostitution. Matt's lasting image of his mother was more often than not with a black eye, a split lip and bruised. Then there were the track marks and bruising on her arms. It wasn't a pleasant vision, and he too had copped a few beatings from some of the visitors, so it was no surprise that as soon as he had the opportunity he ran away from home. Matt got lost in the sorrowful memory briefly, before getting back to counting his money. After another count he was happy that he had enough for a deposit on a flat or maybe even a house. It would be his own, newer and much smarter than the one he currently rented. That would be his next job, to find a new place.

The private detective employed by Brad's nephew Jim was also busy, and he reported to his client. He explained that he had done a bit more digging about Matt, who he had identified as Matthew Briswell, and found that he seemed to be suspiciously involved with a number of police complaints from friends and relatives of recently dead people. There was also the Cortes painting which had actually been seen in his flat. The two of them discussed what Jim wanted to do next. It was decided that the dossier that the private detective had written up on Matt should be given to the police for further investigation.

That evening Matt was due to take Sonja out for a meal. He was buzzing with anticipation and was almost felt as if he was dreaming. The arrangement was to pick her up from a small store close to Valentine's Park. It seemed a strange place to choose, but that was what Sonja had told him, and Matt didn't want to question anything she said. For almost an hour before leaving his flat, Matt had paid special attention to getting ready. He dressed in his best suit, a brand new shirt and put on his most expensive aftershave. He looked at himself in the mirror before making some final adjustments to his hair. It was a quick walk to the lock up before picking her up in the Mustang. As he approached the meeting place, he saw her waiting. She was wearing a stunning black dress, knee high boots and a very smart beige jacket. She looked absolutely fantastic.

Matt hooted, and Sonja waved as she made her way over to the car. She did wonder if it was going to be an old car but she was impressed. The shining yellow Mustang that Matt was driving looked just the ticket. A million dollars.

"Hope you're ready for a great night out, babe?" Matt said as he opened the passenger door and watched every inch of Sonja's legs as she slipped into the seat beside him. He had looked at them many times before, but tonight they looked even better.

"Wow, you look good," said Matt, gulping with amazement.

"You don't look too bad yourself," Sonja replied.

Matt tried to work out exactly what Sonja's real attraction was. Her hair, her face, her eyes? Her gorgeous body, or those endless legs? Every bit of her seemed just delightful, and his mouth was watering at the anticipation of the evening to come.

From the very beginning their date went well, and the two of them ate at a very classy restaurant which impressed Sonja even more. Matt was able to splash some cash around, but not too much, or else Sonja might want to know where he had got his money from. Later, after a couple of drinks, they went back to Matt's flat where she gave him the green light that he had been waiting for. Sonja had been waiting for her marriage to show even the vaguest of signs that it might be back on track, but she had not heard anything from her husband in months now and she was beginning to miss the warmth of a physical relationship.

The two of them couldn't wait to make their way to the bedroom and Sonja knew that Matt was going to be the next man for her. Matt couldn't believe he had managed to bed Mrs Wright, but sure enough it was happening, and he was making the most of it. He had apologised for the poor flat he was living in but said that he was moving into something much bigger soon. Sonja thought that the old flat seemed appropriate for someone on benefits but she could also see that Matt had enough money to back up his story. She was impressed.

The whole evening had been fantastic for both of them, and as they lay in bed in the early hours they chatted for what seemed like ages. The conversation wasn't at all serious, but on subjects that just allowed them to talk to each other although at times both hinted at deeper things without actually saying what they meant.

"How old are you?" Sonja looked at Matt as she asked.

"Surely you know, you've seen my records." Matt was surprised at her question.

"I'm just wondering what a twenty-five-year-old like you wants with an old woman like me?"

"You're not old," Matt told her. "Experienced, but not old." Matt hoped that sounded like a compliment. Sonja didn't really take it as one.

"You mean experienced in bed, you dirty little so and so."

Sonja tried to be serious, but couldn't keep her hands off him as they kissed again and started to make love for a third time. Sonja wanted Matt as a serious partner, and hoped he didn't just see her as a one-night stand. Matt for his part was happy to see Sonja again, but felt a bit lost sometimes with her conversation. Despite that, he was over the moon with her, and hoped this would be the real thing.

Quite soon the dark skies showed signs of brightening as the sun began to rise and send strands of lighter blue through the forest of buildings outside Matt's window. After a few more cuddles and a lot more kissing they eventually said their goodbyes and Sonja called herself a taxi home to get ready for work. Matt gave Sonja one last kiss, and watched her walk down the corridor then went back in and returned to bed. He just couldn't believe his luck.

He lay there looking around at all the scruffy things in his room that reminded him of who he used to be, then thought about who he was now. There were at least three smart suits hanging up in his wardrobe, a whole number of snazzy shirts and smart shoes, and he had money. In fact, he had a lot of money if he was really counting. He also now had a really sexy woman in Sonja. He thought back to Zoe and how they had been, but that was different. Sonja was so much more sophisticated, and Zoe was just no match for her. He knew Sonja was older, but they really clicked, and life was just great. On top of that, he still had the Mustang and he had enough money to find a new place of his own. "Life just couldn't get better," he said to himself.

An hour or so later Matt got up and dressed. He put on more casual clothes than last night but even these were now top of the range. He walked the few blocks to the newspaper stand where he often used to stop and read the papers.

"Howdy, Matt." The newspaper man recognised Matt's face instantly, but it took him a few more minutes to take in the change of style. "Hey, you're looking fine! New clothes today?"

"Yeah, hi, I've managed to get myself a job or two, and thought I should spend a bit on myself." Matt certainly looked very different.

"Well, the new look suits you."

"I'll just have a Times." The newspaper man folded a paper for Matt and handed it over. Matt handed him a ten-pound note.

"Keep the change," Matt said, as he turned round and set off to his flat. It was a bit showy but Matt enjoyed the moment. He walked back going over every minute of last night's date with Sonja. He didn't want to admit it, but for the first time ever he knew he was in love. He slowly made his way back home, entered his flat and sat down to read the paper. It then suddenly hit him. He had not even noticed the numbers over people's heads while he was out. Had Sonja changed him, or was it just a passing phase, he wondered.

Chapter 24
Luther called to act

The Force called another meeting to discuss Matt. It wasn't exactly unusual to hold special meetings just to discuss one human, but this was the third such meeting concerning Matt, to look at what could be done about the problems he was causing. This wasn't good. There were already so many humans setting off alarms because their lives weren't going according to plan, and The Force didn't like that. In fact the list of humans that Matt had interacted with, and caused problems for, was getting longer all the time. There was already a whole string of people whose life plan had altered course because of Matt, and the members of The Force included in this discussion were well aware of each and every one of them.

Grand Counsellor Solon began the discussion but, as always, no words were spoken. Many of the Counsel were of a similar mind, that it was now past the point of no return, and Counsellor Frode had called for drastic action. There was a brief communication about Angel Luther, to decide whether any blame could be apportioned, but all of The Force was behind Luther, and laid no blame on the Angel for what had happened. It was Counsellor Thaddeus who asked that Angel Luther also be included in the discussion, as the Angel had been much closer eye to what had happened in this case.

A call went out to summon Luther, and the Angel duly attended as requested. Luther was a well-respected Angel amongst the Force, even if still relatively young with a lot to learn, but many thought that he would make a good Elder in time. The Force explained the situation to Luther, and asked if there was anything to add to the discussion. Luther was reluctant to go against any decision that The Force had made, and had already been advised of their overall mood, but Counsellor Thaddeus insisted that the Angel give a report on Matt. Luther explained that although Matt was a difficult case, it had now been found that the human's persona had been altered in of the accident, and that the female originally chosen to bring Matt's life on track was now obviously wrong. Luther went on to explain that another female who was a perfect choice had now been found, and their joining had been processed. Luther felt that Matt was now ready to change his life and get back on the right track. The Force listened to Luther's report, and when the Angel had finished they muttered between themselves.

Counsellor Ahura joined Counsellor Thaddeus in believing that Angel Luther should be given yet more time to straighten out this human's life, but Counsellors Frode, Beathas and Zeroun opposed. The Force also looked again at Matt's early life and what he had endured in his younger days. They agreed that he had done well to get where he was today, but then The Force were also well aware that they had taken a massive step in bringing him back from the dead, and this was more or less the final straw.

The discussion was concluded by Grand Counsellor Solon, who decreed that there was no turning back now, and a stop had to be put to Matt's affairs. They all agreed that this task should be given to Luther. The Angel accepted this duty, and the meeting was about to be concluded. Before all of the Elders of The Force dispersed, Luther gave a final contribution to the discussion which was more of an apology, and a request for reassurance that it wasn't the Angel who was being thought of as not being up to the work. Luther outlined a number of previous cases that he had been involved with, where everything had gone to plan. There was no need to have worried, as The Force confirmed that they believed the Angel to be totally blameless. They reminded Luther of the task in hand, which was to finish what had been started. The Force dispersed.

Chapter 25
As it was

Matt was very much walking tall at the moment. His dinner date with Sonja had gone superbly as far as he was concerned, and of course the night that followed it was even better. He couldn't really remember when he had felt so much for a woman before. Sonja was everything he had dreamed of. He knew she was an older woman, but the age difference wasn't that much, and it hadn't been any sort of problem between them. He couldn't wait to see her again, and was happy that they had another date. Sonja said she wanted to be taken to a normal bar for a change, and see the sort of things that Matt was used to. This evening he was going to do just that.

Life was never easy though for Matt, and fortunately he had realised that he had a previous engagement with the red-headed Maureen that evening. After their afternoon in bed the other day he had promised to take her out for a meal, but although he was quite taken by her Irish beauty and charm, he wanted Sonja more than anyone, and this dinner date was indeed more of a bind than anything else. He had to manage the end of this relationship with care, so that he didn't muck up anything he might have going with Sonja. He knew that Maureen probably had less than a couple of weeks left to live, and he didn't want to dump her just before she died. Matt suddenly realised that all through the previous evening with

Sonja, he hadn't looked at the number over her head once. In fact, he began to think that her number had possibly even faded during the evening, so that he didn't notice it at all. He relived some more moments of the date as it also struck him that he hadn't actually looked at anyone else's numbers either. It was quite a relief.

Maureen came back to mind as Matt looked at his watch. He had more or less rearranged things so that he could take Maureen out for a quick dinner but it was not going to be like it used to be. He would make sure he was polite, but put a hold on taking the relationship any further. Having said all that, he had chatted Maureen up for a good couple of months and knew she was fairly well off and ready to part with some of her money, and tonight he would probably lay the plans to deprive her of it. He knew she was happy to invest it with him, and why shouldn't he let her give him the money? There were no relatives who deserved it as much as he did.

Matt thought long and hard about the direction his life had taken. He was fed up with having relationships with dying people. Sonja was a very different proposition. He couldn't wait to see her again this evening. Matt had changed the time of dinner with Maureen to an hour earlier than originally planned, and made an excuse that he had to meet someone later that night to discuss a business deal, but he still wanted to take her out. He picked

339

her up as agreed, and they drove to a decent restaurant where Matt was a perfect gentleman. The meal went well, and Maureen wanted them to go back to her place, but Matt managed to persuade her that he was unable to. They talked about his new business venture, which he said would see him making a good ten or twenty grand and asked if Maureen still wanted to be part of it. She was keen to have a connection with Matt, and agreed to lend him two thousand pounds. "Hey, why not," Maureen said. "I've got the whole of the rest of my life to enjoy the benefits with you so why not spend a little cash now." Matt nearly choked as he listened to her.

After dinner they got a taxi back to Maureen's house. She paid for everything. She wanted to show Matt that she wasn't after him for his money, and Matt was happy to allow her to pay. Matt stayed with her for about half an hour before making his excuses and leaving. Maureen wasn't happy, but he said he would get back to her tomorrow, so she let him go confirming that she was interested in his deal. Matt decided that Maureen would be the last woman he would chat up, as he wanted to concentrate all his future efforts in Sonja's direction. Unlike how it had been with Zoe, he didn't want Sonja seeing him with, or even possibly thinking he had been with, anyone else. There was a distinct change in Matt's life. It was almost as if a curtain had been lifted, and he was beginning to see the right way to live. He thanked Sonja for this.

340

He left Maureen's house and thought first about popping back to his own place to wash off any trace of Maureen before he met Sonja. This was quite unusual for Matt. Washing more than once a day had previously been unheard of, but he wanted to be fresh for Sonja. He also thought it would be nice to try and pay off some of his creditors, so that he could go back to the places he liked to go, and show off his new found wealth and woman. Having washed and dressed quicker than he expected, Matt saw that he had half an hour to spare before meeting with Sonja.

They had agreed to meet at a pub in Ilford near some shops. Sonja told Matt that she would be browsing in the shops and he was to meet her there. On the way, he passed close to Dysans Club so decided to pop in and see if Mikey was about. Almost as soon as he walked in, Mop spotted him.

"Well, if it isn't the new Matt," Mop greeted him.
"Hi, Mop, is Mikey about?"
"He'll be in soon, but he's trying to find someone to take your place. You know, to do those little jobs for us." Matt listened to Mop and felt almost sick at the thought that not too long ago he would have jumped at the chance of helping out Mikey and Mop.
"Matt, wow look at you!" Mikey walked in through a back door, and straightaway saw a smartly dressed Matt talking to Mop.
"What d'ya say Mop, he looks like one of our easy targets now," Mikey continued.

"Stop it, Mikey. I've just got myself sorted out a bit."
Matt could tell that the vibes weren't good, and that
it was probably time to leave.

"Two beers here, barman!" Matt called out as he
turned to Mikey. "I'm grateful for what you did for
me but I'm sorted now. No hard feelings." The beers
arrived and Matt handed them to Mikey and Mop. It
relieved the immediate tension. Matt had more or
less intimated that he would no longer be doing any
jobs for Mikey and although he didn't like the idea,
Mikey had accepted it. Matt decided he should just
depart.

Matt continued to the pub where he was meeting
Sonja. As he approached he looked around the
nearby shops to see if he could spot her, and he did
so immediately. Sonja was casually dressed in jeans
and blouse, with a smart red coat on top, and she
looked fantastic as always. "Sonja," Matt called, as
he crossed the road to get to her. She turned and
smiled as she saw him approaching. He was again
smartly dressed, and looking really handsome.

"Hi, you look good again," she told him. They kissed
and hugged before Sonja put her arm through Matt's
and they walked towards the pub.
"Hope you haven't been waiting too long?"
"No, I've only been here five minutes or so."
"That's good." Matt gave her a smile as he kissed
her again. "Have you had something to eat?"
"Yes, we agreed that tonight was just to visit some of

the pubs where you usually hang out." Sonja almost scolded him with her response.

"I know, I know, but you don't really want to go to some old dossy pub tonight do you?"

"If that's where you usually go, then yes." Sonja was keen to meet some other people who knew Matt. He looked at her and how beautiful she was.

"You're far too well dressed for the old bars I used to go to. So am I for that matter."

"Okay, so where shall we go?"

"Wherever we want to!"

The two of them found a wine bar, chatted, drank wine, kissed and then found a venue that had live music. Matt even got up and danced with Sonja, and that was something he had never done before. The evening became night so quickly that neither realised what time it was until they found themselves being asked to drink up and leave at closing time. They were sat cuddled against each other as it came time to leave.

"Do you want to come back to mine again?" Matt asked.

"I'd love to, or you could come and see my flat if you wanted to?" Sonja surprised herself that she had invited Matt.

"Yes, that would be great, if you're sure?"

"Of course!"

Sonja held Matt's hand as they got up from the table,

finished their drinks and left the bar. They then walked arm in arm through the busy London streets. "Do you want to get a taxi?"

"No, let's walk Matt, it's a beautiful night."

As they made their way through the city they chatted about this and that and generally got lost in each other. Sonja did though have one thing she wanted to talk about that was more serious.

"Matt?"

"Yes?" Matt turned and looked at her. He could see she had a more serious face on.

"Do you think we might make a go of seeing each other?" Sonja didn't really know how to get to the point, and began with this very awkward question. Matt thought before answering as he hoped she wanted to make a go of it and he didn't want to say the wrong thing.

"Well, I think we're good together, don't you?"

"Yes we are, but I know we've only just met, but could we go to the next step and get more serious, do you think?"

"You mean live together?"

"No, I wasn't meaning that necessarily, but it would be nice." Sonja imagined the two of them living in a flat. "No, I just mean going out regularly."

"I hope so, I love you," said Matt, surprising himself as he said it. "Oh, sorry, I didn't mean to say that."

"Ah, it's nice to hear you saying it. I love you too." Sonja smiled at Matt then kissed him again. "It's just that if we were to be going out regularly it puts me in a bit of a situation at work."

"What do you mean?" Matt got worried. "Are you seeing someone else?"

"No stupid, I mean I can't be seen to be dating a client."

"Oh, right!" The penny suddenly dropped for Matt. "Perhaps I could register at another Job Centre."

"No you wouldn't be able to do that, but I could swap you on to another personal advisor's register."

"Yeah, that would be okay."

"Would you do that?"

"For you, Sonja, anything."

They made it back to Sonja's flat still arm in arm, and the night was very much like the first time. They talked. They made love. They talked some more. They were both incredibly happy. Not once had Matt noticed numbers over people's heads throughout the evening, and he hardly noticed Sonja's orange forty-nine although he knew it was there. Matt stayed until the morning, and around nine o'clock left to make his way back to his own flat.

It had been another fantastic night. Matt was just so in love. He felt like a millionaire. He was convinced that he had finally found the one. Sonja was it. She made him feel great, and made him want to get his life in order. As he walked back he decided to try and pay off as many of his outstanding debts as he could. That would be how he could start making things right. He was determined to change his ways.

As he returned to his flat it suddenly hit him just how tired he was, and he was quite pleased not to have a job. He got undressed and fell into his bed, and was asleep within minutes. He dreamed about Sonja. He dreamed about the two of them living together and having a family. It was a nice dream. Matt did very little for the rest of the day. He slept till the early afternoon, and then sat around and watched some television. He wasn't meeting with Sonja and he missed her already. "I've never felt like this before" he said to himself, bored with sitting around. He didn't want to go looking for people with low numbers. He only wanted Sonja. Matt was finding this very hard to cope with, but he knew he had to deal with it. He remembered he owed Dave the DJ some money. Paying him would be another step to putting his life right. He had wanted to go to Bella for ages, but he had been avoiding the place for a while now. Matt was beginning to miss it, so he decided there was nothing for it; it was time he paid Dave back.

He waited until about nine o'clock, then Matt took a brisk walk to Bella and was there within ten or fifteen minutes.

"Hey, Dave, how ya doing?" Matt went straight up to the DJ as bold as brass.

"Matt! Long time no see, and by the look of you it's a much richer Matt than the last time I saw you."

"Not really, I just have this rich old mare I'm taking care of, and she likes to reward my talents by buying me some posh clothes. I suppose you could say I look a lot smarter though." Matt didn't want to expand on his new found wealth too much at the moment, and certainly not in front of Dave. Matt then felt inside his inside jacket pocket and pulled out a big wad of five and ten pound notes.

"You're not telling me the deal has been done are you?" Dave didn't think he was really going to get his money back, but always lived in hope.
"Well, not exactly. I'm afraid the deal went bad and I lost most of the money."
"That's typical." Dave wondered what was coming next.

"But as my friend I don't think it's fair that you should lose out, so I'm paying you back the five hundred pounds you invested, out of my own money." Matt handed him exactly five hundred pounds. The DJ gave it a quick count, saw that there was around five hundred without actually counting it, and was quite pleased and surprised that he had at least got his money back.

"Thanks for that, Matt." Dave thought that Matt made it sound like he had made him take his money in the first place which was never the case, but he was still pleased to get it back.
"And, as I said you would get more back than you gave me," Matt found another ten pound note and handed it to Dave, "there's some extra for you."

"Right, well, I suppose I deserve it." Dave said sarcastically.

"Do you want a drink?"

"That'll be good, just a beer." Dave couldn't remember the last time Matt offered to buy him a drink so perhaps the night was looking pretty good all round. Matt swaggered off to the bar and the barman took his order.

"Three beers!"

The barman returned with the three beers. "Anything else, sir?"

"No that'll be all. These are on the DJ's tab," Matt said as he took one of the beers over to Dave. The barman thought this all sounded okay and added the beers to the tab as Matt wandered around with a beer in each hand. He checked out who was in, and most of the customers were groups of office workers on the usual Friday night binge, or more hardened drinkers who were all men, so Matt found the place boring at the moment. He had moved on from those old days.

Matt didn't want to hang around the club tonight even though the music was good and there was a friendly atmosphere, so having concluded his mission with his DJ friend he slipped out of the back door before anyone noticed. Although it was nearly ten o'clock he thought he might just surprise Sonja by calling at her place. The back door from the club led to an alleyway which reached the main road, so Matt made his way down the dark passage towards the brightness of the street lights. He could see that there was someone stood at the alley exit ahead of him, but this was nothing unusual and he continued towards them, assuming they would move as he approached.

As Matt neared the dark figure, the man turned and looked straight at him. The stare was frightening, and Matt knew immediately it was the man who had visited his flat. Matt stared at him, and in particular at the bright number sixty above his head. Matt was sure it had gained twenty years or so since he last saw him, and was amazed at this fact.

"Oh, it's you," Matt said as he came to a stop, unable to continue as Luther blocked his path. Luther remained in the way. Matt didn't know what was about to go down and a little confused that this man had bumped into him in this alleyway and was obviously wanting to stop him from getting back home. "What do you want now?"

"I'm working."

"Oh, right, doing what?" Matt was a bit confused by Luther's statement, and then wondered if it might be more of a coincidence that the two of them had met.

"I'm checking up on one of my cases," Luther said smoothly, but his voice still somehow boomed in Matt's ear.

"What? Are they in the club, then?"

"No, they aren't."

"Right." Matt was keen to move on and get to

Sonja's, and hoped that Luther would just get out of the way without him having to touch him, but it was obvious that Luther had very little intention of moving at all. Matt started be a little concerned by the situation he found himself in. Luther was a big man.

"I look after people who are down on their luck."

"That's good. Do you help them?"

"I try to, but generally I just make opportunities for them to change their luck."

"Ah, right," Matt replied, as if he understood what Luther was talking about, but in fact he had no idea at all. He looked at Luther again, and recalled that although he could remember him coming to visit him at his flat, he also had a weird feeling that he had met this man somewhere else previously.

"You were down on your luck," Luther continued in his slow smooth voice.

"Well, I suppose I was."

As Matt replied there was a brief pause in the conversation and Matt's mind went back to those days not so far back before his accident, when he was indeed down on his luck. He recalled thinking that there was a time when he was complaining that he had no job, no girl, hardly any money and in fact very little at all to be pleased about, and then remembered telling the newspaper stand guy about his misfortunes when suddenly something clicked in Matt's head.

"You're the..." Matt was unable to finish his sentence

as Luther nodded in the affirmative, almost as if he could read Matt's mind.

"You were that guy I spoke to at the newspaper stand." It was almost as if a veil had been lifted and something that had been hidden from Matt had finally been revealed. "Yes, it was you." Matt spoke in a still half-unbelieving tone. Luther just stared at him.

"You told me my life would change, and I remember now," Matt gasped a bit, "you've been to visit me a couple of times at my flat."

Luther was quiet and didn't seem as if he was going to reply at all, then he suddenly spoke.

"You're probably looking at the number over my head."

This was even better news for Matt as at least there was someone else who was able to acknowledge the numbers, even talk about them. Matt nodded.

"We all have a number, and I can see yours."

This might have been a bit of a threat, but Matt was so dumbfounded that someone else knew about the numbers, he didn't really listen to what Luther was saying.

"I can see your number," Matt finally replied.

"Good, but you mustn't believe everything you see."

Luther opened his eyes even wider and his number began to change. First, it went down sequentially to one, but stayed orange in colour, then it began to count up again to 167 before turning black and starting to flash. Matt wasn't quite sure what to make of it all.

There was a long silence as Matt just stared at Luther and he stared back. Matt was transfixed looking at the numbers changing, whilst Luther was just angry. "You probably don't even realise what's happening, do you?" Luther asked.

"Err, no, not really." Matt was confused.

"I'm not from Earth, but you should have realised that by now. I'm from a sort of…Heaven…I suppose you would call it. It's my job to change the fortunes of unlucky and unhappy people, and I chose to change yours."

Luther continued to speak calmly. "The car accident you were in shouldn't have happened and I sought agreement to keep you alive, do you understand that?"

"Er, yes. You saw the accident." Matt was still unsure about exactly who Luther was, and what exactly he was trying to tell him.

"I felt responsible because of the accident, and brought you back to life, but in doing that I had to grant you a special power; it's just the way it is."

Matt listened, but still didn't really grasp what he was being told.

"The gift I gave you was designed for you to spread comfort and friendship with those most in need of it. Those dying without any friends or family, who needed someone to talk to before their time was up. But you abused your power and brought pain and heartache to even more people. Those up above sent me to try and set you back on the right path, but I'm afraid I failed."

"Yes, but I realise now I need to do things a bit differently."

Matt was just starting to understand what this man was trying to tell him.

"No, it's too late. They won't allow this situation to continue."

Luther closed his eyes and then opened them again. Matt saw them begin to fill up with blood and turn red. The number above Matt's head started to count down.

"What's happening?" Matt felt his breathing become harder. He had an immense pain in his stomach and chest, and his arm and shoulder felt as though they were broken. His throat was blocked, his whole body weakened, and he collapsed on the concrete.

Luther closed his eyes again and turned. Without a word he walked away, leaving Matt dying in the alleyway. Within minutes, Matt was dead.

Luther continued walking, without once turning back to see the scene he had left. He was dismayed that his efforts to change Matt's luck had not worked, but he knew the rules and knew that Matt had really died the night he was hit by the car. Luther stopped and looked skywards.

"I will learn from this, and I will make sure this sort of thing never happens again." Luther walked across the street and disappeared into the night.

On Monday morning, DC Perry was at work early, putting together all the different suspicions surrounding Matthew Briswell, as explained to the Chief. There was also a report given to them by a PI, who had linked Briswell to another couple of deaths. "Chief, do you think we've got enough to question him?"

"It's all pretty circumstantial, but there's a lot of it, so let's bring him in and question him."

"Right, boss."

"If he doesn't come quietly, cuff him and drag him in. Take Barney with you." Given the go ahead, Detective Constable Perry was raring to go.

Jay-Lynne Perry and Barney Jones arrived at Mr. Briswell's address, and hammered on the door of number 37. There was no answer, but Jay knew that someone of Matthew Briswell's age might well have been sleeping in so she persevered with the knocking. After a while, a neighbour opened his door and looked out to see what all the noise was about. Barney went over and showed him his badge. "Everything's okay, you can go back indoors."

"But there's nobody home," the neighbour said, as he turned away. Jay caught what he said, and tried to stop him, but he'd already shut his door.

"Get him back, Barney, let's see what he's got to say." Barney knocked on the neighbour's door, and the old man reappeared.

"You want me now, do ya?"

"You said there's nobody home, how do you know?" Jay asked him.

"He's dead!"

"Dead!" Jay wondered if this was a way of getting rid of unwanted callers. "How do you know he's dead?"

"Saw his old girlfriend, and she told me."

"And where would I find his old girlfriend?"

"I dunno!" The old man started to go back into his flat but then popped his head back out again, briefly, "And I don't know her name, neither." The door slammed shut. Barney and Jay looked at each other.

"Let's go check it out."

DC Perry checked out what she'd been told, and sure enough found that Matthew Briswell had died in a back alley behind Bella Night Club just a couple of nights ago. The doctor's report was a bit odd, as there were no marks, bruises or cuts on the outside of his body, but the autopsy suggested his internal organs looked as if he'd been in a car accident. Jay decided she had to go to Matthew Briswell's funeral, to see who was there, and to speak to a Miss Winfield who had apparently paid for it.

The morning was cold and misty, and apart from DC Perry, there were just three others at Matt's funeral, all women. Zoe and Ruth sat at the front of the chapel whilst a slightly older woman sat nearer the back. The service was short and to the point, and all four stood around the lone wreath in the memorial garden afterwards. Detective Constable Perry identified Miss Winfield, and spoke briefly to her.

"You paid for the funeral?"
"Yes, who are you?"
"Oh, sorry." Jay showed Zoe her badge. "I was going to talk to Matt about some curious deaths he seemed to be mixed up in, and then he died rather suddenly." Jay looked at Zoe closely. "Were you his girlfriend?"
"I was, but we split up." Zoe answered. Sonja listened with interest as Jay continued.
"Did you know a Courtney Thomas?"
"No. Another police officer was asking about her, but I never knew any of the old people he made friends with." Zoe looked at Ruth. "Was she the woman Matt was going out with?"
"Oh, I don't know about that, only that he did know her."
"It's just that I heard that Matt had finally found someone, and I wondered who it was."

Jay asked a few more questions, but seemed satisfied that Zoe was unable to shed any light on the deaths. Zoe did however make a strange comment that stuck in Jay's mind. She said that Matt told her he went after people with black numbers, but to Jay, it made no sense at all. Zoe also explained that Matt had some cash hidden in his flat that she knew about, and it was this money she used to pay for the funeral. The detectives said that they wouldn't query how any money had been spent, but that they might want to recover some property, and they would now take over sorting things out. Zoe was pleased not to be involved any more.

After the detective finished talking to Zoe, Sonja came over and introduced herself to Zoe and Ruth. "Hi, you were Matt's girlfriend then?" asked Sonja. "Well, she was," Ruth replied. Zoe wiped her face. "We split up a few weeks before he died. Who are you, then?" "Oh, nobody important." "Did you know Matt?" Zoe was curious. "Yes, I knew him." Sonja paused, to try and get her words out properly. "I was his personal advisor at the Job Centre." Sonja said nothing else. She shook Zoe's hand and walked away, but then turned back to Zoe. "Deep down, I think he was a very nice bloke."

Stood some distance away, watching the proceedings, was a man wearing a dark overcoat. He looked like any ordinary man, someone who most people wouldn't even notice if they walked past. Luther sighed as the project came to an end. It looked as if things were just starting to come right for Matt, but too late. Luther was annoyed for not taking action sooner, but then knew that if humans were ever to understand how to use their powers properly, Angels had to stand back and give them room to make mistakes. The old days of any number of second chances were gone now. Humans were far too clever for their own good. Luther was annoyed for not getting it right, but knew that whatever action had been taken it probably would have turned out exactly the same way.

It was just over a week later that DC Perry went back to the cemetery to look at Matthew Briswell's grave again. She wasn't sure why she wanted to have another look, it wasn't as if the grave was not going to be there but she went anyway. Not knowing exactly where his grave was she went to the office to enquire, and she had to wait at the counter before a smartly dressed woman came out holding a card.
"Are you here for one of today's funerals?"

The woman placed the card down on the counter ready for the person enquiring to look at, but Jay wasn't interested.
"No, I want to find out where Matthew Briswell's grave is please?" Jay asked, as the woman started to pick up the card again.
"Hold on!" Jay grabbed at the card and stared at it. "Are these today's funerals?"
"Yes," the woman answered.
Detective Constable Perry couldn't believe her eyes when she saw Maureen O'Connell on the list.

Chapter 26
The Force goes on

The Forces were summoned once more, and Luther presented his report of Matthew Ellington Briswell's end. They all agreed that what was done, was done, and that there should be no looking back. Perhaps Luther would try to be a little more careful with future tasks and not let small problems evolve into big ones. This meeting was a typical Force arrangement, with the Elders listening in to the discussion. Any one of them could add any thought or feeling they might have on the subject, and whilst this went on, Luther was expected just to listen without any response. Afterwards there would be an opportunity for him to contribute.

A number of the Force, who had not necessarily been involved in all or any of the initial discussions regarding Matt, were looking at the situation, and how it had got out of hand. They were trying to imagine ways in which it could have been handled better. Some felt that the only conclusion was that Luther might have spent more time checking on Matt, or reacting more quickly to the early signs that Matt was abusing his power. There were also a number of the Elders who had been involved previously, who were happy to acknowledge that Luther had asked for help with this case, and perhaps it wouldn't have mattered who had dealt with it. It would have still gone wrong. The ultimate conclusion of The Force was simple. Luther was to take no blame, but should spend more time on all aspects of any project in future.

After this conclusion had been delivered, Luther was offered the chance to restore the balance. Luther wasn't disagreeing with The Force but wanted to remind them that they, and only they, had the choice to grant special gifts to humans and they also determined what power could be given. There followed further discussion regarding whether the gift of seeing the life clock was indeed something that humans could be trusted to use properly, or whether they were just not ready for any of the powers that The Force could give them. Luther also mentioned that it seemed Matt was getting his life back on target after he had met a proper match as far as a human mate was concerned. It seemed that things could worked out, if only they had waited a little longer. The Force thanked Luther for his valuable comments, and then allowed the Angel to prepare for his next duty.

The Force had finished with Matt, and with Luther for the moment. They called Angel Dominion to receive details of a project in a remote Brazilian village. This was just one of hundreds of thousands of similar projects that The Force were dealing with currently.

THE END

About the Author

David was born in the heart of London 1957, the only son of middle class working parents, themselves both North Londoners. They moved from Euston Road in Kings Cross to the growing town of Goodmayes, but moved to East Anglia when David was a teenager.

He completed his education in Gorleston before joining the civil service in the form of H.M. Customs & Excise in 1973. After nearly 40 years of service he retired in 2012.

He has been writing seriously since 2000 when a football injury left him with time on his hands. David has always been imaginative and enjoyed writing. He is interested in social aspects of future earth societies rather than space travel and alien life forms. He is also interested in time travel too, but his novels are diverse and not easy to categorise, featuring romance, drama and crime.

David has always written in various forms, including poetry, short stories and plays as well as novels but until recently his writing always had to be fitted in around full-time work.

He now lives with his second wife Louise and her son in Lowestoft with the ability to devote more time to writing.

Read on for information about more books by
David E Merrifield.

The Tree Doctor

This book tells the story of a family who move from London to the country, and is in particular about their teenage son and how he struggles to cope with fitting in whilst also dealing with a new love interest.

The story has a twist involving a time-shift, and follows the lives of the family as they deal with the problems which this brings into their lives.

The main character tries to help the family, and has an idea of what they are going through. The book helps to explain some of the changes the family are going through and offers an entertaining and enjoyable read.

We Need a Revolution

Gary Newson is having a mid-life crisis. He lives in an area of Europe that used to be called England which is now under military rule. Poverty and starvation are quite common, but signing up to the military brings its own rewards in the form of a comfortable life.

The Military also reward those who identify to them anyone who speaks out against the establishment, and many people suspect others around them of either being a potential informant or alternatively part of the growing underground revolutionary movement. As such, nobody dares to reveal their true feelings about the current political situation.

This story is set years in the future and sees Gary embroiled in the complicated world of the revolutionary underground whilst keeping a well-respected job. His arrest and torture are the price he pays for trying to serve two masters at a time when no one can be trusted, and every stranger could be the agent of your destruction.

Made in the USA
Charleston, SC
31 July 2016